I0674318

ASGARD'S CONQUERORS

Borgo Press Books by BRIAN STABLEFORD

Alien Abduction: The Wiltshire Revelations * *Asgard's Conquerors* (Asgard #2) * *Asgard's Heart* (Asgard #3) * *Asgard's Secret* (Asgard #1) * *Balance of Power* (Daedalus Mission #5) * *The Best of Both Worlds and Other Ambiguous Tales* * *Beyond the Colors of Darkness and Other Exotica* * *Changelings and Other Metaphoric Tales* * *The City of the Sun* (Daedalus Mission #4) * *Complications and Other Science Fiction Stories* * *The Cosmic Perspective and Other Black Comedies Critical Threshold* (Daedalus Mission #2) * *The Cthulhu Encryption: A Romance of Piracy* * *The Cure for Love and Other Tales of the Biotech Revolution* * *The Dragon Man: A Novel of the Future* * *The Eleventh Hour* * *The Fenris Device* (Hooded Swan #5) * *Firefly: A Novel of the Far Future* * *Les Fleurs du Mal: A Tale of the Biotech Revolution* * *The Florians* (Daedalus Mission #1) * *The Gardens of Tantalus and Other Delusions* * *The Gates of Eden: A Science Fiction Novel* * *The Golden Fleece and Other Tales of the Biotech Revolution* * *The Great Chain of Being and Other Tales of the Biotech Revolution* * *Halcyon Drift* (Hooded Swan #1) * *The Haunted Bookshop and Other Apparitions* * *In the Flesh and Other Tales of the Biotech Revolution* * *The Innsmouth Heritage and Other Sequels* * *Journey to the Core of Creation: A Romance of Evolution* * *Kiss the Goat: A Twenty-First-Century Ghost Story* * *The Legacy of Erich Zann and Other Tales of the Cthulhu Mythos* * *Luscinia: A Romance of Nightingales and Roses* * *The Mad Trist: A Romance of Bibliomania* * *The Mind-Riders: A Science Fiction Novel* * *The Moment of Truth: A Novel of the Future* * *Nature's Shift: A Tale of the Biotech Revolution* * *An Oasis of Horror: Decadent Tales and Contes Cruels* * *The Paradise Game* (Hooded Swan #4) * *The Paradox of the Sets* (Daedalus Mission #6) * *The Plurality of Worlds: A Sixteenth-Century Space Opera* * *Prelude to Eternity: A Romance of the First Time Machine* * *Promised Land* (Hooded Swan #3) * *The Quintessence of August: A Romance of Possession* * *The Return of the Djinn and Other Black Melodramas* * *Rhapsody in Black* (Hooded Swan #2) * *Salome and Other Decadent Fantasies* * *Streaking: A Novel of Probability* * *Swan Song* (Hooded Swan #6) * *The Tree of Life and Other Tales of the Biotech Revolution* * *The Undead: A Tale of the Biotech Revolution* * *Valdemar's Daughter: A Romance of Mesmerism* * *War Games: A Science Fiction Novel* * *Wildeblood's Empire* (Daedalus Mission #3) * *The World Beyond: A Sequel to S. Fowler Wright's The World Below* * *Writing Fantasy and Science Fiction* * *Xeno's Paradox: A Tale of the Biotech Revolution* * *Year Zero* * *Yesterday Never Dies: A Romance of Metempsychosis* * *Zombies Don't Cry: A Tale of the Biotech Revolution*

ASGARD'S CONQUERORS

A SCIENCE FICTION NOVEL:
THE ASGARD TRILOGY,
BOOK TWO

BRIAN STABLEFORD

THE BORGO PRESS
MMXII

ASGARD'S CONQUERORS

Copyright © 1990, 2012 by Brian Stableford

FIRST BORGO PRESS EDITION

Published by Wildside Press LLC

www.wildsidebooks.com

DEDICATION

For my father, *William Ernest Stableford*, from whose example I have learned more than he probably imagines

CONTENTS

CHAPTER ONE

I sometimes have the disturbing impression that the universe is determined to force my life into the mold of an exemplary tale. I have done my best to resist, but I am beginning to believe that resistance is useless. I fear that fate has it in for me, and that destiny has me marked down for something big.

I will explain to you, if I may, how I arrived at this awful conclusion.

There is supposed to be an ancient Chinese curse suggesting that the worst fate that could possibly befall a man is to live in interesting times. I had always been aware of this saying, but had never considered its logical corollaries, the first of which must surely be that one is similarly cursed if one is drawn, moth-to-flame fashion, to interesting places. So I, as a young man, was lured by my good friend Mickey Finn to cross half the known universe to the artificial macroworld that Earthmen had learned to call Asgard: the home of the technocratic 'gods'.

Various members of the galactic community, representing as many as three hundred different humanoid species, had been digging around for technological artifacts in the topmost levels of Asgard for many years. The Coordinated Research Establishment organized the efforts of most of these good people—guided and supervised by the Tetrax, who are very much the top dogs in the galactic community—but I never joined it, preferring to be my own master and go wherever the mood took me into those cold and desolate spaces.

It wasn't me who made the breakthrough discovery that

opened up the warmer and more interesting levels beneath the ones that had caught a dreadful chill in some unlucky cosmic accident. It was my fellow human Saul Lyndrach, who was quickly murdered by evil persons desirous of prizing the secret out of him. It was then that I fell foul of the second corollary of that ancient Chinese curse, which is that one can get into very deep trouble if one happens to become an interesting person. Through no fault of my own, I was suddenly very interesting indeed.

I was interesting to the gangsters who had murdered Saul because I happened to be the only person on Asgard who could read French, the language in which Saul had recorded his notes. I was also interesting to several members of Earth's Star Force, who had come to Asgard fresh from concluding a genocidal war against Salamandra. Their commanding officer, Star-Captain Susarma Lear, was convinced that a large man, to whom Saul had generously given shelter, was actually a Salamandran android mysteriously equipped to take revenge on humankind; she also became convinced that I was the one man who could help her catch and kill this person.

To cut a long story short (you can read about it, if you wish, in the first volume of my memoirs),[1] the android disappeared into the bowels of Asgard, with myself and the starship troopers in hot pursuit. We were tracked in our turn by an assorted rabble of vormyr and Spirellans, bent of mayhem.

And mayhem was what ensued.

When everything was finally sorted out, the star-captain and her merry men set off back to Earth, feeling smug about having completed their nasty mission, and I was left to sell the secret of the gateway into inner Asgard to the highest bidder.

I wasn't used to being rich. All my life I'd lived on the margin, never having to worry about long-term ambitions because it was quite hard enough figuring out where next week's food was going to come from. My lucky strike changed that, and

---

1. See *Asgard's Secret* (Borgo Press, 2012).

suddenly I was precipitated into a premature mid-life crisis, faced with the awful prospect of *making plans.*

Asgard began to seem like a pricked balloon. Its mysteries were far from being solved, but the process had begun, and with hundreds of levels now open for exploration, the contribution which might be made by any one man seemed pretty small. Even though I hadn't really got near the enigmatic center of the world, I felt that my hour of glory had come and gone. I began to wonder what there was in the rest of the galaxy to attract the attentions of a *nouveau riche* recluse like myself. Inevitably, I began to think of home: the solar system, the asteroid belt, the microworlds, Mother Earth.

I'd never actually been to Earth. Asgard, which was more than a thousand light years away from my birthplace in the belt, was the only planet-sized mass I'd ever been on. It began to seem a little odd that I'd come so far from home without ever bothering to visit the homeworld of my species, which was only a lousy couple of hundred million miles away from where I'd started from. The more I thought about it, the more peculiar it seemed.

So I decided to make a pilgrimage to Earth.

Mistral, the ship in which I'd come to Asgard, in the company of Mickey Finn, Helmut Belinski, and Jean Averaud, was still strung up to an umbilical, quietly trailing the Tetron satellite at the top of the skychain. She was evacuated and sealed. No dust, no decay, no wear and tear. She'd been Finn's ship, really, though it had taken our combined fortunes to get her fitted out for the long trip to Asgard. Finn, Belinski, and Averaud had all been killed in an accident downstairs, on one of the trips when it was my turn to stay at home. Under our agreement, I inherited the ship. It was all I did inherit, along with a bill for Mickey's back taxes which the Tetrax kindly forwarded to me.

That had been a bad time for me—to be one of a group of four on a world mostly populated by aliens is one thing; to be a man alone is another. I'd got used to it; in a way, I'd got to like it. In the course of adjusting, I'd pushed *Mistral* into some quiet corner of my consciousness, where she didn't intrude upon my thoughts. But she'd always been there, waiting.

I used part of my small fortune to have her fitted out all over again. I had the fusion reactor overhauled and the space-stresser checked. I don't know the first thing about the tortuous physics of the frame force, which lets us play origami with raw space in order to wormhole ourselves around the universe, and I wanted to make quite sure that the ship would end up back in Sol-space when I pressed the right buttons. I bought new navigational software, and the best troubleshooting programs I could find, just to make sure. Then, relishing the thought that I could splash out without pauperizing myself, I installed some brand new Tetron organics—an integrated thermosynthetic system that would do food, waste-disposal, atmosphere regulation, bioluminescence, and minor electrics with pure organic technology; not an adapted organism in it. When we'd flown out, we'd had to make do with bacterial soup and adapted fungi. The food had been unbearable, the stink disgusting.

When it was all done, and my ship was rigged up for first-class service, I trundled up the Skychain, and I said *au revoir* to dear old Asgard. I wasn't sure that I'd ever be back.

I wasn't sure of anything, much.

Starships are very fast. They make light seem like viscous treacle oozing across a flat tabletop. But galactic distances are not small; in fact, they're unimaginably huge. So the ship's flight back to Earth was no mere ferry-crossing. It took months, and it became very boring.

I had text-discs and I had sound-discs. I had a centrifuge to put weight on me, and various gadgets for keeping various bits of me fighting fit. They kept me occupied for a while, but in the end I was forced to seek some new distraction, some pleasure whose delights I had never tasted before.

That was when I conceived the plan of writing the memoirs to which I referred, and immediately reached for my tape recorder. I won't say that it was an entirely joyful experience inscribing it all, because I am not a literary man, and sometimes found composition hard work. On the other hand, I'm sure that my reconstructed dialogue sounds a good deal slicker than what was actually said at the time; poetic license can be fun! I had no intention of publishing what I'd recorded—not immediately, anyhow—because there was some very sensitive information in there regarding the real fate of the android which Susarma Lear thought she had destroyed, but I took a certain satisfaction in setting the record straight.

I finished the job a couple of days before I had to de-stress in order to enter solar space.

When I came out of my wormhole, I was nowhere near where I actually wanted to be. That was only to be expected. I guess it takes a near-miracle for navigational software to get a ship into such a tiny target as a solar system—you really can't expect to be neatly delivered to a particular planetary doorstep. I wasn't within spitting distance of Earth, or even the asteroid belt. In fact, the only object of any conceivable interest within easy travelling distance was Uranus.

I'd never been to Uranus. To the best of my knowledge, very few people had, although some intrepid individuals had begun poking around the moons and the rings before I left the system. A routine scan by my equipment told me that there was now a microworld in the vicinity of the planet, which rejoiced in the name of *Goodfellow*. My ship was automatically logged in by the microworld's scanners, and my software transmitted all the usual data, receiving the customary cartload of rubbish in return: the size, specifications, population, etc. of the *Goodfellow*. I didn't bother getting my screens to display it, but I got a digest of the essentials. There were eight hundred people aboard, all but a dozen of them civilians. They were supposedly engaged in scientific data-collection and mapping. All very cozy, but not particularly interesting.

They made contact first. I assumed that was because their machines chewed up the data which mine had sent a little more quickly than mine could process theirs, or possibly because the microworlders were more scrupulously polite than me. They sent me an invitation to dock, couched in very friendly terms. I figured that they probably didn't see many strangers out here, and in a small microworld everybody really does know everybody else. A traveler with tales to tell of the mysterious universe would surely be a popular dinner-guest.

I reckoned that I could put up with being a social lion for a while. In any case, the microworld would be spinning fast enough to produce a decent gee-force, and though it wouldn't be very spacious, its walls wouldn't be crowding me quite as closely as the walls of my little star-skipping cocoon. So I decided to visit for a day or two.

It can't hurt, can it? I asked myself.

Which just goes to show that a man can very easily jump to entirely wrong conclusions when he happens to be living in interesting times, and when fate has it in for him.

CHAPTER TWO

It took nearly two days to get to the microworld, with the stresser working very gently indeed. You have to be very careful when you're around large lumps of mass, and you can't wormhole short distances.

On the way in, my software and the microworld's software continued to exchange friendly chitchat, but voice contact wasn't possible while the stresser was functioning. By the time it was possible to start a dialogue, it didn't seem to be worth bothering, because I'd be meeting my hosts face to face soon enough.

So I let the machines negotiate the tedious details of the docking while I cleaned myself up and unpacked my best clothes. I put a thinfilm overall over the top so I wouldn't get smeared climbing through the umbilical to the docking-bay. Civilization is supposed to have left dirt behind in the Earth's gravity-well, but you know how things are.

I squirmed my way through the umbilical, thinking how good it would be to feel the grip of a good spin again. When I came out the other end into the docking bay I was contentedly looking forward to basking in the sensation of fake gravity. The bay, of course, was at the hub of the station and wasn't spinning, but I knew that the reassuring pull would be only a short distance away.

There was no one in the docking bay, which was unusually crowded with equipment. As well as the usual lockers, there were several big steel drums about a meter-and-a-half high and a meter in diameter, with dials and warning notices jostling for space around knots of feeder-pipe connections. I didn't pay them much attention, but made directly for the hatchway that led to the ladder that would take me out into the station's living quarters. I knew that the microworlders would have someone waiting for me at the end of the spur.

I was so preoccupied with the sensations associated with slowly gaining weight as I climbed "down" the ladder that I didn't immediately notice, when I got to the other end and came through the hatchway, that the welcoming party wasn't quite what I had expected.

It took me a second or two to get my up and down properly sorted out, and then I began reaching for the seal on my overall as I looked around for a friendly face.

There were several faces, but they weren't very friendly. I felt a sinking sensation as I realized that the faces were all attached to bodies wearing Star Force uniforms, and the sinking got worse when I noticed belatedly that one of them—a lieutenant—was pointing a gun at me.

Merde, I thought. *I think I've been here before.*

Looking down the wrong end of a Star Force weapon is one of those experiences you never want to repeat.

Reflexively, though I'd no real intention of doing anything as absurd as making a run for it, I turned back to the hatch through which I'd just come. A trooper had already moved round behind me to block the way, and as my eyes met his, he launched a punch at my head. I was too slow, and too unaccustomed to the new gee-force, to dodge. I took it on the jaw, and it lifted me off my feet, sending me sprawling in an untidy heap at the lieutenant's feet. It's slightly easier to take a thump like that in low-gee than in the depths of a *real* gravity well, but that doesn't make it pleasant. The punch hurt, and the hurt was compounded with humiliation. I wanted to hit back, but the muzzle of the lieutenant's gun was now only a couple of centimeters away from the end of my nose.

"Blackledge," drawled the officer, "you shouldn't have done that. "Nobody told you to hit him."

"No sir," said Trooper Blackledge, and added in a stage whisper: "*Bastard!*"

It was obvious that he wasn't talking about the lieutenant.

"Michael Rousseau," said the lieutenant, calmly. "I arrest you on a charge of desertion from the United Nations Star Force. You will be held in safe custody on *Goodfellow* pending the arrival of the Star Force cruiser *Leopard Shark*, when a lawyer will be appointed to defend you and a court martial will be held, according to the provisions of emergency martial law. Your ship is hereby impounded, and is subject to confiscation, according to the provisions of that same legislation."

I was still down, half-kneeling and half-sitting. Absurdly, all I could think of to say was that *Leopard Shark* was a really stupid name for a warship.

I didn't say it.

I also didn't bother to tell them that they wouldn't find it easy to impound my ship. Her inner airlock was programmed to check the retinal pattern of anyone trying to get in, even if they could produce the right passwords.

"On your feet," said the lieutenant. He pointed the gun away from me, obviously having had his fill of melodrama for the time being.

I got to my feet, touching the tender spot on my jaw. The punch hadn't drawn blood, but I suspected that I was going to have one hell of a bruise.

"I don't suppose you'd be interested in seeing my discharge papers?" I inquired. "They bear the signature of one Star-Captain Susarma Lear—almost illegible, I fear, but quite legitimate."

The lieutenant gave me a stony smile. "Every station in the system has been alerted to arrest you," he said. "We knew you were coming back here—you'd have been better to stay out on the fringe, with all your alien friends. And you'd better know that if there's one thing you can do that will make people like you any less, it's to insult Star-Captain Lear. Star-Captain Lear is a hero."

"I believe she mentioned that fact," I said, sourly.

I figured that I had every right to be sour. I hadn't thought Susarma Lear mean-spirited enough to pull a trick like this, after we had parted on fairly good terms. I didn't doubt for a moment that she could get away with it, though.

Why in the world, I wondered, had she posted wanted notices on me? Could she possibly have found out that I'd kept secret what I knew about Myrlin still being alive?

I thought guiltily about the incriminating memoirs sitting on the shelf in my disk-store, and began to regret having recorded them.

Microworlds don't actually have jails, so where I ended up was an ordinary crew cabin with a special lock. It had the usual fittings—a bunk and a pocket-sized bathroom, a food-dispenser, and a set of screens. I soon found out that the screens had a security block on them. I could dial up videos of old movies or library teletext, but I couldn't make personal telephone calls. I was being held incommunicado.

That seemed to me to be adding insult to injury, so instead of meekly sitting down, I tried to get a line to the outside world. I started out by requesting a lawyer, but the system wouldn't let me through, so I tried for a doctor. When the software queried my symptoms, I convinced it that I might well have a broken jaw. It's easy to lie to artificial intelligences, once you can persuade them to take notice of you at all. Within ten minutes, the doctor duly arrived.

"I'm Mariyo Kimura," she said, reaching out to take hold of my chin. "And this jaw isn't broken."

"Really?" I said. "You don't know how glad I am to hear that. It hurts like hell."

I could tell that she didn't believe me.

"Look," I said, "I'm sorry there isn't an emergency, but I did need to talk to someone. I've been cooped up in a tiny starship all on my own for the best part of a year, and the first human being I came into contact with tried to smash me into insensibility. Then they threw me in here, seemingly with every intention of leaving me to rot. In my book, that's cruel and inhumane treatment. I don't know what passes for law around this place, but perhaps you could advise me on what it has to say about my position. I did try to get hold of a lawyer."

"*Goodfellow* doesn't have any lawyers," said Dr. Kimura. "We don't need them."

"You have a platoon of Star Force troopers. Do you need *them*?"

She had opened her bag and she was dabbing something from a bottle on to a wad of cotton wool. She pushed me back so that I sat down on the bunk. I knew that it was going to sting—it's a medical tradition which goes back centuries. When she touched it to my jaw, though, I took the pain like a man.

"Mr. Rousseau," she said, "I don't know exactly what you've done, or why Lieutenant Kramin was ordered to arrest you on arrival here. I don't really approve of the way that you were lured here under false pretenses, nor of Trooper Blackledge knocking you down. But you must try to understand our situation. While you've been out of the system we've been fighting a long war. Salamandran warships invaded system space no less than forty times. Way out here, we were always a target for occupation, or for destruction. Most of us have been here for the whole ten years of the shooting match—it's our home, and transport within the system hasn't been easy. One missile is all that it would have taken to blow *Goodfellow* into smithereens, and we've been very happy to play host to a Star Force defense-system. You'll not find any sympathy here for Star Force deserters."

"Would it affect your attitude to know that I'm innocent?"

"Of course. But that remains to be proven, doesn't it?"

"That's why I need some kind of legal representation. The Star Force is carrying on some kind of weird vendetta against me. I need an advocate from outside, not their court-appointed defender. I'm not a deserter."

No reaction showed in her features as she studied me with her dark eyes. She was very small—no more than a meter sixty-five—and she wasn't looking down from any great height even though I was sitting and she was standing.

"No?" she queried. "Just what *did* you do during the war, Mr. Rousseau?"

It was a dirty question. What was I supposed to have done— rush home and enlist the minute I heard that serious hostilities had broken out? I didn't ask. The answer would probably be yes.

On Asgard, the war had always seemed like a distant affair, and it had been all too easy in that cosmopolitan setting to fall in with the Tetron way of looking at things. In the eyes of the Tetrax, Earthmen and Salamandrans were two gangs of barbarians who ought to know better.

"I need to tell someone my side of the story," I insisted, politely but firmly.

She threw the cotton-wool into the waste-disposal, and sealed up her bag.

"I'll see what I can do," she promised. "But I really don't think it will do you any good."

I had an ominous suspicion that she was right.

CHAPTER THREE

Dr. Kimura's intercession on my behalf brought results of a kind. She must have gone straight to the top, because my next visitor was one of the microworld's top men. His name was Ayub Khan. He was tall and handsome, with a casual grace about his movements. I got the feeling that he'd have been a top man wherever he was, on a microworld or a whole planet.

"I'm very sorry," he told me, with apparent sincerity, "that we must welcome you to the solar system in this manner. We appreciate that you have spent a long time in, as it were, *solitary confinement*, and it is most unfortunate that you should be subjected to more of the same on an involuntary basis. But our hands are tied. The Star Force claim jurisdiction in this matter, and their case is compelling."

"I was drafted on Asgard after being wrongly convicted of a crime," I told him, already knowing that it was hopeless. "My services were about to be sold, under a slave contract, to the people who framed me. Eventually, the truth came out, and under Tetron law, the contract I signed under duress became illegal. The Star Force complied with their directive, and I obtained legitimate discharge papers. I'm not a deserter; they have no right to arrest me."

Khan shrugged.

"Tetron law does not apply here, Mr. Rousseau. The case must be tried according to UN law. I am certain that the court martial will take into account all the relevant information."

"Do they shoot deserters nowadays?" I asked him.

"Very rarely," he assured me. "In the majority of cases, returned deserters simply have to serve out their time in a penal battalion."

"Great," I said, bitterly.

"Hostilities have ceased," he pointed out, "but there's still a great deal of work for the Star Force to do. An interstellar war leaves an unimaginable amount of mess. Our colonies will need rebuilding—and we have to take care of the surviving Salamandrans too. Even in a penal battalion, you'd be doing vital and valuable work."

I couldn't derive much consolation from these helpful observations.

"Mr. Rousseau," he said, kindly, "we are entirely happy for you to consider yourself a guest of *Goodfellow*, in spite of your awkward circumstances. We will make no charge for your food or for the use you might make of our information networks. But the law binds us as it binds you, and we must work within the constraints of the situation."

He reminded me very strongly of my last jailer, 69-Aquila, who had also been scrupulously polite.

"I'm grateful," I said, insincerely. "I would like to ask a couple of questions, if I may. I understand that the Star Force had been told that I was heading for the system, and a general instruction had apparently been issued to apprehend me. Is that right?"

"I believe so."

"Do you know how they found out that I was coming? They couldn't identify my ship until I relaxed the stresser, and I didn't send any messages on ahead. Who told them to expect me?"

"I have no idea," he replied, smoothly. "I infer that a message must have arrived from your point of departure while you were in transit."

I'd inferred the same thing myself. A stress-pulse message would easily have beaten a ship in flight. But stress-pulse messages are very expensive, and are used very sparingly. Susarma Lear couldn't have sent it, because her ship left Asgard long before mine. She must have reached the solar system months ago. She could certainly be responsible for labeling me a deserter, but there was no way she could have known that I was coming home. If the message telling the Star Force to expect me had come from Asgard, then it could only have come from the Tetrax. But how could the Tetrax have known that I was wanted? And why should they have cared?

It didn't make sense.

"Dr. Khan," I said, politely, "I'd be very grateful if you could use your influence to try to find out how the Star Force knew my ship was due. It could be vital to my defense."

"I shall be pleased to do so," he assured me. "*Goodfellow* is a civilized world, and I would not like you to think badly of us."

I couldn't really imagine that I'd be carrying any happy memories away, but I let the matter rest there. When Ayub Khan had gone, I sat down on the bed and tried to make myself feel better by counting a few blessings. At least, I told myself, I was still a rich man.

Then my other visitor arrived.

"Hello Rousseau," he said, as he strolled in through the security-sealed door. "Small universe, isn't it?"

I looked up at him in open astonishment. I hadn't seen him for a long time, but I didn't have the slightest difficulty in recognizing him.

"Jesus Christ!" I said. "John Finn!"

"Around here," he told me, "I'm Jack Martin. I'd be obliged if you could remember that."

John Finn was the black sheep of Mickey's family. I'd known him slightly when we were all teenagers in the belt, but he and Mickey hadn't been close. Whereas Mickey was big, shy, and awkward, John was small, sharp, and too clever by half. He'd come to Asgard once, having left the system for reasons he never fully explained. He'd had money—enough, at least, for a round-trip passenger ticket on a Tetron ship. But Mickey was dead by then. John didn't seem too grief-stricken when he found out—just angry that Mickey had left the ship to me. Maybe if

I'd thought Mickey would have wanted him to have it, I'd have given it to him, but I didn't.

John had stayed on Asgard for six months or so. He had gone out into the levels a couple of times with a work-gang, but the work hadn't been to his taste. He'd done a little work for the Tetrax on salvaged technics, but that hadn't led to the kind of rewards he was looking for. He'd eventually headed back to the system. He hadn't bothered to say goodbye. I hadn't missed him.

"I'll try to remember," I promised, telling myself that at least he was a familiar face, and might even be friendly. "What are you doing here? And how did you get past the security lock on the door?"

"I came to visit," he said, cockily. "And security locks are no problem. I'm the maintenance man around here."

I shook my head in honest bewilderment. He sat down beside me on the bed, and crossed his legs. He seemed to be enjoying himself.

"Stayed in the outer system when I got back," he said, nonchalantly. "Never did like the inner planets much. Belt boy, like you. Was on Titan for a while, and Ganymede. Signed on with *Goodfellow* to have a look at the local sats. Nice people. I do hired-help-type jobs: maintenance work, shuttle pilot, drive the ground-vehicles, that sort of thing. It's not much, but it fills in until I can get some real work. I tell tall tales about Asgard. They say you went to the Center, met the makers."

"Not quite," I said. "I was a long way down. Had a brush with some people who could do very clever things with machines. Couldn't say that we really got much of a conversation going. Still don't know who built Asgard or why." I matched his style of conversation effortlessly.

He sat down on the bed, and suggested a cup of coffee. I dialed up a couple of cups. It wasn't as good as the stuff my Tetron organics produced, but that wasn't surprising.

"You're in trouble, Mike. They still call you Mike?"

"Yes, they do. And I *am* in trouble."

"Star Force really want to nail you. They don't send out

that kind of alert signal for just anybody. Entire system's been eagerly awaiting your return. Don't know what you did, but you sure ruffled *somebody*'s feathers."

"Star-captain named Susarma Lear," I told him. "Funny, really—I could have sworn that we were getting along quite well toward the end. She didn't like me, but she seemed willing enough to let me be. I guess I underestimated her."

"I've heard of her," said Finn. "Got quite a reputation. Ran some bold raids in Salamandran territory. Tits loaded down with medals. I can help you, you know."

I studied him carefully. He had the same pinched face. He was wearing a little moustache now, which made him look like a Parisian pimp out of some old movie. I didn't like his manner, which had always suggested to me that he'd overdosed on assertiveness training in the sixth grade.

"You can?" I countered, guardedly.

"Sure. Can get you out of here and away. Anywhere in the system you want to go—or out of it. If you stay in the system it'll have to be Earth. Nowhere else big enough to hide. Still three billion people down in the hole. Lots of places where they don't have full registration. Your people were Canadian, weren't they? That's not so good. Australia might be a different matter. Biotech desalination plants, desert reclamation...population climbing, lots of work, not many questions. On the other hand, maybe you'd be better off out of the system entirely. For good. Still got friends on Asgard?"

"I guess so," I answered, without much conviction. "I think I could bear to say goodbye to the system forever, if I had to. All things considered, if I were aboard my ship right now, I don't think I'd wait to be court-martialed." I stared him in the face all the while, still waiting for the punch line.

"Rumor has it that you got rich," he said, delivering it.

"Where are these rumors coming from?" I asked him. "All of a sudden, I seem to be famous. Rumor says that I got deep into Asgard, met some funny people. Rumor says that I got rich. Who's doing the talking, John?"

"Star Force," he replied, laconically. "Some of their guys were with you down below, right? Makes a good story, especially with the star-captain featuring. *She*'s famous. You're just notorious. But they do talk about you, Mike. Flattered?"

"Not exactly. I'd rather be inconspicuous."

"I know the feeling. I can get you out of *Goodfellow*, you know. The benefits of knowing the maintenance man, if you see what I mean. Locks don't matter."

"And you were thinking of helping me out for old time's sake, were you?" I asked, with the merest hint of sarcasm.

"No," he replied, bluntly.

"What sort of price do you have in mind?"

"Well," said Finn, "I don't say it's going to be easy. In fact, it could expose me to a bit of risk. I wouldn't be able to stay here, would I? And the Star Force would be looking for me, too. What are you carrying in the way of exchange?"

I had part of my fortune in metals, part in organics, and part in Tetron drafts. Tetron paper money is the only kind you can trust. I told him, without being specific about amounts.

"I can't use the Tetron scrip," he said. "It's registered to user, too easy to trace. But if we were together, we could split everything fifty-fifty, couldn't we?"

I supposed we could. It was a lot of money to pay a maintenance man for fiddling a lock or two, and I wasn't sure I wanted to be partners with John Finn. I *was* sure, though, that I didn't want to serve ten years in a penal battalion. But we hadn't got to the bottom line yet.

"And I'll want half of the ship," he added.

"The ship!"

"Well," he said, patiently, "it's not really your ship, anyhow. It was Mickey's. It always should have come to me. I'm just a little late in claiming it, that's all. I'm only asking half. Half of *everything*. What other options do you have?"

"I'm not sure," I said, sourly. "But I bet they'd be cheaper ones."

"Sure," he replied. "They aren't charging you for the room,

are they? "

I hadn't heard an offer like it since Jacinthe Siani had volunteered to buy me out of jail on Asgard with Amara Guur's money. If it came to a contest, I decided that I'd rather deal with John Finn than with Amara Guur—but it wasn't the kind of choice a sane man would want to be faced with. I was in the frying pan again, and I was only being offered a fire to jump into.

"I don't know yet what the Star Force intend to do with me," I told him.

He laughed. "If you wait to find out, it will be too late to stop them. They only have a dozen men on *Goodfellow*, and they're mostly ones they couldn't trust to do a good job in the real line of action, but they have a couple of hundred combat soldiers on *Leopard Shark*. Once you're in *their* hands, Superman and the Scarlet Pimpernel couldn't get you out. This is your last chance, Mike. Take it or leave it."

It didn't seem to be much of a chance, but there didn't seem to be any others.

"Okay," I said, defeated. "You're on. Spring me, and the ship's half yours. Half the money, too. I presume that I can leave it to you to get the paperwork ready?"

"You certainly can," he assured me. He sounded very pleased with himself. He had every right to be. When I thought what I'd had to go through to earn that money, the idea of cutting him in as a reward for opening a door seemed pretty sick. But if I wasn't free, I couldn't spend my money, could I?

"Get some sleep," said Finn. "I just have to make a few preparations, and then we're away. I wouldn't do this for everyone, you know—but you're nearly family."

I tried to smile. I'd never had a brother, but if I had, I wouldn't have wanted one like John Finn. It was bad enough to have him for a friend. Sometimes, though, friends are in such short supply that you have to take whatever you can get.

It can be an unfriendly universe, sometimes.

CHAPTER FOUR

I can't claim to be the galaxy's foremost expert on jail-breaks—although, as you'll learn later, I have more than a single instance of experience from which to generalize. Nevertheless, I believe that I can confidently identify four criteria that need to be fulfilled if the break is to stand much chance of success. While not wishing to encourage delinquent behavior, I'm prepared to pass on these pearls of wisdom.

Firstly, it helps a lot if make your break at a time when those people who are interested in keeping you locked up are not paying attention. This might be because you have arranged with your allies to create some kind of a diversion, but it's more likely to be because they're all asleep.

Secondly, it helps a lot if you can move around inconspicuously once you're no longer in your place of imprisonment. Darkness helps, but even in darkness it's a good idea not to be instantly recognizable as a fugitive to anyone you might happen to meet.

Thirdly, you need to have somewhere safe and cozy to go—either a vehicle in which you can make a clean getaway, or a place of refuge where you can be securely hidden away while a search is conducted.

Fourthly, never—and I mean *never*—put your trust in the supposed expertise of an assistant who has always seemed to you in the past to be a confirmed no-hoper.

Anyone studying these four criteria will immediately realize that John Finn's grand scheme to liberate me from my secure quarters on *Goodfellow* was bound to be a bit rickety. The fact that he could open the door was merely a beginning, and counted for less than one might imagine.

One problem with trying to be inconspicuous on a micro-world is that it's very small and entirely artificial. It has no cycle of day or night, so the internal lights are never switched off. Another is that everybody knows everybody else by sight, and a stranger sticks out like a sore thumb. Your average microworld has very few hidden and forgotten corners, and in any case is crammed full of sensory equipment and alarms because it has to be perpetually on guard against things going wrong. If the staff are engaged in scientific research, they could hardly work a regular eight hours out of twenty-four, even if twenty-four hours did mean anything special, because they have to fit their personal timetables into the timetables of their observations.

Had I thought about all this very carefully, I would have realized that John Finn's escape plan was far from certain to succeed. Unfortunately, I didn't think about it carefully. I just assumed that he could do it. This was not because I am the kind of person who readily puts his trust in his fellow man, but because I was still feeling benumbed and disoriented by the horrible shock of it all.

I don't know what time it was when he turned up again. I don't even know what kind of time-system the microworld was using. But I was roused from sleep to find that the dimmed light had been turned up a fraction, and that Finn was trying to press some kind of weapon into my fist.

"What is it?" I asked him.

"Mud gun," he said. "Benign weaponry issued to police forces in enlightened nations. Fires wet stuff that goes through your clothes. Skin absorbs some organic that acts as a muscle relaxant. Makes you feel like you do in dreams sometimes, when you want to move but can't. Purely temporary effect. Okay?"

I took the weapon. Then he gave me an overall made out of silvery plastic. He was wearing one just like it. I put it on.

"Right," said Finn. "I reckon we should have a clear run if

we time it right. Keep your head down—if anyone does see us, they'll probably figure you for one of my boys. I daren't dim the lights—any little thing goes wrong makes people very nervous. We're going straight for the umbilical. A few hundred meters. Stay close."

I nodded.

He stood for a while, studying his wristwatch. About three minutes passed before he said: "Let's go."

We went.

He took me along at a brisk walk. My feet kept wanting to break into a trot, but I controlled the impulse and stayed behind him. I wished that he'd brought something to hide me in, but microworlds don't have that kind of mobile equipment. Laundry baskets are rarely seen outside of old movies.

We got at least three-quarters of the way before the unexpected happened and someone came through a hatchway ahead of us. It was a tall, white-haired man and he was seemingly engrossed in studying the display on a small hand-held book-plate. I dropped in behind Finn, trying to keep my face out of the direct line of sight. Finn marched bravely on, and greeted the man cheerfully. The guy with the bookplate barely glanced up, and muttered a reply. I thought we were safe for five whole seconds, until we had to pass through the hatchway ourselves and I spared time for a quick backward glance.

The white-haired man had stopped, and was staring after us, with a look of puzzlement on his face.

"Move it," I said to Finn. "We've got to get out *now*."

I still thought we could make it, with only a short dash ahead of us to the spur that led out to the docking-spindle. They wouldn't catch us from behind, and even if the Star Force had posted a guard in the dock, we had the mud guns. Once we were up the umbilical and into the ship, I thought, all we had to do was detach. I couldn't believe that they'd actually try to shoot us down.

We got to the hatchway leading to the spur without any obvious alarm having been raised, but climbing the spur seemed to take a long time—subjective time always seems to be distorted when you're in a gravity-cline. Finn was ahead of me, and he hurled himself through the far end hatch, gun ready to fire. I hung back for a second, thinking to appraise the situation.

Fantasies were running through my mind in which Finn immobilized the guards and the guards immobilized Finn, so that I could make it to the ship all on my own. I'd have been prepared to take my chances then, and head out of system cheerfully. I still wasn't ready for everything to foul up.

Needless to say, everything did foul up.

There was no guard in the docking-bay. When I came through, after my anticipatory peep, Finn was already halfway to the umbilical. I had time for one quick surge of elation before he bounced back from the wall, rebounding into one of those mysterious metal cylinders, and cursed, with feeling.

The airlock protecting the umbilical was sealed tight. According to the instruments, the umbilical was reeled in. There was nothing on the other end of it.

"They've moved the bastard ship!" he wailed, obviously somewhat put out by the unexpected turn of events. My heart sank.

"They couldn't!" I protested. "There's no way they could get through the lock." I couldn't believe it. But there wasn't any time for further expression of our astonishment. Back in the spur we'd just come along, there was the sound of movement. We were being pursued.

Finn launched himself quickly back to the hatchway that closed off the spur. He shut it, again bracing himself against one of the big cylinders—whose presence certainly made it easier to pull oneself around in the no-gee—and then began to push the buttons on the keyboard beside the lock. All of a sudden, alarm bells began to ring, and a red light began flashing over the hatch.

He turned to me with a toothy grin on his face.

"Created a little emergency," he said. "Station systems think the bay is breached. All hatchways sealed. They can't get in."

"Can we get out?" I asked, ingenuously.

"Not exactly," he admitted. "But we wouldn't want to steal a shuttle, anyhow. Couldn't get further than Uranus in one of those things. We need your ship—which is to say, *our* ship."

Things were still moving a little too fast for me. "So where the hell is it?" I asked.

"Only one place it can be. Inside the belly of a cargo-transporter. They couldn't get into it, so they decided to haul it to Oberon. That's where local Star Force command is."

"They said they'd impound it," I murmured, foolishly. It seemed to me that our goose was well and truly cooked, and that the only place to go was back to jail.

But Finn was still busy. He was punching keys beneath the nearest wallscreen, urgently. He glanced back over his shoulder and nodded in the direction of a locker.

"Spacesuits," he said. "In there. You do know how to put one on?"

"Of course I do," I told him. "So what?"

"Got to create an emergency," he told me. "A *real* emergency."

I opened my mouth to reply, but didn't have time. The alarm bells stopped ringing and the red lights went out.

Finn cursed, and hurled himself back toward the hatchway, stabbing again at the buttons controlling the electronic lock. It was no good. He wasn't the only software wizard around. The microworld was full of them.

There was a telephone strung up beside the keyboard, and Finn snatched it from its perch. He punched out what was obviously an emergency code.

"This is Jack Martin," he snapped. "If anyone comes through that hatchway, you'll have a *real* emergency on your hands. You could be trying to breathe vacuum. We've got suits, and we're not bluffing."

I had an awful suspicion that things were getting out of hand. I wasn't sure that it was a good idea to threaten to sabotage the microworld. I had no idea what the penalty for that kind of sabotage might be, but it couldn't be a minor matter, even by comparison with desertion from the Star Force.

The hatchway didn't open. There was a very long pause. The silence was suddenly rather oppressive.

"Get the bloody suits!" said Finn, impatiently.

"Hell, John," I said, "this isn't something they're going to forgive. Maybe we'd better just give up, hey? Cut our losses."

"You bastard, Rousseau," he said, as it sunk in just how far over the top he'd gone. "This is all your fault."

I felt that the accusation was more than a little unjust. I'd only had the problem, when all said and done. He'd supplied his own greed and his own recklessness. I realized that there must be more to this than met the eye, and that it wasn't just a sudden desire to get rich that had motivated his attempt to spring me. I guessed that he had needed a trip out of the system anyhow. I wondered again what it was that John Finn had done which required him to adopt a phony identity. Nothing trivial, apparently.

He went to the locker, and opened it to expose the neat row of spacesuits inside. There was also a set of lighter suits—sterile suits, I assumed, for working in biologically-contaminated environments. At least one of the spacesuits would be tailored specifically for Finn. He looked at them for a whole minute, then seemed to change his mind, and began fiddling with the sterile suits. He took one out and passed it to me. He took a second one for himself, and began to pull it on.

"It's no good," he complained, in a tone as tortured as if he was chewing on powdered glass. "There's only one thing we can do. We have to get your ship back."

"How do you propose we do that?" I asked.

"Blackmail," he replied, succinctly. "We have to make the threat stick. Trouble is, I can't evacuate anything but the docking-bay. Too many safety-devices. Leaves only one alternative."

He got his suit on, and sealed it. He picked up the mud gun from where he'd laid it down. I could see his eyes staring at me from behind the faceplate. I could tell that he was thinking hard.

The phone beside the hatchway began to trill. Finn ignored it, so I picked it up.

"Martin?" asked the voice at the other end.

"This is Rousseau," I replied.

"Ayub Khan here. What exactly do you plan to do, Mr. Rousseau? I'm sure you know as well as we do that any damage you cause will endanger you at least as gravely as it endangers anyone else. There's nowhere to go, I assure you."

"Mr. Martin thinks we have nothing to lose," I told him. "He thinks that now he's thrown in with me, the Star Force are going to shoot him too. He's not in a very positive frame of mind."

"Martin has a lurid imagination," said Ayub Khan. "This is a civilized world—a scientific research station. The Star Force are not bandits."

"But they won't be pleased with him, will they?"

Finn had undone his helmet again, and he took the phone away from me. "Listen to me, Khan," he said, roughly. "You know as well as I do that I don't have much to lose. I think you already know who I really am, and what I'm wanted for. I'm not going to start blasting holes in your precious microworld, but what I will do is take the plugs out of every one of your bloody incubators. I'll fill the whole bay with your precious bugs— which not only blows half your experiments, but leaves you facing one hell of a decontamination problem. Rousseau and I are already suited up. Now, how would you feel about ordering the cargo ship to turn around and bring the *Mistral* back, so that we can get aboard it? That way, we can all be happy—except the Star Force. Rousseau and I leave the system, your people carry on with their happy little lives and their precious research. Okay?"

I couldn't tell whether there was any reply. After half a minute or so, Finn hung up.

I looked at Finn, and he looked back.

"You'd better suit up," he told me.

"What for?" I asked. "What's in those tanks, anyhow?"

"Ring dust...gunk from the outer atmosphere of the planet... sludge from Ariel and Umbriel."

"What the hell was that about bugs?"

He shrugged. "Stuff's lousy with bugs. Viruses, bacteria... God knows what."

I suppose I must have looked at him as if he was mad. "The rings of Uranus are full of *bacteria*? That's impossible!"

He gave me a filthy look. "Well, I sure wouldn't know about that," he said, contemptuously. "But I'll bet you your half of *our* ship that Dr. Ayub Khan feels a lot more strongly about what's in those tanks than he does about keeping Kramin and his bully boys sweet."

The phone trilled again, and I picked it up.

"Yes?" I said.

"Very well, Mr. Martin," said Ayub Khan, who was obviously no good at recognizing voices. "The cargo-vessel transporting *Mistral* has been directed to turn back. It will dock in approximately four hours. You may board it and depart."

I blinked. I looked at Finn, and said: "You were right. They're bringing her back."

"We win!" His exultation failed to cover up his surprise. He hadn't been at all certain that it would work. But even as I watched him, I saw the mood of self-congratulation build inside him. He was beginning to think that he was a very clever fellow indeed—if he had ever really doubted it.

"Thank you, Dr. Khan," I said into the phone, rather leadenly. "That's most kind of you. We'll be happy to wait."

It was a lie, of course—I was anything but happy.

But I couldn't for the life of me see what else we could do.

CHAPTER FIVE

The best-laid plans of mice and men, so the poet assures us, gang aft agley. The worst-laid plans can hardly be expected to fare much better. You will understand, therefore, that the four-hour wait that stretched ahead of Finn and myself while we waited for our getaway ship to be brought back to dock was not a comfortable prospect.

"You don't suppose they're going to let us get away with this, do you?" I asked of Finn.

"Got a better idea?" he spat back at me. He still had his sterile suit on, but he'd unfastened the helmet so he could talk. I hadn't bothered to put mine on.

I didn't have a better idea. In fact, I didn't have any ideas at all. But I had completely lost confidence in Finn's ideas. He seemed to me to have an overripe imagination, which obviously had a tendency to run away with him. Not for the first time I cursed my luck in running into him. Of all the people I had known in my life who might conceivably be found on a micro-world orbiting Uranus, he was probably the only one who could have compounded my problems to this degree. Everybody else would have had sufficient sanity and kindness to leave me alone.

"Why exactly are you calling yourself Jack Martin these days?" I asked him.

He favored me with a sour expression.

"Because I'm a Star Force deserter," he told me. "Among other things."

It didn't come as a tremendous surprise.

"What other things?"

"Nothing serious. Theft." He paused, then went on: "Was drafted when I got back after my stay on Asgard. If I'd stayed out there, I'd have been okay, but I couldn't stick the place. Creepy humanoids, cold, dark caves—like hell frozen over. Came back, pulled a couple of software frauds, set up the fake identity. Wasn't too difficult. But you can't move about on Earth or Mars these days without leaving a trail like an electronic skunk. Australia got too hot. Had to go back to the belt; had to get out of there, too. Been here for a year. Ayub Khan's on to me, but hasn't turned me in. Not because of his innate generosity, you understand. I'm not even particularly useful to him, in spite of my special skills—but it would be inconvenient to get a replacement. Isn't just the law, either. Got other people looking for me. When you're being hunted from both sides...I'd give a lot to get back to Asgard, even if it *is* hell frozen over. Or a colony world, maybe. Never been to a colony. You?"

"You're quite the little Napoleon of crime, aren't you?" I said. "I always knew you'd go to the bad, even in the old days. Mickey must be turning in his grave."

"I'm not the only one here who's wanted for desertion, am I?"

"You're the only one who's guilty."

"Sure. You're a real war hero, Rousseau. You really did your bit for dear old Mother Earth, piddling around in absolute zero out on the galactic rim. Is it true that your bosses there were peddling android super-soldiers to the Salamandrans?"

These were low blows, but I could see his point of view. The Tetrax *had* sold war-materials to the Salamandrans, including technics they'd developed as a result of our researches on Asgard. Maybe somewhere along the line, one of *my* discoveries had contributed a little. I wondered, though, whether the Tetrax had been selling stuff to our side too. It would be logical. The fact that humans aren't supposed to be biotech-minded probably made Tetrax systems all the more attractive as items of purchase.

"Okay," I said to Finn, "I guess neither of us is Robin Hood. But it looks like we're outlaws from here on in—unless we change our minds and surrender."

"Ho, ho," he said, humorlessly.

"I'm serious," I told him. "You could zap me with the mud gun and claim to be a hero. Tell them I blackmailed you into it because I knew your real name. Or I could zap you with the mud gun and tell them I only just found out what a ruthless desperado you are."

He wasn't amused. "What did you find on Asgard?" he asked, changing the subject back to something less worrying.

I decided that talking was preferable to silence, given the mood we were in. "I found out that the levels go a long way down," I said, without much enthusiasm. "There are thousands of them. There could be more surface area down there than on the homeworlds and colonies of all the galactic humanoids put together. If they were all populated, there'd be an awful lot of people inside that world."

"Know what I think it is?" he asked.

"Probably," I told him. "I've heard just about every theory there is. Hot favorite, by a wide margin, is that it's an interstellar Noah's Ark fleeing from some cosmic disaster that took place unimaginable eons ago in the black galaxy."

I could tell by his face that I'd guessed it in one. Desperately, he cast around for some other notion, so that he could pretend I was wrong.

"It could be a zoo," he said. "Or it could be that they're refugees from our own galaxy, from the time before any of the present-day humanoids went into space. They say it couldn't possibly be coincidence that all the civilizations in the galactic arm should be approximately the same age, and all the humanoid races look so very similar. The guys on *Goodfellow* think we all have common ancestors—that all our worlds may have been terraformed in the distant past by some kind of parent species."

"I've heard people argue along those lines," I admitted.

"So what do *you* think, genius?" he demanded, with a hint of a sneer in his voice.

"I don't know," I told him, truthfully. "But I do think we might find the answers to more questions than we ever dared to ask if anyone does get to the center of Asgard. I saw enough down there to convince me that there are people in the deeper layers who make the Tetrax look primitive. The Tetrax suspect it too. They worry about it—they really like being the neighborhood superstars. They love to call the rest of us barbarians, and I don't imagine they'd like to be shoved into that category themselves. They're very keen to find out what Asgard really is, but I'm not so sure they'll like the answers."

"Like the rest of us to do their spade-work for them, don't they? God, I hated working for them—although I have to admit that they taught me a thing or two about security systems. If it hadn't been for the damned war, I'd really have been in a position to make it big back here. Learned some neat tricks on Asgard. They might be monkey-faced bastards, but they're prepared to share what they know when it suits them. Or did they only open up Asgard to the rest of us so saps like you and me could take their risks for them?"

"That's only part of it," I told him. "If they'd been able to keep Asgard a secret, they probably would have. But they weren't the only ones who knew about it when they began building the first base there. It serves their interests better to encourage multi-species research, and to do their own spade-work behind the scenes. They *are* genuinely committed to the idea of a peaceful and harmonious galactic community. They think it's the only way to ensure that any of us are going to survive. Those biotechnics they sold the Salamandrans—I don't believe that was just profiteering; it was also an attempt to change the way the war was being fought, to quiet it down. They're afraid of firepower, because of the way whole planets can get smashed up. Genetic time-bombs and subtle biotechnics are much more their style, because weapons like that don't cause ecocatastrophes."

My heart wasn't really in the conversation. I'd spent too much time on Asgard concocting fanciful stories about the possible story behind the artifact, and puzzling over the other mysteries of the galactic *status quo*. I'd discussed such matters with cleverer men than John Finn, and I wasn't in the mood to go over old ground for the sake of what I still believed—despite all his claims of expertise—to be a crude and unfurnished mind. I reckoned that if he wanted to be educated, he ought to use his telescreen.

I wondered whether there would be any telescreens where we were going.

If we were going anywhere at all.

"Tell me about these bacteria and viruses orbiting Uranus," I said, deciding that if we were going to talk we might as well talk about something that intrigued me. "Surely it can't be more than thirty K out there."

"About that," he confirmed. "Gets up to one-twenty K in the outer atmosphere."

"Nothing can live at that sort of temperature!"

"Nope," he said laconically. "Bugs are deep frozen. Just like being in a freezer, though—when we thaw 'em out, they're as good as new. Some of them, anyhow."

"How long have they been frozen? Where the hell are they supposed to have come from?"

"That's what these boys are trying to find out. Asgard's not the only mystery in the universe, you know. You didn't have to go chasing off to the galactic rim to find something strange. There are great enigmas even on your own doorstep. We've had Tetrax out here, you know. Was a Tetron bioscientist on *Goodfellow* a couple of years ago, while the war was still hot. Went on out to the halo afterwards."

"Don't tell me the dust in the cometary halo is also full of bugs," I said, sarcastically.

"Not exactly full," he said. "No more than a few. Now *here*, so they say, we've got more biomass than the Earth. Crazy, huh?"

I shook my head in bewilderment. The idea that Uranus had life more abundant than Earth, all of it deep-frozen, was a little difficult to take in. "But where were these bugs before they got deep-frozen?" I asked, again.

I could tell Finn was enjoying this. "Right here," he said, with an air of great condescension . "At least, that's the fashionable idea."

I couldn't work it out. I just stared at him, and waited.

"Wasn't always this cold around here," he said. "Only since the sun stabilized. A few billion years ago, when the solar system was still forming, the sun was super-hot. Was a balmy three hundred K in these parts. Hot and wet, plenty of carbon and nitrogen. Not exactly fit for people, but okay for bugs."

"Jesus!" I said, impressed in spite of the fact that it gave Finn such satisfaction to see it. "There was life out here before the Earth cooled down? DNA and everything?"

"Sure," he said, cockily. "Where'd you think life on Earth came from?"

When I was small, somebody had spun me a yarn about the molecules of life evolving in hot organic soup. They'd implied that the soup was slopping around in the oceans of primeval Earth. Obviously, the story had been updated in the light of more recent news. It didn't take much imagination to push the story back still further. How had the parent bacteria got into the hot organic soup floating around the early Uranus?

From elsewhere, presumably.

It shouldn't have been a surprise. As Finn had been reminding me only a few minutes earlier, the fact that all the galactic humanoids have an effectively-identical biochemistry does strongly suggest a common point of origin. I'd already known—without quite being fully conscious of it—that the story had to go back billions of years. Asgard, apparently, had been deep-frozen for a long time. While studying the ecology that had run wild in one of the lower levels I'd hazarded the guess that Asgard must be several millions of years old. Now, that guess didn't seem so very wild. Perhaps, if I worked hard enough, I could make up a story which would let Asgard be *billions* of years old. Was it possible, I wondered, that all the DNA in the galactic arm had originally come from Asgard?

I thought about it. After all, I had nothing better to do.

All through the four hours, I expected some nasty little surprise package to pop up from somewhere. I thought that the heroes of the Star Force were bound to spring out from some unexpected hiding-place, flame-pistols blazing. After all, Ayub Khan might care far more about the possibility of losing the produce of years of careful research than about the possibility of two Star Force deserters getting away, but the likes of Trooper Blackledge could hardly be expected to give a twopenny damn about Uranian bugs. And what I knew about the Star Force suggested that they wouldn't worry too much about the priorities of intellectual microworlders.

But nothing happened.

I should have realized that that was the most suspicious thing of all, but somehow I just couldn't put it together.

Anybody can be stupid, once in a while. I was having a bad week.

When the four hours were finally up the phone warbled again, and we were told that a ship would be docking momentarily. Finn issued his instructions with all the imperiousness of a man whose right to command is secure. He specified that the men from the cargo-ship should come out of the umbilical one by one, unarmed and unsuited. He told Ayub Khan that he'd have his hands on the precious tanks, ready to let the beasties out at the least sign of anything wrong. We watched the instrument-panels in the docking-bay, following the progress of the ship's approach and the connection of the umbilical. Everything looked absolutely fine.

Finn and I waited patiently, mud guns at the ready. Finn was so confident by now that he still had his helmet unsealed, so that he could talk. Obviously, he thought he'd have time to zip it up with one hand while he was letting the bugs out of the tank with the other. I had my suit on by now, but I left my helmet unsealed too. I wasn't feeling terribly happy, but I saw no immediate cause for alarm.

Finn told me to take up a position beside the hatchway, so I'd be behind whoever came through. I didn't like his giving me orders, but I followed his instructions anyhow. It did seem like the sensible place to be.

We didn't know exactly who was going to appear at the hatchway, because we didn't know who'd been given the job of piloting the shuttle with my ship in its cargo-hold. We were half-expecting a Star Force uniform, though, so I wasn't unduly surprised by the fact that when the lock swung open, the person who stepped through was wearing a trim black suit with fancy braid.

What did surprise me was the fact that it was a woman. She had an amazing halo of silvery-blonde hair, and though her back was to me, so I couldn't see her face, an awful suspicion began to dawn even before she spoke.

She wasn't carrying a gun. In fact, she had her hands on her hips: a posture suggesting total carelessness. I could easily imagine the look of utter contempt that must be on her face as she stared at John Finn.

"Put the gun down," she said, "and stand away from that tank. Open that valve, and I'll personally see to it that every moment of the rest of your life is utterly miserable. The same goes for you, Rousseau, if you're stupid enough to hit me from behind."

It dawned on me that the ship whose docking we'd so calmly followed on the instruments wasn't the shuttle at all. It was the *Leopard Shark.* Ayub Khan had simply asked us to wait around until the reinforcements arrived.

And we had.

"Small universe, isn't it?" I remarked, with a depressingly feeble attempt at wit. "Mr. Finn, I'd like you to meet Star-Captain Susarma Lear."

"Bastard!" said Finn. I charitably assumed that he was referring to Ayub Khan. I saw him reach out to open the valve, to flood the docking bay with vile Uranian bugs. He didn't even bother to seal his helmet.

There was only one thing I could do.

I shot him in the face. He must have got a mouthful of the stuff, because he folded up with hardly a moment's delay. The tank remained inviolate. As he collapsed, the expression of shocked surprise on his face turned gradually to a look of venomous hatred. There was no mistaking the fact that it was aimed at me.

Susarma Lear turned round and relieved me of the gun.

"That's what I like about you, Rousseau," she said. "When the chips are down, you always come through."

CHAPTER SIX

I followed Susarma Lear down the spur to the corridor "below", where three members of the local garrison, headed by Lieutenant Kramin, were waiting. I was relieved to observe that Blackledge wasn't with them. Kramin saluted with enthusiasm. He looked obscenely self-satisfied, and he was wearing a very broad smile.

The smile didn't last long.

Susarma Lear looked me up and down, then gave the lieutenant one of her best gorgon stares.

"Who hit this man?" she demanded.

Kramin looked startled. "One of my men got a little carried away, sir, while we were making the arrest."

"You were told to apprehend him," she said, silkily. "You were specifically told that he was *not to be harmed.*"

That was news to me. I was puzzled, but glad to hear it.

She turned her Medusan expression upon me, then. "Just what the hell do you think you're doing, Rousseau?"

"I was trying to escape," I told her, meeting her gaze as steadily as I could. "We'd have got away with it, too, if some bastard hadn't stolen my starship."

"Lieutenant Kramin," she said, in that same ominously smooth tone. "What happened to Rousseau's spaceship?"

"We put grabs on it and hauled it into the belly of a scavenger," said Kramin, not *quite* certain whether it was safe to be proud of his initiative. "It's on its way to Oberon. Major Kar Ping wanted to...investigate it."

"Are you aware, Lieutenant Kramin, of the regulations concerning looting?" she said.

"*Looting*! This man's a Star Force...." He bit off the rest of the sentence, remembering who he was talking to. He began again: "Major Kar Ping...." He put just a slight stress on the word 'Major', and this time he deliberately let the rest of the sentence hang.

When in doubt, pass the buck. Quickly.

Susarma Lear pulled some kind of printout flimsy from her pants pocket, and handed it to Kramin. "Your orders, lieutenant," she said. "But first—there's a man floating around in the docking bay. We don't want him bumping into anything, do we?" She jerked a thumb in the direction of the hatchway through which we'd come. Then she reached out to put her hand on my shoulder, and said: "I'll take care of Trooper Rousseau."

I expected to be taken back to my makeshift cell, but this turned out to be undue pessimism on my part. Instead, we were shown by one of Kramin's men to a guest cabin. It wasn't so very different from the one where I'd been imprisoned, but it was bigger, with a side-door that connected to a sitting-room. On a microworld, this was what passed for the height of luxury. Star-Captain Lear was clearly an honored guest. She looked around, then told the trooper to get the spare room ready.

"We're having a little dinner party," she told me. "I suppose it's nearer breakfast time, for you, but the microworlders will be pleased to fall in with ship's time. They haven't had this much fun in years. Ayub Khan will be along, and a diplomat named Valdavia. Also a Tetron bioscientist named 673-Nisreen. You do know enough about protocol to handle yourself, don't you?"

By now, I was beginning to realize that things were not quite as they had seemed. Deserters are not often invited to dine at the high table.

"What the hell's going on?" I asked her. "You pull a filthy trick like listing me as a deserter, but now I'm on your guest list. You put the entire outer system on alert to have me arrested, and now you're treating me like a long-lost friend—why?"

"Technically," she said, with affected weariness, "you are a deserter." As she spoke she went back into the cabin and sat down on the bunk. She didn't invite me to sit, so I didn't. "I had the power to sign you on, but I didn't have the authority to discharge you. Technically. Despite what you might think, though, the Star Force is reasonably protective of its honor, and if circumstances hadn't been what they are, the discharge would have been allowed to stand.

"I really am sorry about the alert—it wasn't my idea. If it had been up to me, I'd have waited for your ship to turn up, and asked you nicely for your co-operation, but my superiors weren't convinced that you were the volunteering kind, and in the last few years they've got out of the habit of asking nicely. They just decide what they want done, and then hand down orders. You were needed, so they decided to fish you out of the pond quickly and unceremoniously, using the first excuse that came to mind. By 'they' I mean Star Force Command—and the politicians on Earth. You've become an important man, Rousseau."

She pulled out another batch of flimsies from her pants, and smoothed them out on the bunk. She put aside a sheet for herself, and gave three to me.

"The top one drops all outstanding charges against you," she said. "It restores your clean record with the Force. The second one confirms your reconscription and your assignment to special duties. The third one is your commission."

I shuffled aside the first two to reach the most interesting one. I read it through quickly, and then again, more slowly. I couldn't believe what it seemed to be telling me.

"Is this a joke?" I asked. It was a stupid question. She wasn't given to joking. She shook her head.

"If I'm reading this right," I said, "I'm a Star-Captain."

"As of this moment," she confirmed. "That's the fastest rise through the ranks any member of the Star Force ever had. Faster than any battlefield commission. When I drafted you before, you were just some slob in the wrong place at the wrong time. Now, you're an expert, and the Star Force intends to look after you—after its fashion."

There'd be time to ask what kind of an expert I was at a later time. For the moment, there were more appealing aspects of the situation.

"It means," I said, with a little grin, "that you don't outrank me."

She shook her head again, and waved the flimsy that she'd kept. "As of now," she said, "I'm a lieutenant-colonel. I'm having our new uniforms sent out from the ship, so we can be properly dressed for dinner."

I shook my head, helplessly. "*Why?*" I demanded.

"Mother Earth needs us," she said. "Very badly, it seems. I've been told that the political future of the human race may depend on us. Even allowing for military hyperbole, it signifies that our political masters are anxious for us to play ball. We aren't pawns any more, Star-Captain Rousseau—we've been promoted to pieces."

I could tell that she wasn't trying to be infuriating. She didn't have John Finn's personality defects, though she had a fine collection of her own. I didn't want to stand there repeating the word 'why?' like a parrot, so I just waited for her to get around to giving me the news. She obviously approved of my sense of discipline, because she got straight to the point.

"A matter of days after you left Asgard," she told me, "Skychain City was invaded. The battle, such as it was, lasted a few days—the Tetrax peace officers weren't equipped to cope with a massive incursion of hostile troops. The skychain was smashed. The satellite was badly damaged, and it went into a decaying orbit. Everything that could fly picked up survivors, and a fleet of small ships crammed with people dispersed as quickly as possible. The Tetrax have asked for help—they want everyone who has experience down in the levels. Most of all, they want *you*. Mother Earth wants to make sure they get you. Relations with the Tetrax have been strained because of the war, and the UN men are paranoid about the reduction to zero of our moral credit within the galactic community. They probably see this as a key opportunity to get into the good books of the galactic big boys. There's even been talk of the UN hiring out the Star Force to retake Asgard's surface for them. Where else in the galaxy can they find experienced fighters kitted out with so much heavy metal?"

"They don't like doing their own dirty work," I murmured, recalling Finn's uncharitable observations. "But somehow I can't quite see them going for a deal like that. They have too much pride to want to be seen accepting help from barbarians. How the hell did they get taken by surprise? The Tetrax know everything that's going on in the whole galactic arm. And who could possibly raise a fleet to take Asgard away from them...ah!" Inspiration dawned before I made a fool of myself by having to wait for an answer. "They came from *inside*! We finally pricked the bubble, and we tapped into a hornet's nest. Oh, Jesus!"

"It's rumored," she said, carefully, "that some of the Tetrax think it's *our* fault. Yours and mine, that is. They think that our little expedition into the lower levels was a trifle reckless, and may have given the people we contacted an unfavorable impression of galactics in general."

That sounded ominous. I was quick to tell myself that it hadn't been *my* fault. Not mine at all. Maybe Susarma Lear's, but not mine.

"How many people were killed?" I asked her, my throat a little dry.

"No way to know," she said. "No communication with the invaders at all. We can only assume that they took over the existing political and manufacturing apparatus of the city without undue difficulty and without the need for excessive bloodshed—they can't have met much real resistance, and the Tetrax ordered their own people to surrender as soon as they saw what the score was. The Tetrax will presumably tell us the latest news when we get back to Asgard. *Leopard Shark*'s the fastest ship we have."

"It really could be our fault, you know," I said, unhappily.

"I know," she replied, calmly. She didn't seem quite as arrogant and unrepentant as I remembered her. The success of her mission—or what she *thought* was success—had taken the edge off her temper and allowed her to wind down.

"Are you sure the Tetrax want to enlist us? They might just want to string us up."

"What do you think?" she retorted.

I thought that the Tetrax would be very, very worried. As far as I could judge, the last thing they'd want would be to go to war against Asgard. Not just because it wouldn't be the civilized thing to do, but because they'd be scared of losing. If the builders of Asgard were behind this invasion, then the Tetrax had every reason to believe that they were facing a race whose science was very advanced indeed. Even if it wasn't the builders—because the people Myrlin had fallen in with weren't the builders, if what he'd told me was true—they could still be far in advance of any galactic culture. I figured that the Tetrax would want to tread extremely carefully, and that they might well feel that someone like me, with expertise in the levels, could be very useful to them.

To Susarma Lear I said: "I suppose they'll want to send us back to Asgard. It's my guess they need spies, and they need people who know their way around down there. They'll want to drop us somewhere on the surface, away from the city, so that we can go underground, and make our way back toward the city in level two or three. Then they'll want us to learn everything we can about who, what, where and why."

"That's the way my superiors have it figured, too," she said. "They think we're fortunate to get the job. I suppose there aren't many men with your experience who weren't on Asgard at the time of the attack. Lucky you left Asgard when you did."

I wasn't so sure that 'lucky' was the right word. In any case, I may have left, but I certainly hadn't got away.

"I don't like it," I said. "I don't like it at all."

"They guessed that you wouldn't," she pointed out. "That's why they put the word out that you were to be arrested as soon as you made any kind of landfall. They knew you were already rich. They felt that they had to make you an offer you couldn't refuse."

She had the grace not to look too pleased about it. She wasn't about to issue an official apology on behalf of the Star Force, but she'd made it pretty clear that she didn't agree with her superiors. I wondered whether that was just a bit of diplomatic chicanery—*Sorry, Rousseau, the big men have it in for you but I'm your pal!*—but her expression and her manner implied that she meant what she said.

"Suppose," I said, speculatively, "that I say no."

"Do you have any idea what the penalty is for disobeying orders—given that the state of emergency is still in force?"

I hazarded a guess that I might get shot.

She passed a hardened hand through her stiff, pale hair, and opined that indeed I might.

She pursed her lips, and stared me full in the face with her big blue eyes. I could imagine any number of ways she could have used that stare while building her career—she had a very powerful personality.

"We're in this together," she told me.

A more impressionable man than me might have been quite won over by a remark like that. Some men go for domineering women, and even those who don't can get a certain satisfaction out of having to be around someone as strikingly handsome as Susarma Lear. Personally, I'd been on my own far too long to be suckered by that kind of attraction. Or so I thought.

"In that case," I said, "when I get out of it, I'll think about helping you out, too."

I can make false promises just as easily as the next man.

CHAPTER SEVEN

So there it was.

Fate wanted me back on Asgard and it was prepared to do whatever it had to do in order to get me there.

As soon as our little formal gathering was over, we were hustled aboard *Leopard Shark*, and *Leopard Shark* was hurled into the slickest wormhole she could make, scheduled to make her rendezvous in the inner reaches of the Asgard system in forty days.

I had always thought of space travel as one of the most boring activities ever devised by man. A starship pilot doesn't have to *do* anything, except tell the machines what needs to be done; artificial intelligences in the software take care of the rest. The Star Force was a whole new way of life, though, and the business of learning to be a starship soldier left little time for boredom

I had to learn how to handle dozens of different bits of equipment, including weapons of every shape and size. I had to learn combat techniques, survival strategies, and how to defend myself against all kinds of dangers that my vivid imagination could never have conjured up on its own.

During the remaining hours of each day I had to tell the men who'd be going with us everything I knew about the levels, and I had to train them in the use of cold-suits and all the other items of equipment that scavengers find handy. There was a certain overlap, it's true, between Star Force equipment and the kind of stuff the Tetrax and others had devised for getting by in the upper levels, but the one kind of environment that had never cropped up in all the skirmishes of the war against the Salamandrans was the one we were going into now.

All of the practice, needless to say, had to be undertaken in one gee, and *Leopard Shark* was spun to produce it. I'd been in low-gee, save for very brief periods, for several months, and at the end of every day on the Star Force cruiser I *ached*.

Men of the branch of the Star Force to which I now belonged were only passengers while *Leopard Shark* was in flight, and we had nothing to do with the actual running of the ship. The reason why star-captains are so called is to distinguish their title from that of the captains who command ships, who are of a rather grander species. The man in command of *Leopard Shark* was Captain Khaseria, a white-haired old campaigner of a somewhat acid temperament. His was the 'naval' branch of the Star Force. When the ship was in its wormhole, he outranked everyone. *Leopard Shark*'s crew of thirty, responsible to the Captain, had the duty of defending the ship and making sure it got to wherever it was supposed to be going.

Our 'army' staff had no authority while the ship was in flight—our job began when it was time to come out of the ship and get on with the mission. Susarma Lear was the top-ranking officer on the ship; my old acquaintance Lieutenant Crucero— now a star-captain—was still her right-hand man. We had three junior officers, half a dozen assorted sergeants, and only fifty troopers—less than half the force which the ship had been designed to carry. We were not expected to re-invade Asgard; ours was a special task-force. Even so, training them all was no simple matter, and the more training and aching I did, the less attractive the prospect of taking these men into the levels came to seem.

There were a few petty compensations. For one thing, Lieutenant Kramin and his merry men had been relieved of the not-very-onerous job of guarding *Goodfellow* and had been added to the complement of *Leopard Shark*. That meant that I could give him orders. I could give Trooper Blackledge orders, too. There are, alas, no really *awful* jobs to do on a starship, and if there were, they'd be done by the crew, but I managed to find a couple of small ways of making life uncomfortable for Kramin and Blackledge. The mere fact that I was an officer caused them as much chagrin as anything I actually dropped on them. They had grown fat and out of condition while stationed on *Goodfellow*, and it made my own aches and pains a little less distressing when I knew I could always add a little bit more to the burden of their aches and pains.

John Finn had also been press-ganged into service, saved from a penal battalion by the fact that he had spent time on Asgard and knew a little about working in the levels. With John Finn the situation was different. Kramin and Blackledge didn't like me, but John Finn *hated* me. He didn't seem at all pleased by the fact that he wasn't going to be sent to a penal battalion. Nor was he in the least amused by the fact that he was getting what he had so ardently desired—a free ride to Asgard. He felt himself to be a man much wronged and betrayed, and he had talked himself into an unshakeable belief that it was all my fault. I didn't try to harass or inconvenience him—if anything, I was easy on him—but the mere sight of me was enough to set a peculiar fury seething in his breast. I decided early on that there was no way I was going down to the surface of Asgard in the company of John Finn. Accidents happen too easily in the levels.

My other relationships were easier to handle. My other old acquaintance, Trooper Serne—now a sergeant—was entirely prepared to be amicable. Crucero wasn't in the least disturbed by having to share his new rank with me, and we fell into the role of equals quite readily. The colonel was careful to maintain an appropriate distance from us all—she carefully cultivated the proverbial loneliness of command—but she didn't put any undue pressure on. She didn't try to get heavy when she handed down orders. She didn't talk to me, as she sometimes had on Asgard, as if I were something the cat had dragged in. It made a pleasant change.

I saw very little of our civilian passengers. The diplomat

Valdavia was a thin, lugubrious man with a Middle European accent and an overly precise manner. I guessed that he had landed this job only because he was in the wrong place at the wrong time, but I might have been underestimating him. It's easy to underestimate politicians. The Tetron bioscientist, 673-Nisreen, interested me far more, but he spent most of the time secluded in his cabin.

Once *Leopard Shark* was wormholing we couldn't communicate with the home system or with the Tetrax. A pick-up station had relayed us everything that had come in by stress-pulse, just before we exited from normal space, but it didn't tell us much more than we already knew. Until we reached the Asgard system and talked to the Tetrax, we couldn't make specific plans. All we could do was make sure that we'd be ready to carry them out. Naturally, it didn't stop us having many a heartfelt discussion about what we might be asked to do, and what our chances of surviving it might be.

I wasn't overly optimistic about our chances of becoming successful spies—although we had no official confirmation as yet that the Tetrax did indeed want us to be spies. All those years I had spent poking around in levels two and three, the evidence had suggested that the missing Asgardians were in pretty much the same league as the galactic civilizations—it was their technical *style* that was distinct, not its capability. What I had proved when I went down the dropshaft into the heart of the macroworld was that those appearances were misleading. Deep down inside, there *were* more advanced races, with technical capabilities that made ours look very clumsy indeed. If those races were now coming out of their shell, with hostile intent, the entire galactic community might get swept aside like a house of cards. A handful of human secret agents would hardly be able to achieve much in that kind of game. I had thought, on the basis of what little I had learned about the super-scientists, that they were a shy and peaceable crowd, but this invasion suggested that I might have formed the wrong impression. When contemplating the possibility that they had lied, I found it easy to scare myself with theories about what might happen if they decided to go to war with the galaxy.

I wasn't overconfident about the reliability of my memories of what had happened in the depths of Asgard. After all, the person I'd had my enlightening conversation with was the same person that Susarma Lear remembered having killed. If her memory of what happened was an illusion calculated to reassure her, then so might mine be.

Needless to say, I didn't want to mention this to Susarma Lear, because I didn't want to admit just yet that I knew—or thought I knew—that Myrlin was still alive. I couldn't help wondering, though, whether it might have been Myrlin who had led the attack on Skychain City, maybe in command of a whole army of beings like himself. It was just possible that he was being used in much the same way I was—as a mercenary soldier.

If he was, I sure as hell wasn't looking forward to taking up arms against him. The Salamandrans had built him big and tough, and the godlike men of Asgard probably had the ability to make him tougher still. The thought that we might be sent down to the surface to keep tabs on an army of giant soldiers armed by super-scientists was enough to make anyone's blood run cold.

I didn't feel disloyal about neglecting to confide these fears to Susarma Lear. I preferred to play my cards close to my chest, and keep my head down.

Some people are born interesting, some make themselves interesting, and some have interestingness thrust upon them. But you can fight it, if you try.

CHAPTER EIGHT

I was keen to have a discussion with the Tetron bioscientist, 673-Nisreen, but this proved difficult, partly because I was kept so busy, partly because the Tetron hardly ever left his cabin, and partly because Valdavia seemed to want all communication with the Tetron channeled through him.

Eventually, though, I did manage to speak to Nisreen long enough to arrange an assignation of sorts in his cabin. He seemed as pleased as I was to have the meeting set up, and I gathered that he would have issued an invitation himself had he not been as worried as Valdavia was about the necessity of observing protocol.

I let him ask me the first few questions, as if I were briefing him about Asgard. He'd never been there, and everything he knew about it was from memory chips that were long out of date.

I gave him a selective account of my adventures before moving on to what they implied.

"The people who thought there were no more than half a dozen levels always had a strong case," I observed, "because the technology we were digging out of the top levels wouldn't have been capable of erecting much more than that. The romantics who wanted Asgard to be an artifact from top to bottom had to credit its builders with technological powers far beyond anything known in the galactic community. We still can't say, of course, whether there's an ordinary planet inside the shells, but even if there is, we now know that the levels constitute a feat of engineering beyond anything your people or mine could contemplate. Imagine how long it must have taken to put that thing together!"

"It would seem to have been a remarkable achievement," he opined, in typical Tetron fashion.

"And it begins to look," I continued, "that it might be much older than many investigators thought. That might have interesting bearings on the question of the origin of the galactic races. I understand that your own researches also have some relevance to that?"

"It would be premature to draw conclusions," he said. I didn't intend to let him get away with that. I'd told him my side of the story. Now I wanted his.

"I was told on *Goodfellow* that DNA-based life has been found in the outer system of Earth's star—micro-organisms deep-frozen for billions of years," I said, broaching the matter as forthrightly as I dared, without running the risk of offending him. "The Tetrax must have had a chance to study thousands of life-bearing solar systems. How many are like ours in this respect?"

"Nearly all of them," he said, lightly. "I know of one or two anomalous cases, but we have concentrated our researches on stars of the same solar type, whose planetary systems are roughly similar."

"That seems to indicate that life didn't evolve in any one of them—in fact, that there's no way of knowing where DNA first came from."

"We certainly have no basis for speculations about the ultimate origin of life," admitted the Tetron.

"My ancestors always supposed that life evolved on Earth," I said, carefully angling for more information. "Even when we came out into space and found the other humanoid races, we clung to that idea, and invented theories of convergent evolution to save it."

"Our scientists never supposed that to be the case," he informed me, with a touch of that lofty superiority that the

Tetrax love to display. The best way get them to tell you something is to play up to that vanity.

"How did they work that out?" I asked, trying to sound suitably awed.

"A simple matter of the elementary mathematics of probability. The basic chemical apparatus of life is very complex. It is not only DNA itself, but all the enzymes associated with it, and the various types of RNA involved in transcription of the genetic code. It was easy to work out the probability of such a system arising by the random accretion of molecules. When we compared that probability to the area of our planet and the length of time since its origin, it was perfectly obvious that the chance of life originating there—or on any other planet—was absurdly small.

"It was obvious to us that the chemistry of life is so complicated that its evolution by chance would require vast areas of space and incredible spans of time. Our best estimate is that, given the size of our universe, the length of time for which we expect it to endure, and the kind of life-history we expect it to follow, the odds against life evolving at all were about ten to one against. It would appear that we owe our existence to a remarkable stroke of luck."

I didn't ask him to explain the mathematics of this remarkable calculation, but I took it with a pinch of salt. The trouble with the calculus of probability is that you can easily get silly answers if there are factors operating which you don't know about. Ludicrous improbabilities are ten a penny in scientific research.

"Does that explain why the life-systems of the homeworlds of all the galactic races are so very similar?" I asked.

"Not in itself," he told me. "If your world and mine had simply received the same elementary biochemical system, in the form of bacteria and virus-like entities, natural selection might have built very different systems. The fact that the pattern is repeated so closely, to the point where the insects of Tetra are very similar in their range to the insects of Earth—and so on for all the other major groups—implies that each of our worlds was seeded more than once. We think that new genetic material drifts from the outer to the inner regions of solar systems more-or-less constantly, and that this provides a major source of variations upon which natural selection can work; but we also think that seedings of more complicated genetic packages have occurred two or three times in recent galactic history—within the last billion years, that is."

"So you think that the humanoid gene-complex was actually dumped on the inhabited worlds we know—by godlike aliens using the whole galactic arm as a kind of garden?"

Tetrax can't frown, but I could tell that he thought I was going way over the top, and he clearly didn't want such implications read into his argument. "We could not isolate the humanoid gene-complex as such," he said. "At present, our best theory is that the last seeding may have been done at the time when, in Earthly terms, the dinosaurs died out. That radical break in the evolutionary story is something which recurs on many worlds, but there is no reason to suppose that alien intelligences were responsible for the seeding."

"But you are saying that the mammalian gene-complex came from outer space, not from the DNA that already existed on Earth or Tetra?"

"That seems to be the case," he confirmed. He looked at me carefully for a minute or two, perhaps wondering how much I would be able to understand. I got the feeling that we were now getting close to his own hobby-horse. "Do you know what is meant by the phrase 'quiet DNA'?" he asked.

"No," I replied. I began to suspect that we mightn't get much further. Pan-galactic *parole* is a language designed to be easy to use. It isn't geared up for complicated scientific discourse, and my limited mastery of it might soon come up against its limitations.

"Your gene-mappers, like ours of a few centuries ago, have now succeeded in locating on mammalian chromosomes—including human chromosomes—the genes that produce all the proteins making up your bodies."

He paused, and I said: "Okay—I understand that."

"Those genes," he said, "account for somewhere between five and ten percent of the DNA in your cells. The rest is 'quiet DNA'."

"What you mean," I said, in order to demonstrate my intelligence, "is that nobody knows what it does."

"Quite so. Our scientists thought for some time that it must be made up of genes to control other genes. You see, there is more to building an organism than a mere chemical factory. An egg-cell, as it develops into a whole organism, must not only produce the proteins it needs, but must organize them into a particular structure. For many years our biotechnologists have tried to discover how it is that an egg is programmed to develop into a particular kind of organism. We had always assumed that the answer lay in the quiet DNA. We have failed to solve the problem. Your own biotechnologists are just beginning to be frustrated by that barrier to progress. We have found many practical applications for our biotechnology, and have been able to accomplish many things in spite of our incomplete understanding, but we must reluctantly acknowledge that one of the basic features of the chemistry of reproduction is still a complete mystery.

"What we have discovered, however, is that the quiet DNA of many—perhaps all—lower mammals includes genes which are expressed only in higher forms."

I was having a little difficulty in following this, and had to pause for thought, but I suddenly saw what he was getting at. "You mean," I said, "that virtually all the genes coding for the bodies of humanoids were already *in* mammals when they first appeared on Earth—or Tetra—and that the subsequent evolution of the mammals has been partly a matter of that quiet DNA waking up."

He looked a little surprised.

"That's correct, Star-Captain Rousseau," he said. "In my view, at least, that is a distinct possibility—although it remains as yet unproven. The evolution of mammalian forms is, we think, partly pre-programmed. The program has to be adapted by natural selection to fit local circumstances, but in essence, the evolution of intelligent humanoid life-forms on all the worlds of the galactic community was inevitable from the moment the mammalian gene-complex appeared there. The subsequent millions of years of evolution can be seen as a kind of *unfolding* of potential already contained in the DNA-complex."

I found that a pretty startling thought. 673-Nisreen was still watching me, and I realized that there was something else. Having impressed him with my intelligence, I was now expected to see the next step in the argument. It took me about a minute.

"And the story isn't over!" I said, getting excited. "Ninety percent of human DNA—and Tetron DNA—is still quiet. We have no idea what other possibilities are still locked up in our cells!"

"Indeed we have not," he replied. "Nor do we know what trigger might be necessary to bring it out. Our scientists thought, when they first invented biotechnology, that we had become masters of our own evolution. It is possible that the assumption was premature."

"So the garden isn't in full flower," I murmured. "We might be just the first humble shoots, peeping up through the spring soil. We haven't the faintest idea what it is that we're scheduled to become....or why."

"I must repeat my objection to your assumption that the galactic arm has been *deliberately* seeded for some particular purpose," said 673-Nisreen. "Your image of godlike alien gardeners, while picturesque, has no evidence to support it. It remains conceivable that some entirely natural process was responsible for the spreading of this genetic material through local space."

"Oh sure," I said. "It was probably a fleet of flying pigs on their annual vacation." He didn't get the joke. There isn't a word in *parole* for pigs, and even if there had been, it would have been taking coincidence to ridiculous lengths if the Tetrax had used the phrase "pigs might fly" as an expression of absurd improbability.

Humans came out of their own solar system to find superior aliens already there, in the shape of the Tetrax. It was easy for me to jump to the conclusion that there might be even more superior ones waiting in the wings. The Tetrax had strong ideological reasons for not jumping to any such conclusion. We humans had been anthropocentric in readily assuming that life might have evolved on Earth, making us the product of a special Creation—even though the Tetrax knew better, they had their own anthropocentric, or tetrocentric, tendencies.

"If there are answers to these questions," I said, to cover up for my momentary impoliteness, "I think we might find them inside Asgard. There, I think, there are some very good biotechnologists."

"I think that you might be right," said 673-Nisreen. "And if the evolutionary future of your species and mine is yet to unfold from our quiet DNA, then it might well be that in the lower levels of Asgard we might find that potential already displayed."

He didn't seem to find this an overwhelmingly depressing thought, perhaps because his scientific curiosity was sufficient to outweigh his anxieties as a member of a politically ambitious species. I was willing to bet that some of his compatriots couldn't contemplate the possibility with similar serenity.

When I left him, I had already begun to toy with scenarios in which Asgard could be made to play some crucial role in my hypothetical galactic gardening business.

Maybe Asgard was the gardener's shed. Maybe it was a seed-bank.

Or maybe it was the combine harvester.

It didn't take long for me to get round to looking at the question from the dark and nasty underside.

Suppose, I told myself, *that the galaxy is a garden, and that deep in the heart of Asgard are its gardeners. But just suppose, for a moment, that we aren't the crop that's being raised. Suppose we're only the weeds! And even if we aren't, what can we possibly expect to happen when we come a-calling on the creatures we hope we might become?*

I asked myself what might happen if a legion of Neanderthal men suddenly turned up on the Earth's surface, expecting to be invited to the party.

It seemed a slightly ominous question even then, although I couldn't imagine at the time how soon it would assume a much more peculiar relevance, and what an awful answer might be implied by the example with which I was to be confronted.

CHAPTER NINE

By the time we reached Asgard I had just about readjusted to one-gee, and my muscles—not without a little help from the medics—were ready to go into the levels and give of their best. The men were all trained in the use of cold suits, and had been as fully briefed on the geography of Skychain City as I could manage. I wouldn't in all honesty say that they were raring to go, but the idea of another tour of dangerous duty was hardly new to them. The only ones not combat-hardened were Kramin's little bunch of thieves.

We made rendezvous in the Asgard system with a small fleet of galactic ships—not all of them Tetron. There was a make-shift station providing an anchorage for the group, but it was a thing of thread and patches, not a custom-designed microworld. Months had now passed since the invasion, and the Tetrax had carefully picked up all the pieces, but they hadn't begun to rebuild. Support ships were arriving from the Tetra system, and from a couple of closer ones, but as far as I could judge it would probably take a year or more to put together any convincing base by means of which the Tetrax could establish a respect-able permanent habitation—whether to serve as an embassy in which the galactic community could re-establish friendly rela-tions with Asgard's inhabitants, or as a launching-point for an invasion, remained to be seen.

Meetings with our hosts, including the briefings, took place aboard one of their ships. We had to edge in very close to string an umbilical between the vessels, and ours wasn't the only link they set up. I don't know what we looked like from outside—probably like a lot of wind-blown debris caught in a tattered spider web.

The earliest meetings involved Valdavia and 673-Nisreen, but no Star Force personnel. I had the uneasy feeling that Valdavia was acting as a salesman, dickering with the Tetrax to fix a fair price for our services. I had an even uneasier suspicion that the Tetrax saw it that way as well; their whole social order seemed to be based on elaborate service contracts whereby individuals bought limited control of others. Humans tended to translate the word describing the system in pan-galactic *parole* as 'slavery', but that just made the Tetrax laugh at us for being horrified by the idea. From their viewpoint, selling themselves in whole or in part was quite routine, and there was a parallel system of quasi-feudal duties and obligations which meant that they all stood ready to act as civil servants—maybe even as military personnel too—at a moment's notice. Thus, it was neither surprising nor upsetting to 673-Nisreen that he had been snatched away from his biological work to become a liaison man with the UN nabobs. I couldn't help wondering what Dr. Ayub Khan's attitude would have been had the UN sent him orders to forget Uranus and go to Asgard as a diplomat.

When the haggling was over (Valdavia carefully refrained from giving us the details) the colonel, Crucero, and I went over with him to the Tetron ship, so that we could find out what it was that Earth and Tetra expected of us in the line of duty. The Tetrax, with their usual sharp eye for formality, confronted us with their own committee of four.

One of them, I already knew very slightly. His name was 74-Scarion, and he'd been an officer with immigration control. He'd been the one who'd contrived to get me involved with Myrlin in the first place. He was very much the junior member of the Tetron team, though, and had presumably been included because he and I had already met.

The other three announced themselves as 994-Tulyar, 871-Alpheus, and 1125-Camina. 673-Nisreen wasn't present.

Camina was a female, although it wouldn't have been obvious if she hadn't taken the trouble to tell us. All Tetrax have round faces, wizened features, and black skin with a highly-polished look to it. They do have hair, of a sort, but it's black and very short, and doesn't differ in length or style between individuals. Their dress is unisex and they don't seem to make any attempt to adopt small tokens of individuation. You can tell one from another by the shapes of their noses and the patterns of the markings on their faces, but it isn't easy. They profess a horror of excessive individuation, which is why they give themselves numbers as well as names. I never had figured out whether the names they had were more akin to our Christian or family names, or what kind of relationship was likely to exist between two Tetrax with the same name. I did know, though, that high numbers were in some loose way connected with high status. Four figure numbers were rare, and it wasn't surprising that 1125-Camina turned out to be the chief spokesman.

"We are most honored and very grateful for your willingness to assist us in this tragic hour," she assured us. "This is a time of trouble for all the galactic community, and I know of no homeworld which does not mourn for lost sons and daughters. The Asgard project was one which brought together all races in a common endeavor, and was therefore precious to us all as a symbol of harmony. These have been dreadful happenings."

All of this tripped very smoothly from her tongue in panga-lactic *parole*, which is a language perfectly suited to Tetron mouth-parts. Human tongues, which are flatter and wider, can't quite get to grips with the full range of syllables, and the fact that we have to substitute a couple of non-standard consonants means that we sound very awkward when we try to use the language. Alas, there's no other way to get by in the community. One could hardly expect the Tetrax to learn English.

For this reason, Valdavia's official reply to the greeting was more succinct than his natural inclination would have prompted him to be, and the words did not flow like verbal honey.

"We regret," 1125-Camina explained, speaking directly to

the colonel because Valdavia had presumably already heard the news, "that we have been unable to establish communication with the people who have seized Skychain City. There is, of course, a language barrier, but no attempt seems to have been made by the invaders to begin the work of overcoming it. Our transmissions are ignored. We have sent down unarmed emissaries, but none have returned, though we have no evidence that any of them has been harmed. There are still galactics beneath the surface who have not yet been captured—people who were working in bubble-domes established by the Coordinated Research Establishment. We have been able to communicate sporadically with these groups, although we are wary of attracting attention to them. We did manage to receive communications from our people in the city for some time after the invasion, but we have not picked up any transmissions lately. With your permission, we will summarize briefly what we now know about the invaders."

Valdavia inclined his head, gesturing that she should continue. The colonel simply raised a blonde eyebrow. She was well into her tough-guy routine. 1125-Camina promptly passed the buck to 994-Tulyar.

"The invaders came from beneath the city," he said. "They emerged from at least five different points in levels two and three, using doorways of whose existence we had been quite ignorant. We infer that the invaders must have been grouping in levels three and four for some time before the attack; it is possible that they were there even before Mr. Rousseau first penetrated to the lower levels, and that the attack was in no way a response to that penetration.

"There is one remarkable coincidence, of whose significance we are uncertain. If you will look at these...."

He took some flimsies from a bag beneath the table. They were photographs, presumably taken in the aftermath of the battle for Skychain City and transmitted before communication was closed down.

The invaders looked human.

Of all the starfaring races in the community, about half a dozen are near enough to human for at least some of their members to pass. Humans are pretty various, of course, so it only has to be the case that *some* members of a near-human race could be mistaken for *some* humans for us to be able to speak of there being a coincidence. The invaders in the photographs were all white-skinned—rather pasty-faced, in fact—and they all had light-colored hair. Their features were a little on the Neanderthal side, with heavy brow-ridges and snub noses, but they could have walked the streets of a dozen Earthly cities without attracting too much notice, and on a multiracial micro-world anyone would have been happy to shake hands with them.

I realized that my new-found interestingness was not entirely determined by my experience in the levels.

"The people who once inhabited levels one, two, and three were humanoid," I pointed out. "We've always known that. There's no reason to be particularly surprised."

"Perhaps not," said the Tetron. "It is possible that the coincidence can now be turned to our advantage. Colonel Lear could certainly be mistaken for one of the aliens, and so could you, Star-Captain Rousseau. This might assist in the gathering of intelligence. It might conceivably be the case that the invaders would be more ready to make contact with a race which resembles them so very closely than with the Tetrax, who unhappily do not."

It's difficult to import subtle inflections into pan-galactic *parole*, but he managed to make the word 'unhappily' sound ironically insincere. What he was implying was that the invaders were barbarians just like us, and would probably have more in common with us than with civilized and cultured folk like the Tetrax.

"Is that why we're here—to make contact?" asked Susarma Lear, bluntly, in *parole* that sounded coarse even by human standards.

1125-Camina intervened, quickly but smoothly. "It is our considered opinion that your group should attempt to make contact only if the circumstances seem very favorable. Our own diplomats, aided by members of several races who resemble the invaders closely, are making overt attempts to open a dialogue. Mr. Valdavia will be able to assist us, and he has kindly offered to do so. What we ask of you, if you are willing to help, is that you should help us to reopen channels of communication with the Tetrax in the city. We need the information they have been gathering since our links were cut, and it appears that we will need them to act as intermediaries in communicating with the invaders."

I was trying hard to read between the lines, to judge how anxious she was, and about what. I thought her words overlaid a real sense of urgency, and I guessed that what was worrying the Tetrax was the fear that this affair might not have finished yet— that there might be manpower enough and firepower enough in Asgard's depths to allow the macroworld's inhabitants to carry their campaign out into the star-worlds. I guessed that they were afraid that the invaders wouldn't ever start talking peace, but would instead erupt into the galaxy, guns ablaze, in exactly the same fashion as they had erupted into Skychain City.

"Whose orders are we under, once we're down?" asked the colonel, again defying Valdavia's suggestions by being brutally frank. The diplomat looked annoyed, but she ignored him.

"994-Tulyar will direct operations," replied the female Tetron. "He has lived on the surface of Asgard for some years, and knows the city well. Your own Star Force personnel will of course be under your command, but we respectfully ask that you take no action without careful consultation with 994-Tulyar."

Or, to put it another way, you do as this guy tells you. Susarma Lear didn't challenge the position.

"And what sort of equipment are we taking down?" she asked.

1125-Camina was sharp enough to know that 'equipment' was a euphemism for guns. "We do not consider the circumstances appropriate for the carrying of weapons," she replied. "Our principal objective is to establish friendly relations with the invaders, and your mission is a means to that end. We are determined to make no hostile moves. You should make every attempt to operate in secret, without attracting the attention of the invaders and certainly without trying to kill any of them."

I was slightly surprised when Susarma Lear just nodded, keeping her face quite straight. Valdavia must have warned her that the Tetrax would take this stand, and had presumably instructed her not to protest. She'd already made an effort to show that she might take an independent line if necessary, but she was a colonel now, and colonels have to be extra-careful about expressing their displeasure openly. She had her orders, and she knew that in the end she had to take whatever crap the Tetrax cared to hand out. One more heroic sacrifice for the cause of Mother Earth.

I wasn't a colonel. That meant I didn't have a voice, let alone an opinion. I could make myself heard some other time.

"The interests of both our races—of the entire galactic community—are identical in this matter," added 871-Alpheus, who seemed to be there simply as a yes-man. My old friend 74-Scarion, who was a yes-man of an even lower order, echoed him with the observation: "It is our duty to serve as we may."

I wasn't quite sure how to translate that into ordinary language, but it sounded to me like: "We're expendable, pal— you and me both—and we don't have a choice." I had a feeling he might be right. I gave him a little smile, but I don't suppose he understood it.

"Ideally," said 1125-Camina, now making a show of addressing herself to Valdavia, "we would like to bring some of our people out of the city, and establish routes by which they could go back and forth unobserved. No doubt the airlocks that provide the principal means of egress are heavily guarded, but it should not be too difficult to find covert points of entry into the lower levels."

This clumsy speech was simply to set up a question.

"Could that be done?" Valdavia asked me.

I shrugged my shoulders. "The city sprawls a bit in the lower regions," I said. "The C.R.E. was always reclaiming more space.

They opened up huge factory-fields down there to produce food for the city, so there's a lot of ground for the defenders to cover. The locks are on the surface—down below, the interface between the city's basements and the cold habitats is an extensive and untidy web of pressurized plastic bubbles. Some of the plugs are in dark corners. We couldn't cut in directly without triggering leak-alarms, but if we built our own plastic wall behind us and then pressurized, we could get in. They can't have posted guards everywhere, but they'll presumably be running patrols. What about the C.R.E. people in outlying pockets, though—haven't they been asked to try it? They'd have all the right equipment ready to hand."

"We have been reluctant to order any major project of that kind," 994-Tulyar replied. "In any case, the groups which were not captured were a long way from the city—all but two are actually in different cave-systems. We thought it best not to draw attention to the one closest to Skychain City until we could bring in reinforcements."

That translated as: no way—we were waiting for you suckers.

"One further aspect of your mission," added 1125-Camina, "will be to carry various sophisticated surveillance devices into the city, so that we can continue to gather intelligence of what is happening there even if all else fails. I believe that you have a man with you who has experience of the city, and who has some training in the use of surveillance devices."

I didn't immediately cotton on to what she meant, and was slightly distracted by the implications of her off-hand remark about all else failing. Then I realized that she must be talking about John Finn, and remembered what he'd said about using his time on Asgard to learn something about Tetron "security systems". I was about to make a comment on that, but I was interrupted before I had the chance.

"When do we leave?" demanded the colonel, showing once again her marvelous talent for bulldozing through the bureaucratic niceties.

"As soon as possible," 994-Tulyar told her. "We have already made the necessary preparations here. I am at your disposal. When your men are ready...."

She glanced sideways, at me.

I managed a small sardonic smile, and murmured "Gung Ho!" I said it in English, of course. Pan-galactic *parole* has no need of any such expression. After all, the Tetrax invented *parole*, and they always let other people do their gung-hoing for them.

CHAPTER TEN

We were split into three groups, scheduled to go down in three different shuttles. Each one was to put down beyond Skychain City's horizon, close to a trapdoor which would give easy access to level one. There were plenty of trapdoors like that, painstakingly identified and made functional by the C.R.E. teams that had spread out from Skychain City into the level one habitation at whose hub the city had been built.

Susarma Lear and I were in the same group. Crucero took command of the Star Force personnel in the second; Kramin was attached to his group, and so was Finn, whose temper was dramatically improved by the news that the Tetrax remembered him, and considered his knowledge of bugging devices adequate to warrant giving him further training and extra responsibilities. His self-esteem, which had taken a battering in recent weeks, was boosted back to the level of intolerable arrogance.

871-Alpheus was the Tetron in charge of Crucero's team. Both 994-Tulyar and 74-Scarion were assigned to my crew, apparently confirming that the Tetrax considered us the lynchpin of the mission, and the group most likely to succeed.

Each group of would-be spies had a couple of experienced scavengers allotted to it. My group had me and a Turkanian named—as nearly as I could pronounce it—Johaxan. I'd never met him before, but he was an old C.R.E. hand who'd worked the levels even longer than I had. He'd been on the satellite when the skychain was destroyed.

Turkanians must have been forest-dwellers for most of

their pre-sentient phase, because they still have long arms and bent legs with clever toes. They wear very little in the way of clothing and their skins are lightly furred, the color of the fur being an oddly mottled mixture of greens and browns. Very few humanoid species exhibit that kind of camouflage coloring, because humanoids are usually big enough not to be too worried about hiding from predators. Turkanians, though, exhibit "prey mentality"—they have a wide streak of natural paranoia, and are very shy of fighting, although it would be a mistake to put them down as non-aggressive. In their own way they can be very assertive indeed, and they have the reputation of breeding the best pickpockets in the galaxy.

In terms of equipment, we were reasonably well supplied. We had a cold-suit each, and a couple of spares, and life-support backpacks enough to keep us all going for several months; we were told that further supplies would be dropped when needed. We also had various kinds of cutting-tools, bubble-building equipment, and sleds. Given that we had to travel light, we had everything we needed.

By the time we went down, Susarma Lear had obviously managed to have a meaningful discussion with someone about weaponry, and we *were* issued with guns—but not killing guns. All the weapons training I'd done aboard *Leopard Shark* was for nothing; each and every one of us was issued with a mud gun. Out in the levels, of course, they'd be no more useful than water pistols, but if and when we did get into Skychain City, we'd be able to defend ourselves without doing anyone any lasting damage. This was another little reminder of the fact that our goal was to bring peace and harmony to Asgard, the galactic community, and the entire universe.

Or so we were frequently told.

The colonel did once express the opinion—in private—that the Tetrax were not entirely to be trusted, and that she wasn't prepared to take anything at face value. That was professional paranoia at its finest, but I had to admit to her that the Tetrax were a cunning bunch, who would not shrink from being wickedly underhanded, if they thought the situation warranted deceit. I reserved my own judgment.

The drop was nerve-racking, especially the landing. Atmospheric pressure on the surface of Asgard is low, and there was no way that we could be dropped quietly out of the shuttle to parachute down. The shuttle had to come with us all the way, using its AM jets to soften up the landing. It wasn't a very big craft, but anything zooming around close to a planet's surface blasting away with AM jets can hardly be considered discreet. It's all very well to have a horizon in between you and the enemy once you're on the floor, but when you're coming down from a long way up it's not easy to hide. We were hoping that the invaders hadn't got any spaceship-spotting equipment of their own; certainly they weren't going to get any help from the Tetron satellites. Logic suggested that radar and the like wouldn't be very useful to an army which did most of its fighting under a twenty-meter ceiling, but nerves are notoriously unready to listen to logic.

Once we were down, though, we had reason to be grateful to the efficiency of Tetron targeting; we were practically on top of a hatchway, and it took us less than ten 'hours' (local metric) to go underground.

We abandoned the shuttle entirely; our first mission was to get to another hatchway, two days hike away in the direction of the city, to put up our communications aerial and establish some kind of semi-permanent base of operations. That way, we figured, it wouldn't make too much difference if the invaders did find the shuttle.

Except, of course, that we'd have to hitchhike home if the time ever came to get the hell out.

The first trek was pretty easy. The hatchway let us down to an arterial highway on level one. We sent two troopers on ahead to act as scouts, and then began to haul our sleds right down the middle of the road, skimming over the thin coat of ices. Level one is fairly benign, of course—the temperature rarely drops below two-thirty K, and sometimes gets up almost to the freezing point.

If we had been following the highway to its end, we would have taken a straight-line course smack into the middle of Skychain City, but we didn't intend to go quite that far. Once we were close to the city, our intention was to fade quietly into the forgotten back alleys.

We lit our way with torches mounted on the sleds, conserving our helmet-lights. Everybody took turns at hauling, including the colonel and the two Tetrax. There were no passengers on this trip. We'd already arranged a timetable for rest-periods; whenever we rested, a man would go on ahead to relieve one of the scouts. It all went like clockwork.

We had no trouble at all that first day; the invaders weren't using the highway, and if they had any guards out on it, they were patrolling much closer to home.

On the second day, things didn't go quite so smoothly.

About 37.50 (we were on Skychain City metric time, though there was no reason to take it for granted that Skychain City had retained its old schedule since the new tenants arrived), the scouts reported that they had run into some kind of light-sensitive device on the highway. They said that it was a relatively primitive device, but good enough to do its job. They had every reason to suppose that they had triggered it simply by spotting it, and that it had told Skychain City that we were on our way. It meant that we had to leave the highway immediately.

This was by no means a disaster, because we were so far out it would take hours for an invader patrol to get here even in a fast-wheeled vehicle, and by that time we'd be long gone. But it did seem as if the first point on the board had been clocked up to the opposition.

In the late afternoon we were close enough to go down to level two, where the temperature is mostly an unfriendly one-thirty K. It was as far down as I intended to go. There was no point in risking the men and the equipment in the really cold regions. I thought of level three as a place to retreat to if the going got rough. We had no idea, of course, how well the invaders might be able to operate in three and four. Maybe they were used to moving about in levels which were warm and brightly lit, and had no experience in really cold conditions. We couldn't depend on that assumption, though—their army may have been lurking in three and four for some considerable time before the attack on the city. For all we knew, they might go to the cold layers for their summer holidays.

For me, the return to a world of silvery walls and icy floors was almost like coming home. I felt more relaxed on level two than I had aboard *Leopard Shark*. Joxahan also felt comfortable, and did his bit to jolly along the troopers who found it all very alien and very disturbing. You'd think that anyone who spent the greater part of life aboard a starship couldn't possibly be claustrophobic, but the levels can engender their own special unease. Oddly enough, the person who seemed most uneasy was 74-Scarion, who had spent many years in Skychain City, including the underground parts of the city, but who had never been out in the deep cold.

We pulled our scouts back, and moved in single file across what had once been the 'farmlands' of level two. The ceiling of the level was only fifteen meters or so here, and was ribbed with what had once been very powerful electric lights. In the Golden Age of Asgard those lights had blazed upon carpets of artificial photosynthetic material, interrupted by occasional lakes of photosynthetic fluid. Underneath the carpets and around the lakes there had been processing machinery which had accumulated the products, and below the machinery there had been another active layer of thermosynthetic materials. It all added up to a sophisticated organic technology, in which real organisms had played a very marginal role. There had been no herds of domestic animals—meat-production for the level-dwellers was entirely a matter of organic synthesis from scratch...if you can call the products of that kind of synthesis 'meat' in any but a metaphorical sense.

Now, of course, the whole shebang was in ruins. Most of the equipment had been stripped before the cavies left, and the entire system had been shut down some time before the big freeze-up. What they'd left behind was mostly garbage, although it was still recognizable as the remains of a highly-sophisticated biotechnological production-system. The Tetrax had much that was similar on their homeworld, and I had heard that dear old Mother Earth was gradually making over her useless tropical deserts for the development of this kind of artificial photosynthetic technology. Needless to say, we were buying some of the technology from the Tetrax, but we were having to do a great deal of the R&D work ourselves because we didn't have much that the Tetrax actually wanted in exchange.

On the second night we shopped around for an inconspicuous spot in which to erect a small bubble-dome. We investigated a couple of small 'villages', where residential accommodation was organized in floor-to-ceiling blocks four or five stories high, but I'd always found such places to be poor campsites. The cavies' apartments tended to be untidy, their rooms having been stripped and gutted like everything else, and left in a worse state of dereliction. Opening the doors was always a problem, because the locking mechanisms had long since set firm. I'd had many years of experience cutting laboriously through doors, only to discover that there was nothing of any interest on the other side.

In the end, it seemed most convenient for us to take up residence in a building that had presumably served as some kind of barn or storehouse, where there was a space big enough to erect a comfortable dome, but which wasn't out in the open. We managed to find a place that was clustered around with blocks and pillars, so that it couldn't easily be observed from a distance. Nowhere in the caves is there any open space of the kind you'd find on the surface of a world, because the whole structure has to be protected against the dangers of collapse; but factory-fields are open enough to cause embarrassment if you're trying to hide. We were careful to look for somewhere with plenty of cover.

We had power enough to raise the temperature inside the

plastic bubble to a tolerable level, but we were determined to conserve our air, and didn't want to expend enough to give it an atmosphere. For this reason, setting up accommodation wasn't quite like pitching a tent. We remained in our suits, with the chemistry-sets on our backs feeding our bodies with all the essentials.

We were still communicating with one another on an open channel radio, so there was no real privacy (though I had agreed on a couple of secret wavelengths with my commander, so that we could confer, if necessary, without the Tetrax being able to overhear). It was a relief, though, to be able to lay down the equipment and then lie down ourselves, confident that the environment was as friendly as could be expected.

"Could the invaders track us from the point at which we triggered their alarm device?" 994-Tulyar asked me, once we were cozily set up.

"Very unlikely," I told him. "I don't believe they could figure out where we left the highway. We left traces, of course, but there've been so many other galactics moving about on level one during the last twenty years that there's no way of sorting out our tracks from the others. We're safe here, for now. The traces we leave when we try to break into the lower levels of the city will be a different matter. Then we'll have to take extra care."

"We have every reason to believe that the factory-fields will be operating more-or-less normally," Scarion pointed out. "There will be workers there from many of the galactic races. Once we have stowed away our cold-suits, we will not be conspicuous."

He was obviously trying to reassure himself rather than the rest of us—Tulyar had appointed him to accompany us on our first foray into the lower levels of the city. It wasn't a good time for airing anxieties, so I saved up my less uplifting thoughts. In any case, he was probably right. All we had to do on day one was make some preliminary contacts, try to get a message or two through to the top men in the city, and avoid the invaders. It seemed a sufficiently discreet program, although there was always a danger of our attempts to communicate being inter-cepted, and giving us away.

We'd had a long day, and had worked ourselves pretty hard. In our hammocks, we slept what is euphemistically called the sleep of the just. Just what, I wasn't entirely sure.

CHAPTER ELEVEN

We had no trouble getting close to the city on level two. We'd already picked out a likely point of entry on the map, and our approach was untroubled.

Our means of ingress was to be a narrow corridor on level one, which was sealed halfway along its length by a plastic plug. First we had to put in a second plug behind us, then equalize the pressure, then cut through the original plug. We were going through on level one because the temperature and pressure differentials were far less sharp than on level two—which meant that the plugs we had to deal with would be far less solid and much more easily manageable.

This was the most hazardous part of the operation. Once we'd put a plug behind us, we'd effectively imprisoned ourselves, along with a major part of our equipment. If we attracted attention while we were actually at work cutting, there was no place to go. Once we were inside, there would be a rich selection of bolt-holes, but if we were spotted before we got through we'd be done for. The other big danger was that while we were inside, some wandering patrol might discover what we'd done, thus allowing them to set an ambush for us.

We had decided that four of us would make the first foray into the city, for a preliminary appraisal of the situation. 994-Tulyar and Susarma Lear stayed behind, on the grounds that you don't expose your top personnel on the first run. The Turkanian was out, too, because he'd be the guy entrusted with the task of getting them out again if anything happened to me. That put me in command of the raiding party, with 74-Scarion, Sergeant Serne and a trooper named Vasari. He'd been on Asgard before, but he'd had the plum job of minding the trucks when the rest of us went down into the levels, so he'd never actually been under the surface.

We came back up to level one through one of the usual airlock-type hatchways. The seals on such hatchways were simple mechanical devices, so time and cold hadn't wrecked them, and it had been easy enough for the C.R.E. to make them usable again. Thousands of the things had been mapped within a couple of kilometers of the city boundary, though the vast majority connected levels one and two—getting down into three was a slightly different matter, and in this region it was very difficult get down to four, because there was no major cave-system directly below the city, and the regions of four hereabouts seemed pretty solid, as far as the C.R.E. had been able to establish.

Plugging the corridor was quick work; we sealed ourselves off in a chamber not much bigger than a starship cabin, where we had to jostle for the space to use the equipment. That made it economical to equalize the pressure and temperature, but it increased the likelihood of an accident with the cutting gear. Serne did most of the work—he was quick and neat, and when we were through, he brought the edges of the cut back together so cleverly that you'd have had to get very close indeed to see that anything had been done. We worked by torchlight; the corridor was unlit. We were in what had been a residential district when the cavies lived there, but it hadn't been colonized by the galactics. Out in the factory-fields the lights were on right around the clock, but this was as godforsaken a spot as the city had to offer.

We stripped off our suits and stowed them in the space between the plugs, where we left the equipment. Taking out the tubes—especially the drip-feed injectors—was messy and painful, and in a way it would have been more convenient and more comfortable to keep the suits on; but without them on there was every chance that we could pass for citizens if we were noticed by the new overlords of the city.

We dressed in clothes that we'd brought with us—nondescript khaki coveralls, loose enough to hide the mud guns which we were carrying, and brown boots. The boots were made from Tetron artificial organics, and I was glad to find that they were exceptionally comfortable, designed for human feet. I'd once tried to wear boots designed for Tetron feet, and found them impossible; I'd never seen a naked Tetron foot, but I deduced that they must have very peculiar toes.

When we were all properly dressed, we moved stealthily through the darkened corridor. We played the beam of a single torch along the ground ahead of us.

We'd hardly gone thirty meters before we were startled by sudden rustling sounds. We froze in our tracks.

"There's someone there!" exclaimed Scarion, before I could signal for silence. Serne and Vasari, of course, knew better than to open their mouths in such a situation.

The light failed to pick anything out as we hurried toward what seemed to be the source of the noise. The texture of the sound suggested that to me it was some kind of vermin. Starships are supposedly free from rats, but there are several races in the galactic community that choose to take other life-forms around with them—as pets, I guess. Skychain City had been around long enough to collect a feral population of catlike creatures, which made a living scavenging around the factory fields, skulking at other times in exactly those forgotten corners that had recommended themselves to our purpose.

Further on, we heard more sounds. Again we could see nothing, and I couldn't tell whether the sound was only some small animal scurrying away, or whether it was something—or someone—larger. It might have been a galactic refugee, who assumed we were the invaders.

I looked at Serne for a second opinion, but he just shrugged. There was no point in starting a chase. In the end, we moved on—we had work to do.

Finally, we came to the edge of the darkness, and I switched off the torch. We peered out of a covert at a vast sheet of organo-synthetic material, which looked like a plain of plastic grass, cut up into diamond-shaped sections by railways and walkways. The fifteen-meter ceiling was blazing with light.

Everything seemed to be working normally. Sections of supporting wall interrupted our view, but in between them we could see for several hundred meters. In the distance we could see one of the automated trains which transported the 'crops' ambling along its track, pausing occasionally to pick up cargo. There wasn't a humanoid being in sight.

Although we were carrying flimsies with messages in Tetron script, which we were to pass on to any apparently-trustworthy person, I wasn't at all dismayed by the absence of friendly natives. The longer we had to look around, the better.

"Any chance of hopping on a train?" asked Serne.

"Sure," I said, "but a train might carry us straight into trouble. We have two choices—we can set off on foot along the walkways, which might make us a little conspicuous, or we can go under the carpet, into the tunnels which cut through the thermosynthetic feedways. I favor the walkways—there are plenty of places to duck out of sight, as long as we see the opposition before they see us."

We began to make our way across the food-producing region, heading toward the center of the city, though we had no intention of getting too close. It wasn't long before we caught glimpses of other people. They were workers, servicing the automatic machinery. They looked like galactics—a couple were Zabarans—but I wasn't entirely prepared to take appearances for granted. We didn't know for certain that *all* the invaders looked like human beings. It had crossed my mind that maybe only the shock-troops were human, doing the dirty work for paymasters whose appearance we couldn't know.

We stayed out of sight until we reached a position from which we could see a roadway curving around the outer city limits. It was heavy with traffic—mostly automated transports, but with a number of military vehicles thrown in. We saw armored cars go past at irregular intervals, but whether they were patrols or part of some desultory troop-movement we could only guess.

We moved a little closer, and then, as we moved past a section of wall, we saw a single humanoid standing on a railway, checking the engine of a broken-down train. We studied him from hiding, and 74-Scarion identified him as a Ksylian. I'd seen the species before—brown-skinned and big-eared, with dark eyes that seemed to be forever mournful—but I didn't know much about them.

"You'd better let me approach him," said 74-Scarion. "He's certain to take you for invaders."

"Okay," I said. "Go ahead."

The Tetron moved from hiding and climbed up on to a walkway that took him across to the tracks on which the train ran. The moment the Ksylian saw him, he stopped work and looked furtively around. 74-Scarion talked to him for about fifteen minutes, while I bit my lip impatiently, and then he turned to beckon us over. There was no way to judge from the Ksylian's alien expression what his reaction was to the sight of us.

We were able to crouch down beside the train, so that we were virtually invisible to anyone else who might happen by, while a rapid exchange of information took place.

"He says that everything is quiet in the city," said 74-Scarion. "When the invasion first occurred there was momentary resistance, but the peace officers were ordered to surrender by their commanders, and the killing soon stopped. At first, the invaders brought all the galactics from their homes, lining them up in the streets, but then they allowed almost everyone to return to their ordinary work. They stopped the moving walkways, though, and closed down some of the city's other systems. He says that there must have been at least ten or twenty thousand of the invaders—an enormous force—involved in the initial attack. Since then, he thinks they may have moved another ten or twenty thousand up into the city, but I don't think we can rely on his judgment. They have taken over some of the living-accommodation, and he says that many of the citizens are now living three or four to a room.

"The language barrier was very difficult, he says. It still creates many problems. The aliens need him and others like him, because they don't understand the machines, but he's very uneasy about the fact that they can't tell him what they expect. He says that the invaders have not really managed to figure out who does what, and what kinds of work are essential to the running of the city. He says that they're stupid, and don't understand Tetron technology at all—the Tetrax apparently won't cooperate with them, and they're having great difficulty in keeping things going. He says that their own technology is very primitive."

That seemed puzzling. I'd been assuming that although they looked like Neanderthalers, these Asgardians must be at least as sophisticated as the Tetrax. If the Ksylian was right, it was sheer weight of numbers that had allowed the invaders to overwhelm the city, and now that they had it they didn't know how to run it.

"He thinks that the loss of life was greater than necessary," Scarion went on. "He has heard that thousands of people were shot, though he does not know how much rumor to trust. He says that many citizens, especially Tetrax, have been taken down into the lower levels—no one knows where. This exodus is continuing, although it would take years to transport the whole population of Skychain City. He thinks that the invaders would like to take over the city entirely, but that the galactics are indispensable because they know how things work. He says it doesn't much matter to him whether he works for the Tetrax or the invaders, but he's scared of the invaders."

"What sorts of equipment are they bringing up?" I asked, addressing my question direct to the Ksylian. His *parole* was oddly accented, but we had no difficulty understanding one another.

"Armored vehicles, many guns. They are working hard, trying to understand our machinery. They have many men learning *parole*, and are using many citizens as language teachers."

"Do they all look like me, or are there different races?"

"All those I have seen are your kind. I have heard, though, that they have other peoples working for them as slaves."

"Humanoid?"

"Yes, but I do not know which of the galactic races they resemble most. I have not seen any of these slaves—not knowingly."

"How easy is it to move about on the surface? Could we get up into the streets under the dome without being apprehended?"

"It is very difficult. They try to keep people off the streets. They issue passes, in their own writing—because no one understands their language, such passes are hard to forge."

"Would it be safe for us to use the telephones, or would they be able to monitor our calls?"

"I do not know. They are not clever with the Tetron communications systems, but they do have telephones of their own."

We had already figured that the phones were a bad risk.

"Is it safe for us to move around down here?"

The Ksylian shook his head, but I wasn't sure what the gesture meant in his terms. "Perhaps," he said, noncommittally. They allow the workers to do their jobs—they are desperate to maintain and improve food production. They have found out which food is best for them, and they are trying to produce more, but they do not know how. The Tetrax will not help them."

Most of the food produced in the factory-fields consisted of different varieties of 'manna'—compounds precisely matched to the nutritional requirements of particular groups of galactic humanoids. There were enough different kinds of humanoid in Skychain City to necessitate production of eight or ten brands. If appearances were anything to go by, the invaders would need my old brand, which had been produced in much less quantity than the brands preferred by the Tetrax—or, for that matter, the brands marketed for specialist carnivores like the vormyr or the brands designed for specialist vegetarians like sleaths.

"There's one way we might get a close look at the streets on the surface," said Serne.

"What's that?" I asked him.

"Stop an armored car, zap the guys inside, and steal their uniforms. Then we could drive around to our heart's content."

"It's a bit too melodramatic," I told him. "Maybe later."

"Please go now," said the Ksylian, obviously thinking that if we'd reached the stage when we could talk among ourselves, we could take ourselves off and stop making him nervous.

"Can you get a message to a Tetron on the surface?" I asked him. "Preferably a high-number man."

The Ksylian thought about it. I think he wanted to say no. But his first loyalty was still to the Tetrax, and he probably figured that there was an even chance that the Tetrax would one day be back in charge. When that time came, it would be a lot healthier to be the guy that had helped out than the guy who had refused.

"Perhaps," he said, shaking his head again.

74-Scarion produced the written text which we already had prepared. It was written in a Tetron language, so the Ksylian couldn't read it any more than the invaders would be able to. We figured that it was safe—the Ksylian could probably think up a dozen excuses for having an incomprehensible bit of paper in his possession, if he was asked. He had nothing to lose by trying to deliver it.

I couldn't read the paper either, but Tulyar had told us that it was an invitation to a rendezvous and a request for detailed information about the situation in the city. We were assuming that the Tetrax in Skychain City had continued to gather intelligence even though their ways of beaming information out had been blocked.

The Ksylian pocketed the paper, knowing that it was the price of being left alone.

We didn't want to put all our eggs in one basket, so we went on to make a couple of further contacts in much the same fashion. We didn't find out much more, save for a few items of hearsay that were blatantly untrustworthy, but we did get corroboration of the Ksylian's impressions. Everyone we spoke to was agreed that the invaders seemed to be technologically primitive, and that they were having one hell of a time trying to figure out how to take over the machinery that the Tetrax had used to run the city. We were told that the invaders were not pleased with the Tetrax, because of their unwillingness to help.

This information worried me. The Tetrax who'd briefed us must have suspected this, but hadn't mentioned it. I'd assumed that they were frightened of the invaders because of their probable technological supremacy, but now it looked as if they might be worried because their people were in the hands of reckless barbarians. I'd also assumed that the invasion was a response to my penetration of the lower levels, but there seemed to be no evidence of any connection between these invaders and the biotech-minded supermen who'd taken Myrlin in. Maybe the invaders were just the pawns—but if so, why hadn't the players come forth to help them with their technical difficulties?

We had too much work to do, though, to allow me to spend time pondering such questions. We handed out a couple more invitations for delivery to Tetrax in the city—one to a Zabaran, one to a Turkanian. We didn't see any Tetrax, nor did we get close enough to any invaders to be seen by them.

By the time we set off for home we figured that we could count the day a modest success. We'd spent about six hours in the paddy-fields—during which time we failed to find anything much that Serne, Vasari, and I cared to eat, though 74-Scarion picked up a couple of snacks.

Once we were on the way back we didn't expect that anything much would go wrong. I was already thinking ahead to the next danger point—when we turned up for the meeting we'd arranged, to see what transpired.

As I've observed before, though, plans have a terrible tendency to go wrong.

When we got back to the broken seal through which we'd entered, two of the four cold-suits had vanished.

CHAPTER TWELVE

It didn't take a genius to work out what must have happened.

We'd even heard someone moving around as we came out, and I cursed myself now for having let it go so easily. I looked at Serne, and could almost hear him thinking that we ought to have left a guard. It was all too obvious now, but at the time I hadn't thought about it, and he hadn't made the suggestion.

So much for the value of Star Force training.

"A lone scavenger," I said, bitterly, "hiding out from the invasion."

"Surely there must have been two," said Scarion. "There are two suits gone."

"No," I said. "If there'd been two, we'd have lost the lot. He's taken a cutting-tool as well as the suits—that would be about the limit of what one man could carry."

In a way, we had been lucky—if the scavenger had been cleverer, he'd have stashed the two suits and the tool in some hidey-hole of his own, and then come back for the rest. Maybe he simply hadn't had that much nerve. In all probability, he'd gleefully made his grab and then set off into the distance, making sure that he was as far away as possible from the scene of the crime when we got back.

I realized, though, that his intemperate exit didn't necessarily mean that he wouldn't come back for the rest. It just meant that he wouldn't come back alone.

It was bad enough to find that our doorway to the city was useless. We also had to face the fact that it might now become a magnet drawing all the undesirables in the vicinity.

With two suits left and further trouble in store, our options were limited. We could pick up the rest of our gear and move on, trying to find a safer exit-point, but that seemed rather pointless. It looked to me that we had to split up. Two of us would have to remain in the city, cut off from our base, while the other two took the sad tale back to the colonel and 994-Tulyar.

"What use are the cold suits to him?" complained 74-Scarion. "Unless he belongs to a species closely related to yours or mine, the drip-feed won't be adjusted to his metabolism." On investigation, we had found that 74-Scarion's was one of the suits that had been taken.

The other was mine.

"He might not find it entirely satisfactory," I answered, "but it would keep him alive long enough to make a trip through the levels, if that's what he wants. Any humanoid could get by using your suit or mine for a couple of days. But I don't think he's going to use either suit himself. I think he's got the black market in mind. The stupid thing is that he'll sell the damn things to someone on our side—someone who desperately wants to get information out of the city to one of the C.R.E. bubbles, in the hope that it can then be transmitted to the Tetrax in orbit. If the buyer realizes where he got the suits from...."

"It's not so bad," said Serne. "We have spare suits back at base. Do you want to take my suit? You could have the spares back here in a couple of hours. I'll be safe here for as long as it takes."

"No," I said. "You and Vasari go. But don't come back here—it's too dangerous. The Turkanian will have to guide you to the second of our planned entry points. Scarion and I will go directly there, on the inside—it's on this level and it's no more than ten kilometers away. We'll meet you there at...damn this idiotic City time...at 25.00 tomorrow."

Serne frowned. "We don't know that the second point is any safer than this one," he pointed out.

He was right—we didn't.

"Sometimes," I reminded him, "you just have to guess. Anyhow, with only the mud guns to protect us, we're not really in a position to defend ourselves here. Better to get out. We've spent all day out there, and it's reasonably safe. I'd rather be under the lights than waiting here like rats in a trap."

He still didn't like it, but he conceded the point. While he and Vasari suited up, 74-Scarion and I came back to the city side of the old plug, so that Serne and Vasari could reseal it before opening up the outer one.

"Perhaps you should have gone," said the Tetron. "The sergeant's suit would have fitted you well enough."

"I have a feeling," I told him, "that a star-captain is expected to stay with his sinking mission. It's probably the Star Force way."

I was being sarcastic, of course, but the Tetron thought it a perfect answer. "I understand," he said. Matters of duty and obligation were things that low-status Tetrax understood only too well.

There was a rustling sound close at hand, and when I flashed the torch round the beam caught some furry thing scampering away, illuminating it for a fraction of a second. I let out my breath, slowly.

"Let's get out of the tunnels," I said. "I'll feel better when we're back in the light."

We moved back along the dark corridor, quickly but cautiously.

But we were already too late.

When we got back to the place where the corridor let us out into the fields, and took a look outside, the first thing we saw was a group of humanoids hastening toward us.

"*Merde!*" I said, with feeling.

One glance was enough to tell me that it couldn't be much worse. There were three vormyr and three Spirellans, looking as ugly and as vicious as all their kind, and I had more than a suspicion that our chances of recruiting them to the noble fight against the alien invaders were not good. Clearly, the bastard who'd lifted our cold-suits had made his contact.

74-Scarion and I backed off a short way into the corridor. I wondered whether we had any chance of hiding out, but I didn't like the idea. These scavengers might know the territory, and as soon as they found the rest of our gear gone they'd be after us. Vormyr are said to have good low-light vision, and I didn't fancy playing hide-and-seek with them. Our only possible advantage was the fact that they couldn't know we were back yet. We had a chance to surprise them.

I wished that I had Serne or Vasari with me. They were combat soldiers, who could probably have taken out this gang comfortably. 74-Scarion was a Tetron immigration officer, and fighting was definitely not his line.

"Got to try the ambush," I told him.

He nodded, uneasily.

We waited, mud guns at the ready. I felt anything but confident. My quick glance had told me that one of the vormyr had a needle-gun, and it would be lunatic optimism to suppose that any of the six might be weaponless.

To make things worse, I had a dreadful suspicion that they might know who I was. Amara Guur wasn't the kind of man who had friends, but the vormyr notion of vendetta wasn't based on friendship. If they did recognize me, they'd be all the more enthusiastic to tear my head off.

"Take out the three vormyr first," I whispered to 74-Scarion. "Spirellans are dangerous, but vormyr are worse."

He nodded to show me that he understood.

As soon as they came around the corner, while they were still silhouetted against the light, I let fly at the one whose needler I'd seen. I kept my finger down on the firing-stud of the gun, hoping to spray the knockout juice over as many of them as possible. 74-Scarion seemed to be firing even faster, with panic-driven wildness.

The trouble with a mud gun is that its effects aren't usually instantaneous. I'd shot John Finn in the open mouth, and even he'd crumpled up slowly. It was the shock rather than the anesthetic which had stopped him from firing back while his presence of mind remained.

These guys had very good reflexes, and some of the shots had to soak through clothing. Having just come in from the bright light they were virtually blind, but they didn't need to see in order to react. The one with the needler was hit clean, and didn't manage to fire it—although he did draw it. One of the Spirellans hauled out an old-fashioned pistol, but he didn't manage to get the hammer back before crumpling at the knees. The others, alas, had knives—and they were very quick to lash out with the blades.

A vormyran dived at me, and I brought my boot up very sharply into his midriff, then smacked him sideways with the edge of my left hand. The Spirellan behind him nearly got me, but his thrust went past me into the wall as he tripped over the vormyran. I only had to hit him once before an eyeful of mud put him out.

But I was lucky. It could easily have gone the other way.

74-Scarion wasn't so lucky.

When everyone had gone down, I stopped firing, though my gun was already empty. Scarion was down along with the nasties, and my hope that he'd simply been caught by a little stray mud died almost immediately.

I had to untangle him from a fallen vormyran, and when I kicked the body off him I found that he was bleeding to death from a stab-wound in the chest. He tried to speak, but the blade had ripped his lung, and all he could do was cough up blood. There was nothing I could do to help him, and he died within a minute.

I prized the gun gently from his leathery fingers—it still had a small charge left in it. I put it inside my shirt, and threw my own away.

Then I turned my attention to the six scavengers. They were all unconscious. I stirred them with my boot, not wanting to risk wetting my hands with any mud that might be clinging to their clothing. I picked up the needler and the pistol, gingerly.

I knew that it would be reckless simply to walk away. The logical thing to do would be to pump them full of needles, then drag their bodies further into the dark, so that the vermin could help themselves to a nice square meal. Serne wouldn't have hesitated for a moment, and neither would Susarma Lear. After all, there had to be some sort of chance that I'd run into these beauties again, and they weren't going to say "thank you"— they'd kill me as soon as look at me.

But I couldn't do it. I couldn't just kill them as they lay there. I cursed myself for being a squeamish fool, and I certainly didn't take any satisfaction from my reluctance. I knew that I was a disgrace to my Star Force uniform.

I took the needler and the pistol with me, and left them all to sleep it off.

The brief brutal encounter left me feeling weak at the knees, and I couldn't get the image of Scarion's blood-gushing torso out of my mind. I was glad I hadn't had anything to eat for a long time. I was feeling sick enough, though I knew I wasn't actually going to vomit.

While I walked swiftly along a catwalk we'd crossed earlier, the queasiness gradually changed into a raging thirst, and I had to stick my face into one of the irrigation channels feeding the artificial fields, to suck up some mineral-loaded water. That cleared my head a little, and reminded me that the scavengers weren't the only danger I had to keep in mind. It wouldn't do to forget the invaders.

I ducked down into a ditch at the edge of one of the fields, trying to get everything straight inside my mind. I tried to fix my attention on the memory of the city maps which Tulyar and I had spent so much time poring over.

The place that we'd selected as the second-best site for breaking in was—as I'd told Serne—less than ten kilometers away. I could walk it in a matter of hours, and I was reasonably certain that I could find the exact spot, even in the darkness. With luck, it would be easy—but it would be stupid to be over-confident. If there were scavengers here, there might be scavengers there too—there was no way to know how many people had run from the invaders into the darker corners of the city. In the meantime, I had to stay away from invaders.

I set out again in a more sensible frame of mind, to walk to the place where I'd arranged to meet Serne.

My temper was bad, and it got worse while I silently cursed my luck, asking myself what I could possibly have done to deserve such evil treatment at the cruel hands of fate. The last shreds of my earlier optimism were gone, and I now expected things to get even worse.

Like most of my more doleful expectations, this one turned out to be right.

CHAPTER THIRTEEN

The second place which we'd marked out in advance as a likely point of entry to the city's subterranean regions was very much like the first. It was a sealed-off tunnel in a maze of corridors at the edge of a field-system.

The Tetrax had reclaimed these fields just as they'd reclaimed the ones close to our first entry-point; they'd built their own system on the skeleton of the one the cavies had left behind, but they'd never found any use for the living quarters on the edge, and had left them derelict, without installing lights. By our reckoning, those corridors should have been just as deserted now as they had been for countless years.

But they weren't—the invaders had moved in to occupy them.

I could see from some way off that the walkways and railways in this area were swarming with uniformed neo-Neanderthalers. I went down into the cramped tunnels underneath the photosynthetic carpets, where the stuff they were producing was harvested, and found invaders thick on the ground there too. After sniffing around for a while, edging in as close as I dared without running any real risk of giving myself away, I realized why.

This was one corner of the field-system—maybe the only corner—where the Tetrax had been producing the kind of manna that was best fitted to the human diet. Humans weren't the only species on Asgard who thrived on that version of the one-item diet. Kythnans, who look very like us, ate it too. Many other races, though, found it unpalatable, and in general each species preferred the flavors and textures that were routinely applied to their own kinds of manna.

Our Ksylian informant had told us that the invaders were having trouble with food production. If this was the place that produced the food that suited them best, then of course they would congregate here, trying to figure out how to turn other parts of the system over to the production of human-brand manna.

I guessed that the invaders had one hell of a problem getting food to their troops. Their route up from the levels where they lived was probably tortuous, and their elevator shafts would be overburdened shipping large amounts of food as well as armored vehicles and men. If they wanted to secure their hold on Skychain City and run it efficiently, they would have to produce food locally. It would be a matter of urgent necessity for them to understand both the Tetron biotechnics that were in use hereabouts, and the control-systems governing the transportation and distribution of the manna. A handful of automated trains chugging gently back and forth to the areas beneath the big singlestacks that were the heart of Skychain City's residential district had undoubtedly been sufficient to carry food for a couple of hundred humans, five hundred Kythnans, and a few assorted extras. But the invaders wanted to move in tens of thousands of men, and everyone knows that an army marches on its stomach.

I saw a few Tetrax with the invaders, going around under escort. Their hosts seemed to be trying hard to communicate with them—which suggested that the language lessons were beginning to bear fruit and that at least some of the invaders could communicate in *parole*. What I knew of the Tetrax, though, suggested that those problems in communication would not be easily solved. As the old saying has it, you can drive a horse to water but you can't make him drink. You can learn to talk to a Tetron, but you can't necessarily make him understand. I would have laid odds that the Tetrax were being as polite and seemingly helpful as they could be, without ever getting close to telling their captors what it was they wanted to know.

The more I watched the invaders, and the more I saw of their own technology, the more obvious it became that the Ksylian had been right in telling us how primitive they were. Because they were so nearly human in appearance it was easy to look at them as if they were people out of our own past, and everything told me that they weren't even as sophisticated as contemporary humans. They might have marched out of our twentieth century—the twenty-first at the very latest. A battalion of Star Force troopers with standard equipment could have made mincemeat of a force of neo-Neanderthalers three or four times their number.

That calculation disturbed me. It was easy enough to understand how a barbarian army with the advantage of surprise could overrun Skychain City, which had no defenses to speak of and only a small corps of peace officers, but I couldn't see how an army such as this could possibly hold on to the city if the Tetrax were to organize a properly-planned rebellion. I began to wonder whether our commission to open up lines of communication was simply a way to set up a route by which weapons—maybe chemical or biological weapons—could be shipped into the city to support an armed insurrection.

If that were the case, there was no particular cause for surprise in the fact that the Tetrax hadn't mentioned it to us. I couldn't help being suspicious, though, about the way they had let us believe that the invaders were much more sophisticated than they had turned out to be. They must have known the true situation, given that they had continued to receive intelligence from the city for some time after the invasion. There was something about the way this whole operation had been set up which just wasn't right. There was a distinct ratlike odor about it all.

I found a hiding place behind a stack of empty crates in a gigantic "warehouse" beneath the carpet. It seemed a useful place to be because food was being stored here, and I was getting pretty hungry. Unfortunately, it looked as if it would be difficult for me to get my hands on any, because the place was so busy. At one end of the open space was the terminus where the trains came to load up, and there was a big computer console nearby from which the routing of the trains could be controlled. It was only a tiny substation—the main control center for the entire field-system was thirty kilometers away—but a system that large needs a good many entry-points for information and minor control-points for exactly the same reason that a nervous system needs bundles of sensory cells and ganglia. I wasn't at all surprised to see a party of uniformed invaders in front of the screens, deep in conversation with a couple of galactics.

The galactics were both Kythnans. Ninety percent of the galactic races claim not to be able to tell humans and Kythnans apart, although neither humans nor Kythnans have much difficulty. Almost the first thing I was told by a fellow human when I first arrived on Asgard was that the fact that Kythnans looked like us was no reason to start trusting them. Maybe Kythnans told each other the same thing about humans.

Anyhow, my own experience with Kythnans hadn't prejudiced me in their favor—the last one I'd come into contact with was Jacinthe Siani, who had worked for Amara Guur. Given this, I was quite ready to jump to the conclusion that the Kythnans were probably being a lot more obliging in their dealings with the invaders than the Tetrax.

After a little while of watching the group by the control panels in deep discussion, I guessed that the co-operation the neo-Neanderthalers were getting from the Kythnans wasn't doing them much good. The Kythnans probably didn't understand Tetron technology much better than the invaders. They would have learned how to operate the systems up on the surface that were useful in everyday life, but this would be a new world to them.

I was trying to get closer, in order to overhear what was being said, when another group joined the party. There were two more invaders, in the fancier uniforms which I took to be those of officers, and what I first assumed to be an invader in civilian clothes. It wasn't until I caught a snatch of conversation in *parole* that I realized he was human. I didn't recognize him, but I wasn't acquainted with more than half of the two hundred and fifty of the humans on Asgard, so that wasn't too surprising.

The sight of the human gave my spirits the first uplift they'd had in some time. I hoped, paradoxically, that he would turn out to be a full-blown collaborator and a dyed-in-the-wool traitor to the galactic cause—because if he were, he might have the freedom to walk around on his own, and that meant that I might be able to walk where I wanted to without being seized or shot on sight.

As I strained my ears to catch some of the conversation, though, my enthusiasm dwindled somewhat. The human didn't seem to be in a helpful mood, and what he was trying to tell his interlocutors, not very politely, was that he was a starship pilot, not a biotech engineer, and that he didn't know the first thing about manufacturing manna.

There was an exchange of words between the newcomers and the group that was already there. Then they moved away from me, to the beginning of the underground tracks. There was a passenger-car already attached to the train that was waiting there, and the invaders put the Kythnans and the human aboard, along with half a dozen guards. The two officers who'd come in with the human stayed behind.

I watched them walk back to the console. They seemed to be arguing. I inferred that they couldn't find anyone who could or would tell them how to do what they wanted, and that they were getting very impatient about it. In the meantime, they were afraid to tamper with the computers for fear of accidentally shutting down the entire operation, or otherwise messing things up. So far, it seemed, they'd mastered the manual controls on the trains, and that was about it.

It isn't easy, taking over a highly-automated city, when you don't understand the language or the machines. On the other hand, these guys seemed to have made virtually no progress at all in months of occupation. Stupid, the Ksylian had said. It was easy to see why he thought so. I wondered, though, whether I could have done much to help them myself, if I was actually trying to. You get used to taking technology very much for granted, especially when there's always a Tetron repairman at the other end of the phone. The horrible thought struck me that given his interest in certain kinds of electronic systems, a man like John Finn might have been much more use to the invaders than me.

I looked at my wristwatch, and was dismayed to discover that time had been passing more quickly than I thought. It was 22.50, and my hastily-arranged rendezvous with Serne was not much more than half a human hour away. Was there a chance, I wondered, that I could still make it, and get out of the city without being taken prisoner?

I was seized by a terrible temptation to try something desperately reckless. I had just enough charge left in Scarion's mud gun to drop both the officers.

In an invader uniform, I thought, *I just might be able to walk straight through the crowds and into the corridors.*

There was every chance that the section of tunnel leading to the plug was still dark and unused—or so, at least, I persuaded myself. And I had a golden opportunity here to create something of a diversion. Like the luckless human they'd been questioning, I was no biotech engineer, but it's a lot easier to sabotage an automated system than it is to make it work as you want it to. Like John Finn on *Goodfellow*, I thought I could create a little emergency.

I suppose my commission had finally soaked into my personality; I was thinking like a Star Force commando. Anyhow, I was getting rather tired of discretion. I've always had a submerged reckless streak. If I hadn't, I never would have come to Asgard in the first place.

The two officers were too deep in discussion to see me coming, until one glimpsed me out of the corner of his eye. By then, it was too late; I had two clear shots at their naked faces. One yelped as the stuff hit him in the eye, and they both tried to haul their sidearms out, but they crumpled slowly to their knees as their nervous systems gave up the ghost.

I went to the console first, and studied the keyboards and the displays on the screens. I managed to conjure up a system-map with lights to indicate the positions of the trains both underground and on top. I knew better than to try to arrange a real crash; what I wanted to do was convince the system that something awful had happened, to get each and every one of its emergency systems going.

I typed in a mayday message, and told the machine there was a blocked tunnel just in front of one of the moving trains. The tell-tale light stopped moving, and I knew that the machines had slammed the brakes on. Then I told the system that there was a fire under the surface, that lives were endangered. It wouldn't necessarily believe me—it had its own smoke detectors—but the system wasn't rigged to take risks, and it would take appropriate action pending a check.

Somewhere in the distance alarm bells were beginning to ring.

I tried to think of something else—a crack opening into the cold on level two...a medical emergency involving some workers. But I was already glancing round fearfully at the main body of the warehouse. There were three or four doorways where people were only too likely to appear at any moment.

I decided that there wasn't time for further subtlety. I took out the needler that I'd borrowed from one of Scarion's killers, stood well back to avoid the danger of ricochets, and held down the firing stud. I sprayed the slivers of metal all around the console—keyboards, screens, junction-boxes.

The systems believed *that* emergency, all right. Alarm bells began ringing all around me now, setting up a terrible clamor. Quickly, I dragged one of the officers behind the crates, to buy me an extra couple of minutes when the crowds began to arrive, and stripped off his jacket and trousers. It was more difficult than I had expected, because he was a dead weight and an awkward shape. By the time I was able to start pulling the garments on—without bothering to remove my own first—people did start arriving, over by the tracks and from the farther region of the warehouse as well. I left all the weapons behind except the stricken man's sidearm, and walked out of hiding with a purposeful stride. There were soldiers everywhere, plus a couple of neo-Neanderthal civilians and a handful of galactics. I just walked to the side door and went out. Nobody said a word, and I doubt that they even saw me—all their attention was focused on the wrecked console and the unconscious officer.

Up on top, no one had a clue what was happening. There were people running along the walkways in several different directions. I didn't want to be left out, so I ran too. The only difference was that I knew where I was going. I got out of the fields and into the corridors that crisscrossed the solid mass which was holding up the topmost of all Asgard's layers. I ran purposefully past dozens of invader troopers, trying my very best to look like a man with an urgent mission, who must at all costs not be interrupted.

It worked like a dream for fully nine-tenths of the distance I had to cover, but then—in a corridor far too narrow to allow me to pass—I ran into a whole bunch of the enemy, including two men with such fancy decoration on their torsos that they had to outrank the poor sap whose uniform I'd stolen.

One of them—a big, bald man—barked an order at me. I don't know what he said, but all I could do was stop and look foolish. There was nowhere to go—I couldn't get past and as I half-turned, the man in charge barked again. I was grabbed, and pulled forward.

I could tell by the way he stared that the bald man had jumped to the right conclusion. My brow-ridges obviously weren't prominent enough, given my inability to respond in any way whatsoever to his challenge. It probably helped that he'd been shipping humans down here to try and help his own boys out. He was quick to conclude that I was a member of the species *Homo sapiens*.

I had been feeling very good about my boldness until that

moment—high on my own adrenalin, and pleased to take credit for my brilliance. Now, all of a sudden, I began to feel nauseous and extremely foolish.

The guns came out, and suddenly I was in the middle of a very hostile crowd. I stuck my empty hands up into the air, hoping fervently that they could recognize the symbolism of surrender. I let them take the sidearm from my belt, having made no attempt to reach it myself.

There was nothing very gentle about the way they hustled me along. Stupid they might be, but they could put two and two together well enough to figure out who was responsible for all the alarms that were ringing. They had no way of knowing where I'd been headed, so Serne should be safe enough, but I was going to be treated as a saboteur.

I wondered, as they hustled me along, what they did to saboteurs. On good old Earth, I remembered, they used to shoot them.

CHAPTER FOURTEEN

Eventually, having removed my stolen uniform, they threw me into an ill-lit room with a table and a couple of chairs. They hadn't handled me too roughly—somewhere along the line, I guess, they'd found out that I hadn't killed the man from whom I'd taken the uniform. They searched me, but I wasn't carrying anything to give them a clue as to who I was or where I'd come from.

The questions finally began after an hour or so. I couldn't tell whether the temporary chaos that I'd caused was still giving them trouble. A Tetron system wouldn't have gone down in its entirety because of such a brutal assault, but I assumed that the Tetrax wouldn't be keen to assist their unwelcome guests in the vexing task of putting Humpty Dumpty back together again. I knew that I would still be very unpopular, especially as I had struck at what they must consider a vital target.

Two men came in to do the interrogation—not because they intended to play Mutt and Jeff, but because the one guy who could speak *parole* had to report everything back to the other, who didn't. I didn't mind that—it slowed things up. Despite the fact that the interrogation had to be conducted at a leisurely pace, though, the atmosphere was far from relaxed.

They obviously weren't above a bit of calculated drama. Before they began, they threw the empty mud gun on the table, to show me that their clever little minds had at least taken step one in figuring out who I was, what I'd done, and to whom.

"What is your name?" asked the *parole*-speaker. He was

about my age and height, with pale skin, very blond hair, and weak blue eyes. His companion was older, with white hair, but his eyes were a darker blue. I'd never seen Earth's sea or its sky except on video, but I began thinking of them nevertheless as the man with sea-blue eyes and the man with sky-blue eyes. Otherwise, they might have been brothers.

"Jack Martin," I replied, almost without thinking.

"And where do you live?"

"I used to live in a singlestack in the third sector, but I haven't been home in a while."

"Where *have* you been?"

"Down here. I figured after the tanks rolled in that I'd hide out."

They both looked at me solemnly, but they didn't immediately call me a liar.

"What is your job?" asked sky-blue.

"I used to be a scavenger—I used to go down into levels three and four, hunting for artifacts. The bottom seems to have dropped out of the market, though. I don't suppose you'll be maintaining the Coordinated Research Establishment now you're in charge."

As the blond man relayed this to his companion, they both remained very poker-faced. I didn't know whether they could understand sarcasm. Almost all humanoid races have some such concept, but it's difficult even for two humans from different cultural backgrounds to be sure when they meet it. Sea-blue took some flimsies from his pocket, and the two of them scanned the pages for a minute or two. I practiced staying calm, reminding myself that the Star Force way was to maintain grace under pressure.

"Are you a human?" was the next question.

"Yes," I replied.

"Your race is very like ours," said Sky-blue, "but I am told that you come from a world very distant from here."

"About a thousand light-years," I told him. I didn't suppose the term 'light-year' would mean a lot to him, given that his kind must have had a very different idea of what the universe was like, but he didn't query it. He must have heard it before.

"We have drawn up a list of all humans known to be resident in the city. There is no Jack Martin on the list."

I met his eye steadily. "Nobody knows how many humans there are in the city, and nobody knows all their names. Scavengers come and go."

Actually, the Tetrax probably knew exactly how many humans there were in Skychain City, and all their names, but I had to gamble that the invaders hadn't been given free access to Immigration Control's data. They didn't press the point. I began to feel more in control of the situation, though they were still frowning with displeasure.

"Why did you steal the uniform and destroy the computer?"

"I wanted to get into your stores here, and I had to create a diversion. I needed food, weapons, clothing. I was getting desperate. It's not easy, living wild out there. A lot of the other people running around are pretty nasty characters—vormyr, Spirellans, and the like. I take it you've met the vormyr?"

They had a brief conference about that.

"Are there many others...living wild, as you put it?" asked the man with paler eyes.

"Hundreds, probably. The city sprawls over a big area down here, and there are many dark regions where the Tetrax hadn't really got anything going. Plenty of places to hide."

"Is that where the resistance to our occupation has its head-quarters? Where sabotage is planned?"

"I doubt it," I said, calmly. "I steer clear of other races. There's a grave danger of being mistaken for one of you. They'd probably be just as enthusiastic to kill me as you are."

After another brief exchange between themselves, they turned to stare balefully at me again. "We do indeed shoot sabo-teurs, Mr. Martin," said the man with pale eyes. "In the past, we have treated members of your race generously. We believed—perhaps wrongly—that because your species is so very like our own, we might easily develop a sense of kinship. We have been told that the Tetrax are oppressive rulers, and that your species has no reason to feel loyalty to them. In spite of these assurances, humans have given us little real help—and now we find you trying to destroy the trains which carry our food. Can you give us one good reason why we should not execute you?"

It was nice to be given the chance, but I wasn't entirely sure that I could.

"You came into the city shooting in all directions," I told him. "I've heard rumors that you're shipping people away to some kind of concentration camp way down below. Sure I hid out. If I'd been sure that you'd treat me well if I was useful to you, maybe I would have volunteered—but how could I be sure? I thought I'd try to make it on my own, at least for a while, and see how things turned out. I was doing what any one of you would have done in my situation. But if there *is* any help I can give you, I'd naturally prefer that to being shot."

As I said it, I couldn't help feeling that it was a weaker argument than I'd have liked to produce. But it was all that a Jack Martin could reasonably be expected to produce.

"Were you hiding in the hope that the Tetrax would launch some kind of counter-invasion?" asked my interlocutor.

"Not really," I replied, laconically. "The Tetrax aren't the type. They'll try to talk you into being friends with them, and they'll probably succeed. They talk everybody into being friends, in the end."

"Do *you* have many friends among the Tetrax?"

"I don't have many friends at all. I'm not a friendly person."

I was trying to put on a show of being harmless and utterly insignificant, although I didn't want them to be entirely convinced. It might have been the wrong tack—perhaps I should have been trying to worm my way into their affections by telling them how much I could do for them, but my reasoning was that it might only make them suspicious. I wanted them to make me some kind of offer. I had a suspicion they might, on account of what I'd seen in the warehouse. They were obviously shopping for collaborators among the races who looked most like them—exhibiting a kind of chauvinism that the Tetrax would undoubtedly have considered barbaric. I wondered what that implied about the variety of races in the levels below.

Meanwhile, Sky-blue and Sea-blue were having a another conference. They didn't seem to be entirely in harmony. From what little I'd seen, the invaders certainly seemed to be a quarrelsome lot.

"This gun is of human manufacture?" asked Sky-blue, when the quiet row was over.

"That's right," I said.

"It does not kill."

"It doesn't kill people with our kind of metabolism. Some of the more peculiar races react badly to the anesthetic."

"Although you did not kill the officers you shot," said the blond-haired man, carefully, "you are still guilty of a crime which carries the death-penalty. Under our law, I should have you shot."

I was grateful to note the word 'should'.

"Well," I said, with the air of one determined to be brave at all costs, "it was difficult to see much future anyway. I knew the risk I was taking. *C'est la vie.*" The last, of course, I said in French. He asked me to explain it, and I did. When he reported back to his companion, I thought the white-haired man seemed to be impressed by my fatalism. I began to congratulate myself, unobtrusively, on having laid down some good bait. I daren't get too confident, though—there was always a chance that they'd take me at my word and shoot me.

The man with the darker eyes delivered quite a long speech in his native language, while his companion just nodded and made affirmative grunts. Then Sky-blue turned to me, and said: "This is a very strange place to us, with many strange people. We understand that your invasion of our world was carried out in ignorance, and we have been restrained in trying to repel it. The Tetrax and all the other races from the star-worlds must accept, though, that Asgard—as you call it—is *ours*, and that we are prepared to defend it. We intend to establish friendly relations with the races of the galaxy, if we can. We will need assistance in order to do this. Although you have committed a crime against us, we are prepared to be lenient. If you cooperate with us to the full, you will not be shot. But I warn you that we expect you to help us to the best of your ability, in order to cancel out your evil actions. Do you agree?"

"Why not?" I said, lightly. "Certainly I agree."

"Do you know how to repair the damage that you have done?"

"Not entirely," I said. "But I've been using Tetron technics routinely for several years, and I'm not stupid. I can help you get to grips with the city and its systems, and I know the Tetrax well enough to help you deal with them."

"We are already finding ways to make the Tetrax tell us what we need to know," he said, in tight-lipped fashion. I guessed that to mean that they were sick of being gentle and were adopting more violent means of interrogation. The Tetrax feel pain like everyone else, and it could only be a matter of time before the invaders began to get on top of the situation here. I wondered if the Tetrax planned to react to save their people from being maimed or executed, or whether their notion of the individual's duty to his fellows was powerful enough to let them sit back and continue to attempt to make friendly contact through diplomatic channels. I didn't know the answer.

"The first thing we require of you," said the man with blond hair, "is that you should answer many more questions that we have. We are confronting a situation which is new to us. Nothing in our previous experience prepared us for what we have found in this city, and what we now know to exist beyond the dome. We know that we have much to learn, and there is much that you can teach us. But I warn you that our patience is now worn thin. We do not care very much whether you live or die, and if we find that you are not helping us to the very best of your ability, we will shoot you. We have many other people to help us, and the more we learn from them, the less useful you will become. Do you understand that?"

"I understand," I said, flatly. "But I answer questions better when I'm not so hungry."

He wasn't entirely pleased by the tone of my voice, but his displeasure was tempered by understanding, and I thought I'd just about won my case.

"You are hungry, and would like to eat?"

"Yes I am," I told him. It was perhaps the first entirely honest thing I had said.

"Then I will take you to a place where we can eat. There you will meet some of the other people who are helping us. Afterwards, you will begin the work of repaying us for our generosity."

The man with sky-blue eyes stood up, and spoke for a couple of minutes to the white-haired man, who remained seated. Then, having apparently obtained approval for his proposals, he gestured to indicate that I should precede him to the door.

When I opened it, I found myself looking down the guns of a couple of guards, and I stood back to let my inquisitor pass. He spoke to them, and they relaxed, but they didn't put the guns away. They fell into step behind us as we went along the corridor.

The electric lighting system the invaders had rigged up here was makeshift, and the light was much yellower than the brilliant white favored by the Tetrax. I looked up at the bulbs strung on a cable pinned to the ceiling, and the man with sky-blue eyes took it as a criticism.

"It is very poor," he admitted. "But these are the disconnected levels, where we cannot use the power-systems left to us by our ancestors. Very regrettable. You will find things very different closer to the Center, where the ancestors' power is the motor of our civilization."

I would have liked to continue that conversation, because there were at least as many questions that I wanted to ask him as he wanted to ask me, but we were already arriving at a larger room kitted out as a refectory, with a dozen long tables and hundreds of folding chairs. It was very noisy—the room was full of invader troopers. I guessed that they must be eating in shifts. Hot food was being dished out from big tureens—flavored manna with a few trimmings, which presumably made it seem a little more like the stuff their mothers used to cook for them.

The odor of the food made my mouth water furiously. Tetron cuisine never had that effect on me, even when I was pretty hungry, and it seemed grounds for concluding that the invaders really did have a great deal in common, both physically and biochemically, with my own kind. I hadn't had a decent meal since leaving *Leopard Shark*, and although a cold-suit will feed you, it can't satisfy your aesthetic sensibilities. I could feel my stomach muscles churning in anticipation, though I knew I'd have to take it easy until I got back into the habit of eating.

The crowd was so big, and my mind was so preoccupied, that although I saw the group of Kythnans sitting at one of the tables I didn't really pay them much attention until one of them suddenly stood up. She stared at me, and I looked at her dazedly, not really knowing what was happening until the accusing finger was pointed. She took the man with the sky-blue eyes by the elbow, and guided him away from me, talking furiously into his ear in a low voice.

I just stood still, knowing that there was nothing else I could do. The muzzles of the guards' guns swung once again to point at my chest, and I knew that yet again my luck had turned completely, and gone to the bad.

The Kythnan woman was Jacinthe Siani—a ready-made collaborator if ever there was one—and she knew only too well who I really was. She might also know that I'd left Asgard before the invasion, and that my presence here now was a real twenty-four carat surprise.

The sky-blue eyes no longer seemed weak as they fixed me with an astonished gaze when the hurried whispering was over. They seemed very, very hard.

"Well, Mr. Rousseau," said Jacinthe Siani, vindictively. "This time, it seems, my evidence hasn't acquitted you."

"No need to be so smug about it," I told her, with as much

bravado as I could muster. "I don't think I can give you much of a character reference, either."

But I couldn't conceal the fact that I was very frightened indeed. All that trust I had carefully built up was smashed to smithereens, and it now looked odds on that I was scheduled to be shot—or worse.

CHAPTER FIFTEEN

This time, there was more urgency about the way I was manhandled. Surprisingly enough, though, they didn't march me back outside again. They took me to a corner of the room, sat me down, and gave me the food they'd promised. But Sky-blue didn't sit down to eat with me—he went buzzing off like a startled hornet, with Jacinthe Siani in tow. The guards watched me eat; the fact that they didn't relax suggested that they'd had stern orders to look after me very carefully.

Long before I'd finished, Sea-blue was back again, and so was an even older, smaller man with brow-ridges that looked big even on an invader. This one looked to be a real top man. I carried on eating while they discussed the situation, because I figured that if I was going to die, I might as well do it on a full stomach. My appetite wasn't very powerful, though, and I hadn't finished when they indicated that it was time to go.

I was rushed through the corridors and into the open, where there was a passenger car waiting on the nearest section of track. I was shoved in, unkindly. Sky-blue, the old man and Jacinthe Siani followed, plus a couple of troopers.

As we got under way, I said to the man with pale blue eyes: "Wouldn't it be easier to shoot me right here?"

"We are not going to shoot you, Mr. Rousseau," he said. "You have far too much information which would be valuable to us. But we can only assume that you are a spy, and hostile to our people."

That sounded ominously like a threat of torture.

"I came back because the Tetrax asked me to come," I told him, quickly "but I'm an ambassador as much as a spy. The Tetrax are very keen to open up a dialogue. They want to make friends, and they don't understand why you won't respond to their signals. When we get up to the surface, I'll be more than happy to act as an intermediary, if you wish."

"We are not going to the surface, Mr. Rousseau," he told me. "We are going in the opposite direction. And we have no desire to hurry in making contact with anyone outside Asgard. There will be all the time in the world to deal with the Tetrax, when we are ready. At the moment, much more pressing matters concern us. What you can tell us will be most interesting—and you *will* tell us everything that you know."

By this time I was getting used to being interesting. It seemed that everyone in the universe was keen to talk to Michael Rousseau, and were exceedingly reluctant to take no for an answer. I realize that Jacinthe Siani hadn't just fingered me as a Tetron spy. She'd fingered me as the guy who'd penetrated the lower levels—the man who'd talked to the super-scientists.

Everything I had seen of the invaders suggested that they were, by galactic standards, country boys. They must know, by now, just how unsophisticated they were by galactic standards. They knew that the Tetrax were a long way ahead of them, although they seemed to be making what efforts they could to stop the off-world Tetrax finding that out. But Jacinthe Siani had told them that they had neighbors inside Asgard who were even more advanced than the Tetrax. That had to be the main reason why they were playing for time in refusing to talk to the Tetrax. They were hoping to find allies who would help them keep the universe at bay!

And they were convinced that I could help them, once they had persuaded me to talk. Unfortunately, they probably weren't going to believe me when I told them that there wasn't a lot of help I could offer...and their unbelief might cost me dear if they really got tough in the business of persuasion.

I wondered how troubled and confused these would-be

conquerors of Asgard were. It must have been quite a shock to them, first to discover the universe, and then to find out that they weren't by any means the most powerful parasites in the guts of the macroworld.

"You don't have any idea who built Asgard, do you?" I said, looking into the pale eyes of the blond-haired man. "How many levels can you operate in? Ten...twenty?"

"Do not underestimate us, Mr. Rousseau," he replied, calmly, looking away to watch the factory-fields going by beyond the windows of the carriage. "We control hundreds of habitats in more than fifty levels. It is true that we had not been able to calculate the size of Asgard until we unexpectedly reached the surface, and even now we have no way of knowing how far down the levels extend. We know, though, that our ancestors were the builders of Asgard, and that it is only a matter of time before we regain access to the knowledge they had. It may well be that our ancestors were your ancestors, too, and that you too have lost access to what they knew just as we have. If that is true, then your interests and ours are alike, and you must make every effort to help us contact our cousins—those you have already met in the depths of the world."

I glanced at Jacinthe Siani. Like most Kythnans, she had olive-tinted skin and jet black hair. Her eyes were a very dark brown. She was very much the odd one out in the car, though there were many Earthborn humans who looked less like Sky-blue and his friends than she did.

"Are your ancestors *her* ancestors too?" I asked.

"It seems likely," conceded Sky-blue.

"And the Tetrax?"

"That seems *un*likely."

"I'm afraid not," I told him. "We have good reason to believe that we're all brothers and sisters under the skin. Any common ancestor that you or I had is just as remote from us as the common ancestor linking either of us to the Tetrax." *Or*, I thought to myself, *the common ancestor I share with a pig, non-flying variety.*

"I don't know about such matters," he told me. "I'm only a soldier. You will have the chance to speak to people who do know."

Again, there was a threat in his tone of voice.

"The Tetrax know," I assured him. "If you were only prepared to make proper contact, you could fix up a nice dialogue between your own wise men and theirs. If you and the Tetrax pooled your resources, you might well be able to figure out who did build this thing, when, and why. It's something we'd all like to know."

"It is not for me to decide such matters," he said, terminating the exchange. Then he had to report back to the older man everything that had been said. I turned my attention to Jacinthe Siani.

"Are they treating you well?" I asked.

She smiled, in a strangely catlike fashion. "Quite well," she said. "I like them better than many of my old friends."

Knowing what I did about the company she used to keep, I didn't find that at all surprising. "Hell," I said, "you don't have to take such an obvious relish in landing me in it. I never did anything to you, did I? You were the one who was trying to shaft me, remember?"

"I remember everything," she assured me.

I decided that she just didn't like me very much. Some people don't. I can live with it.

From the train-car we transferred to a road vehicle, which whisked us across country with considerably greater alacrity. It was silent, and presumably ran on fuel cells of some kind. I suspected that the invaders hadn't invented the fuel cell themselves; in fact, I had now begun to suspect that they hadn't invented very much at all. It occurred to me that they were real barbarians, and that their home-level technology consisted mainly of ready-made items that they'd discovered—or rediscovered—how to use. Giving their ancestors the credit for ordering the world in which they found themselves was a face-saving exercise. Even inside Asgard, they were little boys lost—no matter how many environments they had "conquered" in the course of their explorations.

Given that they were so primitive themselves, it was easy to work out how mediocre things had to be in those levels of which they had taken control.

Once I had reached this conclusion, I wasn't at all surprised that our trip down into the lower levels was anything but smooth. There was no huge elevator shaft going all the way down to wherever they were taking me. We could drop three, or sometimes four levels at a time, but then we had to transfer to a car or a train again, and hurtle across country to some other point of descent. There was heavy traffic all the way, and I began to realize what an awesome task it must be to move the invader armies around—and, by implication, how vulnerable their troops in Skychain City must be.

By the time we were down to level twelve—assuming that my counting was correct with respect to the levels we skipped past—I didn't see any more groups of galactic prisoners. Wherever we were, there were only invaders—legion upon legion of them. All but a few were males in uniform. All, without exception, were pale of skin. I couldn't help remembering Myrlin and the biotechnics that had been used to shape him: an accelerated growth program and some kind of mental force-feeding. The perfect way to grow your own soldiers. I wondered briefly whether these soldiers could have been made that way, and fed with illusions about their own nature and origins. But it didn't make any sense—these neo-Neanderthalers certainly didn't behave as though there might be some mysterious master-race behind them.

On the way down, I got to see small areas of about thirty different levels. I think we eventually ended up on level fifty-two, give or take a couple. The top few levels were all dead—no sign of life at all. Five and six were like one and two: very cold, but not as cold as three and four. There was no way to be certain about the temperature outside the tightly-sealed vehicles which we used to cross territory on those levels, but it must have been way below freezing.

Seven and eight I didn't see, but nine was alive, though pretty desolate. It reminded me strongly of the level much further down, to which Saul Lyndrach's dropshaft had initially led us—which is to say that it looked like an ecology that had once been balanced but had run wild. Certainly there was no sign of the machinery of artificial photosynthesis—if there had ever been any, it had long since rotted away, to be replaced by real plants eking out their existence under an enfeebled and ill-lit sky. The terrain looked like tundra, bleak and sub-arctic. There was no sign of native humanoid habitation, or of colonization by the neo-Neanderthalers.

Eleven and twelve were alive, too, but looked much the same. If anything, their bioluminescent skies were even further degraded, so that their light was even weaker.

What we'd eventually concluded about the worldlet Saul had found was that it had initially been set up with very sophisticated biotechnology, which had gradually gone completely to pieces. Its energy supply had initially been electrical and thermal, and the light-producing systems had been organic—although they were not *organisms* capable of independent life. Over a very long time—possibly running to several millions of years, entropy had done its work, and the carefully engineered artificial organics had gradually given way to *real* organisms, which did retain some of the features of the artificial system, but not so efficiently.

What had happened, therefore, was effectively a devolution or degeneration from artificial systems to living ones. I know that seems almost crazy, given that we generally think of living systems being far *more* ordered than non-living ones, but the builders' biotechnics had been more sophisticated than living systems. Even something as primitive (in these terms) as the Tetrax artificial photosynthesis systems up on level one would, if left to its own devices, eventually give way to 'natural' grass. Think of it not so much as non-life degenerating into life, but as the delicately-bred plants in a garden, adapted not simply to reproduce themselves, but also to serve the purposes of the gardeners, gradually devolving into coarser—but inherently hardier—weeds.

A mixture of guesswork and inference suggested to me that some of the old inhabitants of Skychain City were being relocated to lower levels, where they were being herded into the ruins of ancient and long derelict cities to begin the work of refurbishing them for their new would-be masters. For the Tetrax, especially, it must have been like being sent back to the Stone Age. As we crossed a particularly bleak plain on twelve I wondered whether there was some kind of testing going on. Maybe the invaders wanted to see whether the Tetrax were clever enough to find out how the systems built into Asgard's structure could be made to function again, even after a vastly long period of disuse and decay.

Further down, the rot that had claimed the higher habitats seemed not to have set in—or not to have progressed so far—but there were other complications.

Until we reached fifteen I had assumed that all the levels would have much the same atmosphere. The atmospheres of almost all humanoid homeworlds are very similar indeed, the relative percentages of nitrogen, oxygen, and carbon dioxide being a cleverly-maintained optimum. Planetary atmospheres, of course, are the creation of life, and because all the humanoid homeworlds share the same chemistry of life, they share the same ideal conditions. Their ecospheres adapt to produce and conserve those conditions, in much the same way that homeostatic mechanisms within endothermic organisms produce a constant internal temperature.

There are one or two galactic humanoid species who breathe air that the rest of us would find uncomfortable, but for precisely that reason they aren't fully integrated into the galactic community. There are life-systems which have alternative chemistries, but they shape up very differently from the kind of life-system which produces humanoids. You do get life, of a sort, in the atmospheres of gas giant planets—even gas giants as cold as Uranus—but it doesn't produce anything like the range of organisms that DNA can produce, and as far as I knew no one had ever found evidence of anything in such a system as intelligent as an insect, let alone a man.

Thus, I was very surprised to find that in a big airlock on level fifteen, our little party boarded a vehicle which looked more like a gigantic bullet or a wheeled starship than a car, and that when we went out into the open, we found ourselves in a real pea-souper of an atmosphere.

For a few minutes, I simply watched in astonishment as the colored fog roiled around the thick windows, stirred into activity by the velocity of our passage. It was a dingy green color, lit from above by a sky no more than fifteen meters above us. The green wasn't uniform, though: there were coiling wraiths of purple and indigo, like gaseous worms, and bigger, paler shapes that reminded me of old-fashioned images of immaterial spooks and specters.

I could tell that Jacinthe Siani had seen it before, but not often enough to get entirely blas, about it. Sky-blue and the troopers were as bored as they could be, though.

"What is it?" I asked Sky-blue.

"Mostly methane, hydrogen, and carbon oxides," said Sky-blue, morosely. "Some helium, many longer-chain carbon molecules. Very high pressure. We have to be careful with the locks. If the atmospheres get mixed, they react. Sometimes explosively. We don't know any other way through. Our maps are incomplete. We were fortunate to be able to locate a way up as quickly as we did; an environment like this might have been a barrier for many generations. The first one our forefathers discovered was the boundary of their empire for a long time, but we can now move about freely in such habitats, and we find certain uses for them."

"Is there life here?"

"Of a sort. Nothing that troubles us."

"I don't suppose you have a theory as to why your ancestors should fill some of their cave-systems with alien atmospheres?"

Before he could answer, the older man cut in with a few

sharp remarks in his own tongue. Sky-blue favored me with a dirty look, and I figured that he'd just been reminded that I was a spy and an enemy. I decided that it would be diplomatic to ask fewer questions.

By the time we left fifteen, I was ready for more surprises. Indeed, I was eager for them, if only to take my mind off what might be awaiting me below. For that reason, all the levels I numbered in the twenties were disappointments. They certainly weren't dead, and I didn't get the impression that they were markedly decayed, but the territory we crossed was empty. The skies were bright, and the vegetation seemed reasonably lush, but there was no evidence of sophisticated machinery except for the vehicles on the road, and the only sentients I saw were the pale-skinned invaders.

I could see plenty of pillars holding up the ceilings, but I couldn't see any blocks filled out with doors and windows. I knew, though, that we were seeing only the tiniest slice of each habitat, and that every one of them would surely be as big, and might well be as various, as an Earthly continent. It was as though I was trying to judge the nature and complexity of the Earth from a twenty-kilometer drive across a randomly-chosen part of Canada. The best sights these levels had to offer might be awesome indeed, but it was entirely possible that the invaders had never yet caught a glimpse of them, having only skated quickly across the surface, more eager to find doorways to other levels than to explore fully those which appeared harmless and useless to them.

When we stopped to sleep, at a way-station on what I took to be level twenty-nine, I was beginning to fear that Asgard might not have much more to show me. Wouldn't it be ghastly, I thought, if the Center turned out to be no more exotic than Skychain City—or the microworld *Goodfellow*? There is no more horrible way that any mystery can be resolved than by a dissolution into ironic anti-climax.

I consoled myself with the thought that we were a long, long way from the Center yet—and with the knowledge that the reason I was being taken on this little trip to the heartland of Invaderdom was that I had already been shown proof that there were more things in Asgard, as in Heaven, than had hitherto been dreamt of in the invaders' poverty-stricken philosophy.

But could I, I wondered, interest them enough to persuade them to let me live?

CHAPTER SIXTEEN

The levels which I numbered in the thirties were much brighter and more crowded than those in the twenties. Every time we emerged from one of the buildings that housed the connecting shafts we came out into thriving city streets—wide roads with floor-to-ceiling façades, pavements, shops. This, I inferred, was the heartland of the invader empire; these were levels they had colonized in the distant past. I couldn't tell which of them was their home level, and my companions weren't answering questions. Sky-blue and the senior officer had been arguing again, and Sky-blue was rather tight-lipped. Jacinthe Siani was keeping her distance from me, probably because she wanted to impress upon her new friends that she was solidly on their side.

I saw very few people on the streets who belonged to any other race than that of the invaders themselves, though there were far more females visible now, and far more civilians. The range of physical variation within the neo-Neanderthaler species was unusually small. I guessed that they were all descended from a relatively limited gene-pool; that would fit in with the popular theory that Asgard was some kind of Ark, whose many habitats had been set aside to be populated by the descendants of a favored few individuals. Maybe all the invaders were descended from a single Adam-and-Eve pair, though they had now such a vast population that they had filled up several other habitats in addition to their allotted Eden.

Obviously, such colonization hadn't been a mere matter of moving into empty space—they would hardly possess armored vehicles by the million and an army that seemed to involve ninety-nine out of a hundred of the adult male population if they had only discovered virgin territory. What I could see in the streets didn't give any indication of what had happened to the conquered races. The few exotic individuals I saw might conceivably have been slaves—or the enfranchised relics of populations that had been all but wiped out.

As we cruised the city streets I amused myself with a little speculative mathematics.

Suppose, I thought, that the pale-skinned pseudo-Neanderthalers currently filled twenty cave-systems, each with a land area not much less than the land area of Mother Earth. With abundant food production they could be doubling their population every forty or fifty years. That implied that they would have to take over another sixty cave systems in the next century, and another four hundred and eighty by the end of the following century. How long would it take them to fill Asgard? How long would it take them to bump into someone who would put a stop to their game? And if Asgard was really millions of years old, why hadn't one of its races already expanded to fill the whole macroworld?

I tried raising such issues with my captors, but the man with blond hair was sulking, and refused to talk. He had been forcibly reminded that his job was to transport me, not to enlighten me.

Below forty, things began to change again. The invaders seemed to have had every bit as much difficulty going downwards from their local area as they had going upwards. Once again, their cities were replaced by much more limited roadside developments in less promising territory. But these lower levels weren't all dark and they weren't all bleak. On the contrary, many were brighter, hotter, and full of life. If the topmost levels could be reckoned tundra or steppe, these were jungle, swamp, and savannah.

On one particularly long trip—at least sixty kilometers—from one downshaft to the next I sweated so much that I longed for my lost cold-suit, with its careful temperature control. We were using an armored car here, as we did on most of the levels that weren't fully civilized, and the way the hot light beat down on the metal from the thirty-meter ceiling made it feel like an oven.

The area on either side of the road had been sprayed with some kind of herbicide, and new growth was only just beginning to creep back into an area whose earlier plants were all browned and desiccated. In the distance, though, we could see trees that reached up almost to the ceiling, spreading vast palmate leaves in a horizontal array to soak up the intense radiation almost at source, so that what got through to the lower layers was a crazy zigzag of thin shafts. I couldn't believe that the lush, strange undergrowth beneath the trees was wholly sustained by the interrupted light, although it was certainly well illuminated by it, and I concluded that much of the ground-hugging vegetation was thermosynthetic, leeching energy from the ground itself.

I'd never seen natural thermosynthetic organic systems before, and was surprised to see that they were not fungus-white, as I would have expected, but patterned and multicolored in all kinds of bizarre ways. Like the flowering plants of Mother Earth, these thermosynths had evolved in collaboration with insects, and they signaled to their pollinators in every possible way, appealing both to the visual and olfactory senses.

That one was a very noisy forest, full of fluting sounds which I initially assumed to be the calling of birds, but in a rare few minutes of conversation Jacinthe Siani remarked that in the ecosystem in question even the plants had voices, so intense had the competition to attract insects become. Here, she said, there were fat flightless birds which mimicked flowers both physically and musically, in order to entice their prey into their hungry beaks.

I wondered whether the invaders had located the machinery that controlled temperature in these habitats, and why they hadn't simply turned down the thermostat to make them more hospitable. I couldn't believe that the neo-Neanderthalers had simply decided, like good conservationists, to leave this system the way it was in order to avoid precipitating an ecocatastrophe. It seemed much more likely that they had left it the way it was because they didn't know how to change it. They really were like a bunch of Neanderthalers on the streets of twenty-first-century New York; they could pass for locals by putting on clothes, and could make a living as muggers with their own rough-hewn weapons, but they didn't know how anything worked.

But where were the zookeepers who should have made sure that these savages couldn't break out of their own allotted cage? Where, oh where, were the Lords of Valhalla?

As we traversed another of these tropical demi-paradises, I wondered what kind of sentients lived there. I was reluctant to conclude from the fact that I hadn't seen a single humanoid flitting among the bushes that these systems were just gargantuan vivaria. Clearly the invaders hadn't colonized these levels to any significant extent, but they could easily have built themselves a reputation for violence sufficient to make the locals very discreet. I fantasized about peaceful pygmies, tribes of lotus eaters, and about clever fellows who had invented musical instruments in order to charm the butterflies and the bees.

Further down, things got stranger still. I was glad to find that there wasn't a simple temperature cline determining the distribution of levels. Had it been the case that the levels started at absolute zero and had got so hot by fifty that they could no longer sustain life, I would have become pessimistic about the prospect of finding much more of interest. But the gravity had barely begun to weaken here, and I knew that the balmy arena in which I'd fought my duel with Amara Guur was much lower down.

Below the tropical regions there were cooler ones whose life-systems seemed much less fervent. Some looked ripe for colonization, but showed even less evidence of invader penetration than the tropical hothouses—and the invaders we did see were mostly wearing masks and protective clothing. We weren't— but we were in a vehicle that I judged to be very tightly sealed.

My companions wouldn't tell me what it was about levels forty-three and forty-five that made them so hostile to invasion, even though they looked so innocent, but the masks and suits brought to mind rumors of galactic explorers who'd found lush worlds that turned out to be biochemically booby-trapped in some way. Where many humanoid species are gathered together, travelers' tales are a penny a hundred, and only one in a hundred has a grain of truth in it, but I'd listened to a lot of them, partly because they were fun and partly because they did at least convey some sense of the strangeness of the universe.

You might think that because all "Earthlike" planets have the same biochemistry, and a very similar range of major-groups of life-forms, one would be pretty much like another. That's true—up to a point. I've been told that even a seasoned galactic traveler might never see anything to convince him otherwise. (Although few humanoids ever visit one another's homeworlds, they visit one another's home systems, but in a civilized solar system there often isn't any real need or incentive to go down into a deep gravity well. A well-travelled galactic might have visited twelve or fifteen systems, but it's a very rare tourist who has actually set foot on more than three actual planets.)

The really exotic worlds are, of course, those on which humanoid life failed to evolve, or on which it evolved in a very different ecological context—and those worlds are very often hostile to visiting humanoid life at a very basic level. It's not just that the locals will throw spears at you—it's that the local organics are poison through and through. The habitats through which we passed on what I took to be levels forty-three and forty-five might have belonged to that type, although I couldn't, for the life of me, see any obvious clues as to why they were so dangerous. The vegetation was still green, and most of it still looked like trees, bushes, grasses, and flowers.

Forty-seven and forty-nine had been extensively colonized, and there were thriving invader communities beside the roads on which we drove, though the temperatures were still on the high side. Fifty, though we saw only a brief stretch of it, was a real wonder. It was very dimly-lit, although the light was uniform—resembling a very cloudy twilight rather than a starlit night—but it was very warm, and it was home to a rich life-system, which was presumably almost entirely thermosynthetic.

It wasn't easy to imagine a kind of planet—or a locale on a planet—where these kinds of conditions could occur. Maybe on a planet with perpetual fog and a steep axial tilt, in a region of considerable volcanic activity, there could be something like that, but it was difficult to imagine any such region being stable long enough to develop a rich flora and fauna.

One would expect there to be no color in that kind of ecosystem, with the dim light encouraging only shades of gray. But that wasn't the case. Many of the plants there produced colored fruit and flowers, which they lit up themselves; it was a world of Christmas trees, with inbuilt bioluminescent fairy-lights. Many of the insects, too, carried around their own lights—wherever I looked there seemed to be clouds of fireflies, and the ground was beribboned by the lights of glowing worms.

In a way, I realized, what was happening here was a curious inversion of the characteristic pattern of life on Earth. There, light provided the fuel for the ecosphere, and sophisticated organisms made their own heat. Here, heat was the basic fuel, and the cleverest organisms made light for communication—perhaps as casually as Earthly creatures made odors. I had never heard rumor of anything like it, and I found it entrancing, but my bored fellow travelers hardly gave it a glance through the sealed windows of the car. There were a few buildings along the road we traveled, but no pedestrians. I guessed that it was probably another of the habitats where the invaders needed filter-masks to breathe safely.

Neither the man with pale blue eyes nor Jacinthe Siani volunteered any information about the place, and I realized that the Kythnan's single comment about the musical plants was a true gauge of what it took to awaken her curiosity. As for the invader, even though he was "only a soldier", he seemed nevertheless to be remarkably insensitive to the beauty and the inherent fascination of what Asgard held. He took all this for granted—it meant nothing to him, in terms of inspiring theories about what Asgard was, and the godlike beings who had designed it.

The savage mind, I thought, *fixated on the wisdom of imaginary ancestors, uncaring about the progress of its own wisdom. And yet these people might succeed in driving the Tetrax from Asgard, and in bringing desolation to vast reaches of the macroworld.*

If ever I had thought seriously about throwing in my lot with the invaders and betraying the Tetrax, I was sure by now that I couldn't do it. I needed to pin my colors to the mast of some cause whose partisans were actually interested in penetrating Asgard's mysteries.

After catching only the merest glimpses of the ecosystem on level fifty, I was enthusiastic to see more. Our next drop took us to what I judged to be level fifty-two. This was another weird one, and I knew when we changed vehicles before we went through the complicated locks that it would be another with a reducing atmosphere. The car we got into was like a miniature spaceship, sealed very tight.

There was more life there, though, than there had been in the earlier hydrogenous environment. Up there, everything had been vaporous save for a kind of swampy sludge at ground level. Down here, there were many dendritic forms—I hesitate to call them "trees" because they looked more like corals, and certainly didn't have any leafy foliage—coiling and branching tortuously. They didn't form much of a forest, because they mostly kept their distance from one another, but some of them—after the fashion of the cloudy habitat on level fifty—bore what looked like luminescent fruit.

There were flying creatures, too—or, to be strictly accurate, gliding creatures, because I couldn't see any evidence of fluttering wings as they floated from one dendrite to another. There was a sort of undergrowth, consisting mostly of globular entities of assorted sizes, many of which were associated in clusters. I couldn't imagine what kinds of metabolism the things must have; I knew there were bacteria in conventional ecosystems which could only grow in the absence of free oxygen, but I knew of no metazoan entities with anaerobic habits. Here, I assumed, some fairly radical revision of the basic DNA support-system must be necessary—if indeed this life was at all akin to our own.

Our drive across this territory was another short one—barely a couple of kilometers. We came then to a big windowed wall curving away in either direction into the murk. We crawled through a second system of airlocks, but instead of coming to another big elevator, which could lower our vehicle down to the next level, we parked in a bay. As we disembarked, and were met by more armed troopers, I realized that we weren't going any further. We had arrived at our destination.

The wrist-timer I was wearing was showing Asgard metric time, but in human terms our journey had taken the best part of two days. While there had been plenty to look at, I hadn't been entirely aware of how tired I was, but now it came home to me that I'd only slept for about six of those forty-eight hours.

I was initially surprised that our destination had proved to be located in such a hostile habitat, but I soon perceived the logic of it. What better place is there to put a maximum-security prison than a building surrounded by an alien atmosphere? It would certainly help to discourage would-be escapers.

Now that we'd arrived, I could no longer distract myself from the extremity of my plight. Fifty levels down, there could not the slightest hope that the Tetrax could do anything to free me. Susarma Lear would have not the slightest chance of ever finding me, even if she were disposed to bring the Star Force to my rescue.

As if that were not trouble enough, I was morally certain that my captors were going to demand far more information from me than I actually had to give, and that they were not going to take at all kindly to the inadequacy of my answers.

CHAPTER SEVENTEEN

I later discovered that it was a pretty crowded prison camp, but that was by no means obvious when I arrived. The corridors were all empty—the inmates were locked up in the cells. There weren't even many guards about; I suppose they didn't need very many, given that there was little future in dreams of rebellion or escape.

The accommodation offered by the camp seemed somewhat basic, as far as I could judge while being marched through its corridors. The walls were polished, coldly metallic in appearance, and the cell doors were all identical—row upon row of them, a mere six meters apart.

It seemed a bleak prospect, as they hustled me to my appointed place, but when they opened the door and shoved me in, I was grateful to find that it wasn't quite as bad as I had begun to fear. The inmates of this curious institution were housed two to a cell, and our captors were considerate enough to match up like with like, placing members of the same race together. As it turned out, at the time of my arrival there was only one other human in the camp, so I was taken immediately to his cell.

As the door banged shut behind me, he looked at me in open astonishment, as if the fact of my appearance was almost a miracle. I was pleased to see him, figuring that he was probably the next best thing to a friendly face that this godforsaken spot could offer.

"Hello Alex," I said. "Small universe, isn't it? What time do we eat around here?"

It was pleasant to see the expressions of utter surprise crossing his face, one after another.

"Rousseau!" he said, almost as if I were Santa Claus—or maybe the devil incarnate.

"You can call me Mike," I said.

"But you left before the invasion," he complained, foolishly. "You should be back on Earth by now." He was speaking in *parole*—English wasn't his first language, and he tended not to speak it unless asked.

I looked around warily. "Is this place bugged?" I asked, in English.

He shook his head tiredly, more in amazement than negation. "Hardly," he said, answering in the same language. "As far as I can tell, these people are barbarians. Apart from technology they've taken over without really understanding it, they're about as sophisticated as early twentieth-century humans."

"Well," I said, "it probably doesn't matter anyway. It's just that I'm not entirely sure how much the Neanderthalers know about me, or how much I should tell them. Jacinthe Siani fingered me as the guy who went down Saul Lyndrach's dropshaft, and blew a cover story I'd invented on the spur of the moment. They're interested in me on account of what I found down below, and I suspect that's the only thing which is inhibiting them from shooting me as a Tetron spy. I'm being as discreet as I can, but I don't know what they have planned. How much have you told them?"

"I can assure you," he said, stiffly, "that I have told these people absolutely nothing, and have not the slightest intention of doing so. They might regard me as a first cousin to their race, due to a superficial similarity of appearance, but that only betrays their crudity of mind."

I nodded. Alexandr Sovorov could always be relied upon to stand on his dignity. He didn't go in for half-measures, either. If he had decided not to talk to his captors, he was perfectly capable of remaining silent until doomsday.

I sat down on the unused bunk, and wiped my forehead with

the back of my hand. I felt slightly feverish and my throat was a little sore. Until that moment, I had attributed the fact that I didn't feel on top of the world to tiredness, but now my sinuses were beginning to trouble me.

"Have you got a spare handkerchief?" I asked. "I've got a cold coming on, and I was traveling light. I don't suppose the medical facilities around here are up to Tetron standards?"

"Hardly," he said. He found me a handkerchief and passed it over to me gingerly. There didn't seem to be much point in avoiding physical contact—if we had to share a cell, we would also have to share our viruses.

"I suppose one of our fellow humans identified you as the man most likely to know how Tetron technology works?" I speculated. "So they asked for your help, didn't like your uncooperative attitude, and sent you down here for a bit of re-education."

"Quite probably," he said.

"Have they tortured you yet?"

"No. So far they have only tried to seduce my support with arguments and bribes. I think they believe that my knowledge is very limited. Their worst threats have been directed at the Tetrax."

"That's a relief. I only hope they use the same tactics on me. Arguments and bribes I can stand."

"I hope," he said, frostily, "that you do not intend to cooperate with these vicious murderers."

"That depends," I told him, "on what they want to know. I do have a certain authority to negotiate. Who's senior Tetron here in the camp?"

"There is an individual named 822-Vela," said Sovorov, a little suspiciously.

"Do we have any opportunity to talk to him?"

"Certainly. There are two exercise periods per day, when prisoners associate quite freely. Do you have any particular reason for wanting to communicate with him?"

"I told you. I'm a Star Force spy. The Tetrax hired me, along with Susarma Lear and a ship full of troopers, to investigate the situation down here, and to open up lines of communication."

"How do you expect to be able to report back?" he asked, sarcastically. "Security in the camp is lax, but it hardly needs to be tight. Even if you could get an atmosphere suit, there is nowhere to go except the elevator shaft, and even if you could get up or down the shaft, there are invader-occupied levels at the other ends."

"So nobody escapes?"

"Nobody even tries," he assured me.

"In that case," I told him, "I'll probably have to talk my way out. And if that means telling them some of what they want to know, I'll do it. We all have to make sacrifices." I hadn't realized until I spoke that I would have to make plans along some such lines—in fact, I hadn't been planning at all—but Alex Sovorov was a man who'd always been able to provoke me with his marginally insufferable manner, and I wasn't about to tell him that I hadn't a clue what I could or should do.

He looked at me uncertainly, not entirely sure whether it was appropriate for him to disapprove. That was a new dilemma for him—in all our past dealings, he'd been quite certain that I merited disapproval.

"You're working for the Tetrax?" he queried.

"That's right. They're having difficulty making contact with our genial hosts, and they sent down three teams of snoopers to find out what's going on. I was unlucky, and struck out before getting past phase one. Hopefully, some of the others have been enjoying better luck while I've been in transit. For my own satisfaction, though, I'd appreciate it if you could fill me in on what you know—assuming that your determination not to communicate hasn't extended to seeing and hearing no evil as well as speaking none?"

"Of course not," he said. "Unfortunately, I have not been able to gather much information here. Much as I would have liked to talk to the natives of Asgard who are imprisoned here, the lack of a common language has proved a barrier. Some of them are as keen to learn *parole* as the invaders, but their opportunities are more restricted. Some have made progress during the exercise periods, but the invader linguists are busy round the clock with collaborators, and have mastered the language much more fully."

"That's okay," I said. "I don't expect miracles. Let's start with the camp. How many people are here, and who are they?"

"I have not been able to make an accurate count."

I found his pedantry a little hard to cope with. I wondered whether it might be better to go to sleep now, and try to hold a more sensible conversation in the morning. My head was beginning to ache. But I persisted.

"Come on, Alex. I just want to know the score. What kind of a place is this?"

"Well," he said. "I think there are about two thousand people here. The great majority are members of non-galactic humanoid races—I estimate that there are at least a dozen different species. Perhaps a tenth of the prisoners are galactics. Most are Tetrax, but the invaders seem to have brought down at least one specimen of each of the races represented in Skychain City. This is as much a center of learning as a place of imprisonment—it seems probable that anyone the invaders wish to interrogate for an extended period of time is brought here. There seems to be no routine mistreatment of prisoners, but I'm not in a position to observe the whole range of the activities that go on here. Until I have more data, it would be premature to draw too many conclusions."

"Oh *merde*," I muttered. I should have known what to expect. I lay down, with my head on the pillow, and looked up at him.

"You're tired," he observed. It was nice to see that he wasn't entirely incompetent in the business of drawing conclusions.

"You never did tell me what time we eat around here," I reminded him.

"We operate a day cycle slightly shorter than the Tetron norm," he told me. "The invaders appear to use a forty-unit division. I have no idea why. The lights go on at the zero point and off at twenty-five. We eat during the first, the eleventh, and the twenty-first periods. We exercise during the fifth and sixth, and during the fifteenth and sixteenth."

"I'll try to remember," I promised.

After a pause, during which time it might have sunk in to his thick skull that he wasn't being very helpful, he said, in a softer voice: "What's going to happen to us, Rousseau? Will the Tetrax succeed in securing our release?"

"Now why should the Tetrax worry unduly about you?" I asked him, returning a little of the malicious sarcasm. "In spite of all your sterling work with the Coordinated Research Establishment, they probably don't give a damn about you, and now that I've failed in my mission, they probably care almost as little about me. If I were you, Alex, I'd start wondering how I could help myself. That's what I'm doing."

"Oh," he said flatly. "In that case, I wish you the best of luck."

I can tell when a man isn't sincere. Unfortunately, I thought I might *need* the very best of luck—and a bit more. I shut my eyes, and tried to figure out how I should play it when the questions began again—as they undoubtedly would. I couldn't get my thoughts straight, though. I was tired and I was sniffing continually in a hopeless attempt to clear my sinuses.

Of all the stupid places to catch a cold, I thought, furiously, *I have to do it in the one place in the universe where I can't get proper treatment.* Fate still seemed to be dealing me the worst cards it could find, and I realized that what I'd said to Alex was probably true. In all likelihood we were out of the game for good, and nobody would bother to make the slightest effort to bring us back into it. If I didn't play my cards exactly right, I might be stuck here for a very long time.

CHAPTER EIGHTEEN

The second phase of my interrogation started in a more polite fashion than the first. My new interlocutor spoke far better
parole than my old acquaintance with the sky-blue eyes, and
he obviously wasn't "only a soldier". He even began by telling
me his name, which was Sigor Dyan. He was dressed in black,
like all the uniformed men, but he wore no insignia of rank
at all—which implied, in subtle fashion, that he was important
enough to stand outside the hierarchy. He had the customary
white skin, and his white hair was commonplace, too, but he had
curious eyes, which were a purplish color somewhere between
light-blue and albinoesque pink. His brow-ridges weren't very
prominent and he had a comparatively steep forehead, which
made him look very human indeed.

He received me in a pleasant room, and invited me to sit on
a sofa, though he sat on a more angular chair whose seat was
elevated—with the consequence that he could look at me from
a higher vantage-point, even though I was a good three centimeters taller than he. There was a low-level glass-topped table
between us, with two cups and a pot of some kind of hot drink.
Without asking, he poured us each a cup, and pushed mine over.
I tasted it carefully. It was green and sweet, like sugared mint
tea. It soothed my throat, which had become very sore. It was
obviously velvet glove time—but I knew I'd have to look out for
the iron fist.

"Your name is Michael Rousseau?" he began.

"That's right," I croaked.

"And you are a native of a planet which you call Earth?"

"It's the homeworld of my species. I was born on a micro-world in the asteroid belt. That's a thin scattering of big rocks somewhat further away from our star than the homeworld. You know about stars and solar systems?"

"We are learning. I believe that Asgard is a very great distance away from your homeworld—a distance so great that I can hardly imagine it. We have grown used to figuring distances in rather small units. We have discovered that our conceptual horizons were narrower than we could possibly have supposed."

"I hope your soldiers aren't agoraphobic," I commented.

He smiled. "I fear that they are," he told me. "Many have experienced difficulties in working on the surface. Even the dome of Skychain City seems to us to contain an unusually large open space. Beyond the dome...perhaps you can imagine what a vertiginous experience it is for our people to look up into that sky for the first time."

"Perhaps I can," I admitted. I couldn't—when you're born in the asteroid belt you grow up with a sky that makes all others seem comfortable.

"What brought you to Asgard, Mr. Rousseau?" He spoke gently, and I certainly didn't want to discourage him. I felt too poorly to get into an argument, though I was trying to put on a brave face and keep my symptoms under control.

"A spirit of adventure," I told him. "You get to a point in life where you can afford to buy a starship, and suddenly the whole galactic arm is open to you. The microworld began to seem intolerably parochial, and the asteroid belt seemed to have very little to offer—just millions of orbiting boulders. I had a friend who was keen to head for somewhere Romantic. Asgard is Romantic, with a capital R: the biggest, strangest world in the known universe. News of its existence had only just reached the system, and it was the great mystery—the ultimate puzzle. The space-born tend to look outwards...they rarely go back to Earth. To them, Earth is the dead past...the galactic community is the future. What brought *you* to a place like this?"

"A certain talent for learning languages. Perhaps, though, you do not mean the question personally—perhaps you are asking what brought my people to this environment?"

"It would be interesting to know," I answered.

"Initially," he said, "the need to discover more space than was provided for us in our original habitat came from simple population pressure. Our habitat was some thirty million square kilometers in extent, but there were no significant checks on our population growth. We do not know how many of us there were originally—not very many, perhaps—but by the time we discovered a way to penetrate other environments there were six billion of us, and we faced the prospect of doubling our population again in the space of a man's lifetime. For most of our history—I should say *pre*history, as we had no written records for what must have been the greater part of our time here—we took our environment for granted. Only in recent lifetimes have we begun the business of learning to exploit the technologies that lie behind it.

"We thought that we were making very rapid progress as we moved up and down from our native level. We found no other inhabited level as advanced as our own, and we found many levels effectively uninhabited. Levels like this one posed severe problems in downward expansion. There are others like it beneath us. It seemed easier and more rewarding to go upwards, until we met the cold levels. It looked as if they would be an insurmountable barrier, until we found the lower levels of your city. It seemed to us a very welcome loophole—we could not know until we had already committed our forces what unwelcome revelations awaited us there."

He paused, expectantly. I didn't like to disappoint him, so I took up the threads of the argument. "So you discovered that you weren't the lords of Creation after all," I said. "And now you don't know what to do."

"We are...undecided," he admitted. He seemed to be waiting for me to respond further, and I decided there was no harm in it.

"At a guess," I said, "you don't know much about Asgard, let alone the universe. You have no idea how you got here. When your great-grandfathers first began to find out what kind of world they were in, they naturally assumed that it was all built for them, laid on for the convenience of their expanding population. They credited it to their own ancestors. Your expeditions and conquests might have made some of you skeptical, but there was nothing to overturn your faith in your own position of privilege...until you moved into Skychain City. You went in expecting to make mincemeat of a few other barbarians living parasitically on the technology of the ancients, and suddenly realized that it was an entirely different kettle of fish. It must have been a shock."

"Kettle of fish" didn't translate too well into *parole*, but he got the drift.

"You're a perceptive man, Mr. Rousseau," he said. He seemed genuinely pleased. Perhaps he'd been starved of intellectual conversation because Alex Sovorov and the Tetrax wouldn't talk to him.

"Why don't you negotiate with the Tetrax?" I asked him, bluntly. "They're not given to grandiose gestures of revenge. They'd forgive an honest mistake. In fact, they're really rather keen to arrive at a peaceful settlement beneficial to all parties."

"So our Tetron guests have assured us," he said. "But you must try to see things our way. What would happen if we were to make peace with the Tetrax? They would want access to the levels we control, in order to pursue their peaceful researches. In return, no doubt, they would offer us their own technology, their own knowledge. They would become involved in our projects, interested in our environments. They already believe that Asgard is theirs, because they have the technology to built cities on its surface, and explore its depths. If we give them leave to go where they wish, do what they will, Asgard *will* become theirs. They will be the ones who learn to use and control the technology of our ancestors. That would not be right. We are the inheritors—all this is ours. We must do everything in our power to keep control of it."

Again he paused, expectantly. I played fair, and tried to see things his way. I had to concede that he had a point. "If you let the Tetrax have the run of your levels," I said, slowly. "They'll certainly be in a far better position than you are to figure out how Asgard is put together. The technology of the builders— which is incarnate in the very architecture of the macroworld and in the systems that supply energy to the life-sustaining habitats—is very much superior to Tetron technology, but if you and the Tetrax are both trying to figure it out, the Tetrax are bound to get there first. I can see why you want to keep it all to yourselves. You're sitting on the most high-powered technics in the known universe...if you could only learn to understand it, you'd be ahead of the Tetrax—ahead of *everybody*. But the fact is that you don't understand it—you don't even understand the technology you've captured from the Tetrax in Skychain City, do you?"

"Asgard is ours," said Sigor Dyan. "We belong here. I think the people of Skychain City refer to us as 'invaders', but that is not correct, is it? It is, in fact, the inhabitants of your city who are invaders of our world. Is that not so?"

"I can see that it must look that way to you," I conceded, carefully.

"I understand that your own race has recently fought a war against another species, which you won," he said. "Is that not so?"

"It's true."

"And why did you fight that war?"

I gave him a wry smile. "Territorial disputes," I admitted.

"Your opponents were humanoid, I believe—but I am told that they did not resemble you as closely as we do."

"That's true too," I confirmed, warily.

"If they *had* resembled you as closely as we do, do you think your two races might have resolved their differences more amicably?"

"I doubt it," I said, dryly. It was an interesting question, though, and I couldn't pretend to know the answer for sure.

"Your own race is, I believe, technologically inferior to the Tetrax. You are no doubt more advanced than we are, but you have had to find your place in a community of races dominated by the Tetrax. Do you think, given what you know of that community, that humankind will ever catch up with the Tetrax? Do you think that the Tetrax would ever allow any other race to catch up with them, given their present position of superiority?"

I swallowed a gulp of the green stuff. He was sounding altogether too reasonable. His questions were the sort that is best answered with more questions.

"What chance do you think you'd have against the Tetrax if it came to armed conflict?" I asked him. "They take great pride in not being violent, but I'd be willing to bet that they could draw upon some awesome firepower if they had to."

"I have no doubt of it," replied Dyan. "If half of what humans have told us about your own Star Force is true, I have no doubt that you could blast Skychain City into dust, and that we could not defend it. But would the Tetrax really want to bomb Skychain City when there are so many of their own people there? What good would it do them, in the long run, if they did? We have twenty billion people in the lower levels. If they tried to retake Skychain City without destroying it, they would find it very difficult—I do not say impossible, but I cannot think of a way that it could be done. And if Skychain City were to fall...what then? We still have twenty billion people in the lower levels. How long do you think it would take your invading armies to take the tenth level down...let alone the fiftieth?"

He had obviously had more time to think this out than I had. His arguments looked suspiciously strong. If the galactics tried to take the invaders' little empire by force, they would have a real job on their hands. It might be easy to retake Skychain City—but what then? Could the Tetrax really send their explorers down into the levels with a vast population of hostile aliens standing against them? I knew only too well how difficult it had been for the C.R.E. to make headway in the task of learning about the people who had once lived in the outermost layers of Asgard, even when their only enemy was the cold. Maybe, I thought, the neo-Neanderthalers could buy themselves the time they needed to catch up. Maybe they could keep the Tetrax at bay, not just for years but generations, while they fought as hard as they could to master—really master—the technics that were all around them, built into the fabric of their enclosed universe.

"Okay," I said. "You can keep the Tetrax out of Skychain City...and the levels you control. But you don't have any way of controlling what happens on the other side of the macroworld, do you? Your empire's straight up and down. If it's to be a contest, the Tetrax are going to start digging in all the other habitats on level one. And they'll bring in a great deal more manpower than they ever lent to the C.R.E.—you might still outnumber them by millions to one, but you've already conceded that they're clever. They could still win the race, and if you go all out to stop them, it will cost you an awful lot of lives. Maybe even twenty billion. Do you really want that kind of war?"

"We are used to war," he told me, coldly. "It would be a foul betrayal of our ancestors to surrender to alien beings the inheritance which they left for us."

I was tempted to challenge his assumptions about his so-called ancestors, but I didn't want to antagonize him. I kept quiet, nursing a headache that was getting rapidly worse in consequence of the taxing discussion.

"In any case," said Sigor Dyan, silkily. "There are other factors in the situation that still remain to be considered, are there not? We know that there are other inhabitants of Asgard more advanced than the Tetrax or ourselves. It is entirely possible that our ancestors are still alive, far beneath us in the depths of our world. If our ancestors were now to emerge, to assist us in our hour of need, it would transform the situation dramatically, would it not, Mr. Rousseau?"

I realized then—perhaps belatedly—exactly why the invaders had been so very pleased to see me when Jacinthe Siani pointed me out. The way Sigor Dyan had things figured, I was the man who had talked to their ancestors...the messiah who had been in touch with their gods. I had been thinking in terms of alliances, assuming that the invaders were interested in their downside neighbors as potential allies. It hadn't sunk in that their way of looking at things made me much more important than that.

I didn't relish the idea of being cast as a messiah. It's a dangerous job, by all accounts.

I nearly blurted out the fact that Aleksandr Sovorov and at least a dozen of their Tetron prisoners must also know the location of Saul's dropshaft, but I bit my tongue.

I didn't know how much they had already been told. If all the information they had came from Jacinthe Siani, it would be woefully incomplete. They probably had no idea what kind of deal I'd made with the C.R.E., and they also might not know that the way down to Myrlin's biotech supermen had been very solidly blocked. I had to keep in mind the maxim that careless talk costs lives, and that one of them might easily be mine. I had to tread carefully until I found out exactly what they wanted from me, and exactly what they thought I could deliver.

"You don't have any real reason to believe," I began, tentatively, "that the people down below are your ancestors. They could be just one more race planted in their own habitat just as you were. The fact that they're technologically superior doesn't mean a thing. Ask yourself, Mr. Dyan—if they're just another captive race, would you be any better off becoming their underlings than you would becoming the underlings of the Tetrax?"

"That is exactly the kind of question, Mr. Rousseau, that we hope you can answer for us," he said, his voice as sweet as the stuff he was feeding me...which, now that I had finished it, had left in my mouth a strange and not altogether pleasant aftertaste.

CHAPTER NINETEEN

During the next exercise period, while I was temporarily let loose—presumably to think over everything that had been said to me—I got my chance to talk to 822-Vela for a while.

We met by one of the observation windows, and as we spoke I was able to alternate my glance between his wizened face and the alien wilderness outside. There was a kind of swirling oily mist, which made it difficult to see further than ten or fifteen meters, but there was a cluster of the dendritic structures close to the wall, and it was possible to make out, albeit vaguely, the small creatures fluttering amid the branches. The colored lights that dressed the branches of the dendrites insinuated their soft radiance into the mist, creating rainbow hazes through which the fireflies danced and darted.

Why is it here? I wondered. *Is it something so very unusual in the great universal scheme that it came to seem precious?*

822-Vela was explaining to me the policy that the Tetrax of Skychain City had decided to adopt. "Essentially," he said, "our strategy is one of calm reason, with a measure of stubbornness and a certain seductive appeal. We are trying to make clear the benefits that both the galactic races and the races of Asgard would obtain from a meeting of minds and a joining of resources. We stress the standards of behavior that are required if a complex galactic community is to exist in peace and harmony. We have refused to tell the invaders anything about our technology, or about our discoveries on Asgard, or about the position of our other subsurface bases, unless and until they make some kind of treaty with us and allow us to restore effective communication with the starships in space."

"Well," I said, deciding that I could make a bid for prestige by name-dropping furiously, "1125-Camina and 994-Tulyar deduced that you would follow that policy, and are planning their own overtures to fit in with it. The problem is that the invaders won't respond in any way to their calls, and without more information it was difficult to decide how to continue. With luck, one of our groups will have managed to renew communications, so that the people in orbit will be fully informed, but it's not easy to see what will happen next. You can probably judge better than I whether 1125-Camina would think it appropriate to order some kind of military action."

It's no good fishing for information with the Tetrax. They're too good at it to fall for any bait mere humans can deploy. All he said in reply was: "No doubt 1125-Camina will make the best decision. Can we assume that you, like Dr. Sovorov, will follow our directions in this matter? Many of your species-brethren are actively collaborating with the invaders—mercifully, few humans or Kythnans are in a position to offer effective assistance to them."

I couldn't tell whether he was implying that I was in no position to offer effective help to the enemy either, but I didn't care. For a few moments I just looked out at the swirling mists, wondering whether this habitat, too, contained tens of millions of square kilometers of territory, and wondering what awesome variations the life-system might exhibit over the full range of its terrain.

When I did answer him, it was to say: "There might be gains to be derived from collaboration. As you say, my fellow humans are not in a position to explain Tetron technics to the invaders, so they can do little harm. They might, however, succeed in winning the trust of these people. We must remember that the discoveries they made in capturing Skychain City have upset their entire world-view. By the time my race ventured outside our solar system, we already knew a great deal about the universe, and were forewarned of the fact that it was inhabited. Contact with the galactic community was not entirely surprising. These people have suffered a shock of far greater magnitude. It might be that they are reassured by their close resemblance to us, and that, through contact with humans, they can gradually become accustomed to contact with galactics in general. My species-brethren may be building vital bridges."

I was proud of myself; I thought it a speech worthy of a Tetron in its delicacy and guile. No doubt 822-Vela wouldn't agree, but a Tetron never will agree that anyone can play his own game half as well as he does.

"That would be a dangerous policy," observed 822-Vela. "And we must remember, Mr. Rousseau, that you humans are not practiced in the ways of diplomacy. Better, perhaps, to say nothing at all than to attempt a policy of friendliness that might easily do more harm than good."

Or to put it another way: *don't try to be too clever, human—you're not up to it.*

"I'm not sure that they'll be prepared to be polite indefi-nitely," I told him, not without a certain vindictiveness. "I think members of your own race might be in grave danger of harm. I think that it might be necessary to give these people some answers—and the answers we humans can give them may help to discourage them from attempting to extract information from you by violent means."

Tetron faces aren't expressionless, but they're very difficult to read, even for a human who has spent a lot of time around them. I couldn't tell whether he was disappointed or annoyed, or whether he was telling himself that this was just what you'd expect from a lousy barbarian.

Somehow, Aleksandr Sovorov materialized at my elbow. He seemed to know what I'd just said, though he certainly hadn't been in earshot when I said it. "It's important, Rousseau," he said, sternly, "to figure out exactly where your loyalties lie. Your past recklessness has already cost us one chance to communi-cate with the advanced race that apparently lives in the lower levels. It would be unfortunate if further recklessness were to damage our standing in the galactic community irreparably."

I deliberately turned away from both of them to stare directly out of the window. They edged round slightly, lining up on either side of the view like a pair of curtains.

"The thing is, Alex," I said, with all the condescension I could muster. "You aren't really in a position to see the big picture. Anyhow, I'm in the Star Force now, and recklessness is my profession."

Sovorov and the Tetron exchanged glances, and the Tetron bowed slightly before withdrawing.

"Vela and I were chatting yesterday, while you were being questioned," explained Sovorov. "We tried to establish what would be the best thing for you to do."

"Very kind of you," I murmured, hoarsely. "The Tetrax must be really proud of you, Alex. Their number one human yes-man. They're fond of yes-men. They'll probably give you an honorary number one day. Maybe as high as thirteen."

"I find it difficult to believe," he said, frostily, "that the Tetrax chose you to spy for them. They must have been desperate."

"They were," I assured him. I was still staring past his shoulder at the twisting dendrites with their colored lanterns, and the whirligig points of light that danced between their branches.

"Is this life-system DNA-based, Alex?" I asked him. He barely glanced behind him.

"I suppose so," he said, with the stiffness of one who does not appreciate the subject being changed.

"Come on, Alex, you're a scientist. You must find it rather intriguing. It's amazing, and it's very beautiful. You may have been here long enough to get used to it, but you can't have lost your curiosity entirely."

Sovorov shrugged. "It's pretty," he said. "But we can only look at it. If you want more data about its biology, you'll have to ask your new friends. That's assuming that they've bothered to investigate it themselves. I get the impression that whatever doesn't shoot guns doesn't interest them much."

"Sometimes, Alex," I told him, "you can be less than intelligent as well as less than charming. I believe you're in danger of losing sight of the reason you came to Asgard in the first place. You came to figure things out, right? You came to learn. I know you get impatient with all the fantasizing about the Center, but your impatience seems to have closed off your own imagination completely. Don't you ask yourself, ever, what Asgard is *for*, and what part it plays in the great scheme of things?"

"There's no point in posing questions until you have data that permit the formulation of answers," he said, defensively. Personally, I thought he was dead wrong. You have to formulate the questions first, and the bigger you pose them, the better they are.

"Did you know," I asked him, "that there's a microworld orbiting Uranus right now, dredging organic matter out of the atmosphere and the rings. They've found tons of stuff—DNA in all kinds of packages. According to a Tetron scientist I talked to, it's been there since the earliest days of the solar system, when it was briefly warm out there. Life antedates the solar system, Alex—maybe the galaxy. It's in the dust clouds between the stars. Sometimes it gets frozen for billions of years, but it doesn't care. It just hangs about until local conditions become conducive to reproduction, and then it gets going again. It rains down all the gravity wells in the universe, and wherever it finds somewhere that it can get along, it multiplies and multiplies as fast as it can, letting natural selection sort out the most efficient forms for local use. Wherever it can give birth to an ecosphere, it does. It negotiates its energy-economics with the prevailing physical environment, working out some kind of chemical compromise.

"My Tetron reckons that the DNA must have evolved spontaneously in the *very* distant past—and I'm talking about ten billion years here—and has multiplied and multiplied to the point where its creative efforts permeate the entire universe. He reckons that the fundamental humanoid gene-package evolved a long time ago, in some distant corner of the universe, and that it drifted into the galactic arm in some kind of vast cloud a few hundred million years ago to seed all the local stars at much the same time.

"On that basis, Asgard must be the product of a separate Creation, made in some other galaxy at some unimaginably distant point in time. And yet, its inhabitants—maybe even its builders—are first cousins to us and first cousins to the Tetrax. But if that's so, what can it be doing here? Was it sent to seed the galaxy? Did it bring those initial packages that were scattered all over the galactic arm? Or was it sent here to escape something? Is it saving specimens from the ecospheres of a thousand worlds from some unimaginable menace? And in either case—where are the builders? Why is their whole beautiful macroworld being allowed to run wild, with whole levels dead or deserted, and tinpot emperors appearing with dreams of illimitable conquest? What's going on here, Alex? You do *care*, don't you?"

At least, after all that, he had the grace not to stick out his black-bearded chin and reply with an obstinate: "I don't know." Instead, he said: "I didn't know about Uranus. It does cast new light on the question of whether the galaxy was seeded with life. The convergent evolution theory begins to look rather sick."

I nodded toward the alien forest with its marvelous fairy lights. "Not much convergent evolution there," I said. "That is some...."

I broke off in mid-sentence, and gulped. Sovorov had been watching my face, not the forest, and he had to turn around to look for what I had seen. By the time he was facing the right way, it was no longer there.

"What is it?" he asked.

"If it was what I think it was," I said, "it's probably a case of convergent evolution. I thought I saw a humanoid figure, out there among the trees."

"No," he said. "There's nothing like that out there. It's a low-energy ecosystem. It couldn't possibly sustain anything motile that's bigger than your little finger. Insufficient ecological efficiency—very weak food chains."

His comments proved that he had done a little bit of thinking about his surroundings, which served to restore some of my faith in human nature, curiosity-wise—but I still was convinced that just for a moment, I had seen something humanoid. It was difficult to judge distances because of the mist, and that made it difficult to judge size, too, but I had got the distinct impression that what I had seen was big and bulky—more like a giant ape than a human.

I opened my mouth to ask Alex whether the guards were in the habit of wandering around outside in pressurized suits, but I didn't get the chance. Two Neanderthaler troopers came over and beckoned unceremoniously. Sigor Dyan was obviously expecting me—and this time, I figured, he was going to want some answers.

Unfortunately, I still wasn't at all sure what answers I could give him, and my head throbbed mercilessly every time I tried to force myself to come up with a sensible strategy.

I was just about ready to fall unconscious, and leave the whole sorry mess behind. Instead, I walked with my escorts back along the corridors to my appointment with the inquisition.

CHAPTER TWENTY

When they brought me back to Sigor Dyan, everything was the same, except for the stuff he gave me to drink. The new liquor was brown and turbid, and reminded me a little bit of mussel soup. I had drunk quite a lot of mussel soup in my youth, because the closed ecospheres on asteroid microworlds—unenlivened in those days by imported Tetron biotech—frequently used engineered shellfish as a key element in their recycling processes. Mollusks, it seems, are clever in ways that other kinds of organisms aren't. They don't taste very good, though. I had never learned to love mussel soup.

I took a couple of sips from the cup, and then laid it down for good. I was still feeling queasy, and my temperature was way above normal. I had hoped earlier that I might be on the road to recovery, but the fever didn't seem to be clearing up and my nose was still runny. The headache seemed to be getting steadily worse.

"Personally," I told him, "I don't have any strong feelings about who I work for. I'm not altogether keen on the way the Tetrax do business, but I can work with them. I guess I can work with you, too. I'll tell you where to find the dropshaft into the lower levels which Jacinthe Siani has told you about. Say the word, and I'll even lead you to it."

He smiled with pleasure. "Actually," he said, "we already know the location of all the bases established by the Coordinated Research Establishment—including the one built around your shaft from level three downwards. We might be savages, in the eyes of the Tetrax, but we're not stupid. We can understand the maps we found at C.R.E. headquarters."

So much for secrecy.

"Why do you need me?" I asked him, bluntly.

"Because we don't understand much apart from the maps. We can't read Tetron script and we can't cope with the Tetron data-storage systems. All we know about what you discovered in the course of your adventure is what the Kythnan told us. Why have the Tetrax not established contact with the advanced race you encountered—if that is indeed what happened?"

"They didn't want to be contacted. Like you, they were somewhat surprised to discover the universe. You can probably appreciate what a shock it was far better than I can. Like you, they wanted time to figure out what to do about it. They had been in contact with the level we reached at the bottom of the dropshaft—an ecology run wild, its humanoid inhabitants regressed to *real* savagery—but after meeting us, they decided to withdraw, and seal themselves off from it. So they told me, anyhow."

"What did they look like? They were humanoid, I presume?"

"I presume so too," I told him. "But I only spoke to an intermediary." Rapidly, I sketched in the story of Myrlin, and explained that he had been adopted by the underworlders. I tried to keep the story as simple as possible, but there were several matters of detail that I had to fill out in response to his questions. I told him no lies, and by the time I'd responded to all his questions I'd told him virtually all the truth as I knew it—which didn't necessarily mean that he believed it all.

"As far as you know, then," he said, taking up the thread of the argument, "these people have no more idea than we do who built Asgard?"

"So I was told," I assured him. "And there's not the slightest reason to believe that they're your ancestors. It's entirely possible that they're another race like your own, who have simply made more progress in understanding the technology they found all around them."

"So you say. You also say that you know of no way to establish contact with them. It is all very convenient—as if you were trying your utmost to persuade me that we have nothing to gain from what you can tell us."

"I don't know whether you'd have anything to gain by making contact with these people—or with any other races who may be living in the deeper levels below your empire. Maybe you could find allies to side with you against the Tetrax. Maybe you could even find your ancestors—but I think you already know that there are no guarantees. You have no god-given right to come out of this situation the winners."

I think he did know that. Certainly, he didn't want to get into a heavy discussion about his hypothetical ancestors. As far as the origins of his species were concerned, he seemed to be an agnostic, no matter what the rest of his people might believe. After a pause, he brought the discussion back to more practical matters.

"This weapon they used, which you call a 'mindscrambler'— do the galactics have anything similar."

"Yes. The Tetrax certainly have a similar device, and so do one or two others. It doesn't work on all humanoids, and sometimes has to be attuned to the particular brain-characteristics of a species, but it's basically a matter of using a rapid-fire sensory transmission to trigger a protective withdrawal-response from the victim. It's the visual equivalent of a shot of anesthetic. A messy and somewhat indiscriminate weapon, though—you can't target a particular individual, and you can't just put it on a TV screen: you really have to blast it out. It was neat the way they used the entire sky on the second occasion—the first time, they used some kind of robot to deliver the punch."

"Where would large-scale versions of such weapons be found in Skychain City?"

"You probably won't find them now. There were mindscramblers incorporated into the anti-sabotage devices protecting the skychain itself and one or two other places. I suspect that you probably reduced those defenses to rubble, mindscramblers and all, when you blasted the skychain."

"I am suspicious of one part of your story," he admitted. "I wonder why it was that you were brought back to consciousness in order to hear what your friend had to say. Is it possible that they lied to you?"

"I don't know," I told him. "It could be all lies."

"It could indeed," he observed, in a fashion that suggested that he wasn't entirely convinced of my honesty.

I'd never been entirely happy with the story either, though I didn't like to admit it. I had come back from the depths convinced that I was cleverer than everyone else, exuberantly proud of my little secret. They might have fed me that happy feeling in much the same spirit as an adult bribing a child with a sweet. Maybe Myrlin *was* dead, and I was the dupe.

I blew my nose, and ran the back of my hand across my brow. I was sweating quite heavily, and I felt as if my brain had been hit by a mild dose of mindscrambling.

"Another thing puzzles me," said Dyan, after a pause during which he sipped his mussel soup. "If these people are so much more advanced than we are, *why* did they not know about the universe? Why have they not explored Asgard thoroughly, if they have been able to move about in the levels for so much longer? It seems too much of a coincidence to imagine that despite their sophistication, they have only been exploring for much the same time as ourselves, and had penetrated only a limited number of levels."

"Not necessarily," I countered. "Remember that they started from a home base a lot further down than yours. Myrlin suggested that they're immortal—that might imply that they long ago stopped multiplying; I doubt that an immortal race would be troubled by something as petty as Malthusian population problems. If their population within their own level is stabilized, they'd have no practical interest in expanding into others. Scholarly curiosity isn't such an urgent driving force as lust for conquest. They might have been exploring for tens of thousands of your lifetimes before they penetrated as many levels as you've invaded."

He nodded, abstractedly, and sipped more of his drink. "You should try to take some," he said. "While you have a fever, you should drink plenty of liquid. Shall I ask the doctor to look at you? He may be able to help."

"It's okay," I muttered. "Only a cold in the head."

"Are you well enough to answer a few more questions?"

"I think so," I said—and then wished that I had said no.

"I shall try to keep to essentials. I am grateful that you have decided to tell me all this, but there are other matters with which you might be able to help us, and about which I must question you. I'd like you to record for us, if you will, all the details of the plans that you and your employers made before you returned to Asgard. We'd like confirmation of what we already know about the groups of spies which were dropped from orbit—their personnel, their objectives, the bases they intended to use and the places at which they planned to enter the city. Can you do that?"

If I hadn't been feeling so awful anyhow, that might have been one to set me aback. As things were, I cared somewhat less than I might have.

"So Jacinthe Siani did know I'd left Asgard," I said, resignedly.

"No. But you were only the first member of your group to be apprehended. We have captured others, some of whom have been cooperative. Information about your mission reached me this morning. Some of your companions will be joining you tomorrow. I think that our people have enough information to round up all the invaders, but just by way of checking, I would be obliged if you could tell us all you know."

I looked at him sulkily, wishing that I felt in better shape to make a decision.

"As an officer in the Star Force," I said, finally. "I'm not able to tell you anything that might imperil my companions. It's a matter of military honor." I was only being slightly sarcastic. Susarma Lear might not have been my favorite person in all the world, but I was hesitant about betraying her.

"As you wish," he said, in an easy tone which suggested that he did indeed have the information already. "In fact, you do not seem to me to be well enough to undertake such a laborious task. I think that I will ask the doctor to see you again. After all, we do not want you to...."

Suddenly, the easy manner evaporated, and he was looking at me with a very different expression. I thought I could read him exactly as I would another human, and he had the appearance of a man who had been struck by a distinctly unpleasant idea.

I swallowed. My throat was sore, and I was becoming dizzy. The sweat was trickling from my forehead into my eyebrows, and running into the corners of my eyes to gather like bitter tears. I had to lie back, lolling against the leathery material of the sofa.

"Is it possible, Mr. Rousseau," he said, in a deadly voice, "that your Tetron masters *intended* that you should all be captured?"

I opened my mouth to say no, but the denial wouldn't pass my lips. It wasn't just the sore throat—it was the awful possibility dawning in my own mind.

I had asked myself more than once how the Tetrax might plan to go to war against the invaders of Skychain City. I had tried to weigh up the possibilities in my mind. But I hadn't really kept it in mind that the Tetrax aren't like humans. They aren't heavy-metal-minded. They're biotech-minded. They would always think first in terms of biological weaponry and biological warfare.

Now—very belatedly indeed—it occurred to me that the best way, and maybe the only way, to get a virus weapon into a domed city would be to use live carriers. And if the virus in question had to be carefully tailored to a particular biological pattern, so that it would hurt the enemy far more than the Tetrax themselves, then the carriers would have to be as similar as possible to the targets.

Suddenly, lots of little pieces of the puzzle seemed to fall into place. The Tetrax had received messages from the surface for some days after the attack. They had photographs of the invaders. Maybe they even had the results of gene-analysis of invader tissue. Maybe they had all that they needed to plan a swift and efficient counter-attack—everything except a group of clever carriers, to take the disease into the city for them.

They knew how primitive the invaders were—how unprepared they were to fight off a virus epidemic. They knew how easy it would be for their own people to seize control of the city again, if only the occupying forces could be comprehensively weakened.

And so they had used us. They had hired the Star Force, and they had hired me, feeding us that halfway plausible story about needing us to open lines of communication, to gather intelligence...when all they really wanted to do was use us as a bunch of Typhoid Marys.

"Oh *merde!*" I said, with a great deal of feeling. "The lousy, rotten *bastards!*"

But I could see in Sigor Dyan's face that he didn't believe that I was innocent.

It seemed the perfect time to give up the unequal struggle and let go, so I let the dizziness and the fever take control, and I fell into insensibility.

CHAPTER TWENTY-ONE

My memory of subsequent events is understandably a little
hazy. The fever didn't make me delirious in the sense that I was
afflicted by crazy dreams, but it did put such pressure on my
brain that I suffered continual lapses into semi-coma.

They tried to ask me more questions, and I tried to answer
them, but I wasn't terribly articulate and I don't suppose they
got much joy out of it. I wasn't taken back to my cell, but was
instead removed to some kind of isolation unit. All of a sudden,
everybody who touched me was wearing rubber gloves and
surgical masks. Even in my dilapidated state I knew that they
were locking the stable door with the horse long gone. Since I'd
slugged my first invader I'd been manhandled by an awful lot of
soldier boys. The disease would be peacefully incubating away
in a great many bodies by now. If the Tetrax really had planted a
biological time-bomb inside me—and I didn't doubt it—they'd
made sure that it had a nice long fuse, so it wouldn't show up
too early. I was still cursing myself for not having realized how
perfidious they were.

Tetron biotech makes for very good medicine, and a weapon
like this one would have been useless even against the likes of
human beings. The invaders, by contrast, could do very little
even to treat the symptoms. And I, poor hapless weapon, had to
suffer alongside them.

I must have lain in my new bed suffering the ravages of the
fever for several days. At first, I didn't even notice when they
wheeled in the other patients, and the realization dawned on

me only by degrees that there was only one person I knew who possessed a shock of bright blonde hair like the one adorning the head that was tossing and turning on the pillow five meters away.

There had been no need to worry about betraying Susarma Lear to the invaders. She'd already been betrayed—probably by order of the Tetrax, so that she could start the serious business of spreading her germs far and wide.

I remember thinking to myself, not altogether coherently, that it was a great pity, because now there was no U.S. Cavalry out there to ride to my rescue.

At some stage I must have been able to take a good look at the other two people who'd also been moved in, because by the time I became *compos mentis* again I knew who they were.

They were Sergeant Serne and Trooper John Finn.

I would like to report that I was tough enough to recover before anyone else did from the ravages of the sickness, but I wasn't. Truth to tell, I was still very much under the weather when the others were beginning to recover, and it took a lot of effort on the colonel's part to get me to pay proper attention when she woke me up in the middle of the night.

"Come on, damn you," she said, shaking me in a most unkind manner.

"Just leave me to die," I told her, in a croaky voice.

"You're not going to die, you stupid bastard. Would you rather I slapped your face or poured cold water over you?"

"Neither," I told her, aggrievedly.

"Then you'd better pull yourself together, hadn't you?" She still had a grip on the collar of the nightshirt which our hosts had provided, and she was bouncing my head around, apparently in the hope of shaking some sense into it.

"For Christ's sake, stop it!" I told her. She did, and the relief was very welcome.

She'd switched on a bedside lamp in order to see what she was doing, and she pointed its tiny light straight at my face to check that I was present and paying attention.

"Okay now?" she said. "Serne's still out for the count, but it looks as if he and that rat Finn will live. Did they tell you that they think the Tetrax used us to carry the virus into the city?"

"I was there when they reached the conclusion," I told her.

"Is it true?"

"You know as much as I do," I assured her. "But I believe it. Don't you?"

"Is this place bugged?"

"Jesus, Susarma, I haven't a clue. Alex Sovorov reckons they aren't clever enough, but he doesn't know his ass from his elbow. They don't know English anyway—don't be so bloody melodramatic! Have we any secrets left?"

"Only one," she said. "Before we left the solar system, I was told to investigate the possibility of making a deal with the invaders, to support them against the Tetrax, if that looked like a better deal than the Tetrax were offering. If they really did use us to start a bio-war, I'm inclined to wonder seriously which side we should be on."

"What I feel just now," I told her, "seems to me to be evidence that it's not a good idea to take on the Tetrax. The invaders are not going to win this war, even if there are twenty billion of them."

"The Salamandrans tried tricks like this all the time," she assured me. "We learned to cope. If you know what you're up against, it's not so difficult. Maybe the invaders could win—if they had our help."

"Not against the Tetrax," I told her. "It could have been worse. It's flu, not bubonic plague—it might be a dirty trick, but they could have played even dirtier. They've aimed to incapacitate, not to kill."

"You think it was intended to be a warning shot across the bows—to let the invaders know how far outclassed they are?"

"Who cares?" I complained. I wondered whether she'd just woken me up for a friendly chat, or whether she had something important to discuss. My body felt as heavy as lead, and my head hurt.

She must have seen that I wasn't in a good mood, because she got to the point. "We were shipped straight in here," she told me. "We didn't see much on the latter part of the journey, either. How much did you see? What are the chances of getting out of here?"

I managed a hollow laugh. In retrospect, I guess it would have been difficult to manage any other kind.

"They don't keep much of a watch on the doorways," I told her. "We could walk right out. Trouble is, the atmosphere outside has no free oxygen. Even if we had suits, there's nowhere to go but the shaft we came down. Beyond the shaft—invaders by the million."

She didn't seem particularly daunted by this news. "If we can pass for invaders...." she began. She left the sentence hanging. Then she said: "How many other humans are down here?"

"Only Alex Sovorov," I told her. "And he's next to useless. Anyhow, he's scheduled to get very sick in a day or two—we were sharing a cell. He's never going to forgive me."

She looked round at the other beds. "How far can we trust *him*?" she asked, nodding toward Finn.

"About as far as you can throw a feather into a headwind," I told her. "He probably already told the invaders everything he knew, and they probably sent him down here with us to make regular reports back. They might not understand bugs, but with Finn around they don't need to. Turncoat through and through."

The expression that crossed her face was one I'd seen before—determination mixed with disgust. Then she looked at me again, and I was surprised to see the expression change. It wasn't exactly a friendly expression—she didn't have one of those in her repertoire—but it showed traces of concern for my welfare.

"Get some sleep," she said, sounding very tired herself. "In the morning, play dead. I don't want them to know that we're recovering."

I didn't think it would be very difficult to pretend to be ill. I hadn't much faith, yet, that I was recovering.

In the morning, though, I really did feel a lot better. I woke up to a welcome absence of pain and disorientation. I can't say that I was brimful of *joie de vivre*, but I no longer felt as if I'd been through a document-shredder. I felt almost capable of coherent thought, and began to notice things.

I noticed for the first time the nurse who spoon-fed me breakfast, and with a gently practiced hand tipped water on to my tongue for me to sip. She wasn't an invader—she belonged to one of the other Asgardian humanoid species, as did most of the prison's menial workers. She didn't say a word, although she must have noticed that I was paying attention for once. It was unlikely that she spoke any *parole*, although she seemed to understand when I thanked her for her help with the food.

I noticed the doctor, too, when he gave me my morning examination, taking note of my temperature and pulse-rate before lifting my eyelid to shine a light at my pupil. I did the best I could to be ill, but I guess my body couldn't lie, because as soon as the doctor went out, Sigor Dyan came in. He barely glanced at the colonel before drawing up a chair to the side of my bed.

"I'm glad you're recovering," he said, flatly.

"Thanks," I said, weakly.

"It gives me hope that our own people will recover. The virus is already decimating the troops in the City. I am beginning to feel the effects myself. In two days, I will be in that bed, or one like it."

"Where will I be?" I asked.

He shook his head to indicate that he hadn't quite decided that yet.

"We didn't know," I told him. "If the Tetrax really did send us down here just to start an epidemic, they did it without our knowledge."

"I would like to believe that," he told me. "But I cannot be completely sure. If our people begin to die...."

I could see his point.

"We would like to strike back," he said. "We are very angry

about what has been done, and if you are telling the truth, you must be just as angry. If you want to redeem yourselves in our eyes, you must tell us how to attack the Tetrax."

I could understand his attitude. In all probability, I could understand it better than the Tetrax could. When they had planned this strike they would have thought of it not only as a way to facilitate a counter-coup in Skychain City but also as a way to make the invaders see reason and acknowledge the inevitability of coming to terms. That wasn't too bright. The Tetrax were always jeering at the stupidities of barbarians, but when it came to calculating the way those so-called barbarians might react to circumstances, they weren't very clever at all.

On the other hand, understanding his attitude wasn't quite the same thing as agreeing with him. It wasn't going to do anyone any good to start taking reprisals against Tetron prisoners, or trying to slaughter the Tetrax in the city.

"That's not such a good idea," I told him. "You fired the first shot, remember. Why not call it quits now? They're not going to let you ignore them. This is a matter of pride for them too. If you lash out at them, there's every possibility that they'll crush you. They may talk a lot about the joys of peace and harmony, but that's because they know full well that they have nothing to fear from violent opposition."

He looked at me bleakly. I could tell from the sweat on his brow that he wasn't feeling too good. Maybe his judgment was distorted. But an empire of twenty billion people spanning fifty levels is quite some juggernaut, and I could see why he might think that the idea of surrendering to a few thousand Tetrax wasn't too appealing.

"Mr. Rousseau," he said. "You had better decide whose side you are on. And you had better be prepared to show it. There will be no surrender."

After he left, I looked across at Susarma Lear. She pulled herself up on to her elbow, and stared at me pensively. Behind her blue eyes, there was a lot of hard thinking going on.

"If we're not careful," I said, "we'll be caught like a handful of corn between two millstones."

"You have to play the game from where you stand," she said. "We might have to look as if we're on their side, but we're on nobody's side but our own."

It was the only possible point of view. She would get no argument from me.

A little later, the nurse came back with another cup of water. I sat up to drink it—there didn't seem to be any further point in play acting. She stood patiently by the bedside, waiting. She had bluish skin and big eyes, with pointed ears and a cap of mousy fur where humans and invaders have hair. She seemed to me to have a friendly kind of face, and she also seemed to be the one person around from whom I had absolutely nothing to fear. I gave her a smile of gratitude and a respectful nod as I passed the cup back to her.

When she took it, she switched it for a folded flimsy. I blinked in surprise, but had sufficient presence of mind to clutch it in my fist and put my hand under the blanket. I unfolded it carefully and covertly, without having the least idea what to expect.

The message was simple enough. It said: *Four suits and a homing device will be in airlock nine, three periods after the lights go out. Someone will come for you. Two Tetrax will be with you. Do exactly as you are told, and all will be well.*

It wasn't signed.

That was hardly surprising.

What was surprising was that it was written in English.

CHAPTER TWENTY-TWO

You will, no doubt, remember my four criteria for maximizing the success of an attempted jailbreak. You can imagine, I am sure, how confusing it was trying to weigh up our situation in the neo-Neanderthalers' prison camp hospital in terms of those criteria

I could see immediately that criteria one and two would be fairly readily met. The invaders, unlike the inhabitants of *Goodfellow*, were sufficiently slavish in their devotion to habit to maintain regular hours, and didn't take the trouble to be overly vigilant in the hours of darkness. In addition, the epidemic which we'd brought with us was just beginning to break out among our genial hosts, and would presumably be causing a reasonable measure of chaos in the ranks. I had every faith in our ability to reach the relevant airlock easily and safely.

Criteria three and four, however, were the jokers in the pack. Did we have somewhere safe and cozy to go? Did we have *anywhere* to go? What sort of anywhere could there possibly be? It was all very well for our cryptic correspondent to assure me that a homing device would be provided, along with suits to protect us from the alien atmosphere—but where was 'home' supposed to be?

In addition to all these puzzles, I had also to worry about the identity of the man who had undertaken to assist us. As far as I knew, there was only one person outside of our sickroom who could write in English, and that was Aleksandr Sovorov. I couldn't think of any less likely person to mastermind a jailbreak. In the no-hoper stakes, Alex could have given John Finn a hard race, and maybe beat him. At least Finn was devious; Alex hadn't even got dishonesty to recommend him.

At the first opportunity, I slid out of bed and passed the note to Susarma Lear as covertly as it had been passed to me. I glanced in Finn's direction, to indicate my suspicion that we needed to be discreet even among ourselves. Finn had not yet raised his ugly head to take notice of the rest of us, but I had observed when he took his food that he did not seem to be in any worse state than I was, which presumably meant that he was only pretending to be unconscious. Deceit came as naturally to him as breathing.

While the colonel read the note, I moved into a position where I was between her and Finn, so that she could move her lips without being in his line of sight. That way, I figured, a whispered conversation could not be overheard.

She began with the obvious question: "Who sent this?"

"I don't know," I muttered. "Unless they've shipped more English-speaking prisoners down in the last couple of days, it can only have come from Aleksandr Sovorov. I can't believe that he's behind it, but he might be the middleman. If I had to guess, I'd say the Tetrax have arranged the break, and he's relaying a message from them."

"Why should the Tetrax want to spring us?" she asked.

"Who knows? Gratitude, maybe. They do have a strong sense of obligation, even to their slaves and other assorted cat's-paws."

"You really believe that?"

"It's not easy. I've met 822-Vela, and he didn't seem to be a mastermind. But who can tell with the Tetrax? Anyhow—*somebody* sent it. Do we really have all that much to lose?"

She pursed her lips. There was more than one possible answer to that.

If we jumped, we'd be leaping in the dark. We had to ask ourselves the usual questions: how bad was the frying pan we were in? And what sort of fire might we end up in?

"Do we go?" I asked. For once, I was looking for a second opinion. I guess being in the Star Force was beginning to pollute my soul. Instead of making up my own maverick mind, I was actually waiting for guidance from my superior officer. It can really take it out of you, being ill.

"Damn right we go," she said. "How the hell else do we find out what's going on? I'll tell Serne."

"What about...?" I tossed my head slightly to indicate the guy behind me.

She favored me with one of her best smoldering glares. "I don't think we can trust the bastard," she opined, in a fashion which suggested that Finn might be too ill to travel, whether he had recovered from his fever or not.

"It might be better to take him with us for precisely that reason," I pointed out. "If he's with us, we can keep an eye on him. If we leave him behind...who knows what he can get up to?"

She shrugged her shoulders. "I guess he's still in my command," she said. "But I don't know how long he was in their hands before they shipped him down here, and I don't know how much he might have told them. We should never have brought him, in spite of his experience in the levels and his supposed knowledge of Tetron surveillance devices. We should have sent him to the penal battalion, where he belongs."

I wasn't about to quarrel with that. Had we but known why the Tetrax really wanted us....

"What do you think is happening up above?" she asked.

"At a guess," I said, "a pitched battle. The Tetrax in Skychain City—and anyone else they can trust—will be making the most of the epidemic. They've had months to figure out where to cut the invaders' supply-routes. Starships will be landing to give support. For all we know, the Tetrax have plans to take control of ten or twenty of the levels below the city. Maybe they even know a way to get down here, and bring us out. I'm not prepared to underestimate their ability to wage effective war—not any more."

"And we thought they might want to hire the Star Force," she said, regretfully.

"We always knew what they thought of the Star Force," I reminded her. "Clumsy barbarians." I didn't add that we now knew what they thought the Star Force was fit to be used for—there was no point in rubbing it in. I could imagine the kind of feeling that must be roiling around inside her. She was Star Force through and through, and the insult which the Tetrax had hurled at us must hurt her far worse than any mere physical injury. Her pride would make her hate the Tetrax for this—and that hatred would be increased rather than diminished if they casually secured our release now. There was no point in my pointing out to her that the Tetrax had done what they had done entirely because of their own sense of pride.

I returned to my bed with a disturbing feeling that we might all be in the process of being led up the garden path. It was hard to make sense of this proposed jailbreak, and thinking about it threatened to renew my headache. I decided to get some sleep and recuperate as fully as possible. There was, after all, a certain truth in what Susarma Lear had said. If we wanted to know what the hell was going on, we had to follow the bouncing ball.

Just before I went off to sleep, I remembered the figure I'd seen from the observation window while I was talking to Sovorov. All of a sudden, the idea that it was a man in a space-suit began to seem rather encouraging. Was it possible that we had *friends* out there?

I woke up again for the evening meal, and for once found myself with a ravenous appetite—a sure sign that I was well and truly on the mend. The nurse seemed grateful to be able to hand me the bowl and spoon, instead of having to help out. I saw that all three of my fellow patients were now sitting up and taking notice. The food was the same kind of broth they'd been serving to us all along, with lots of unfamiliar vegetables and lumps of third-rate meat, but for once I wasn't too bothered about the taste.

Afterwards, I stayed sitting up, wondering whether it would

be possible to have a harmless conversation. Serne got out of bed, looking ridiculous in a nightshirt that barely came down to his thighs. I wondered what our chances were of getting hold of some decent clothes before we made our break.

I checked under my bed, and was pleased to see that my comfortable Tetron-issue boots were there, but my one-piece was nowhere to be found. It was probably in the laundry. The idea of having to make our great escape clad in nightshirts, boots, and spacesuits was sufficiently incongruous to be funny, but not too attractive. I hoped that the someone who came for us would bring the proper accoutrements.

Serne went over to talk to Susarma Lear. Finn got out of bed too, and wandered over to join in. Then the door opened, and he started guiltily. Serne just looked round, his face impassive, as a couple of orderlies wheeled in a fifth bed. Following behind it, looking ready to collapse at every step, was Aleksandr Sovorov.

He gave me a poisonous look of pure resentment as the rubber-gloved attendants helped him off with his trousers and on with the nightshirt. Unintimidated, I waited calmly until the coast was clear, and then hopped out to visit him.

"Sorry Alex," I said. "How was I to know?"

"There's a rumor going around that this is an act of war by the Tetrax," he croaked. "Are you responsible for that?"

"Not exactly," I told him. "They worked it out for themselves."

"It's not true," he said, defensively.

"Oh sure," I told him. "Finn and I probably picked up the virus on *Goodfellow*. It's probably been lurking in the Uranian rings for four billion years, waiting for someone to come along and be infected. And now it's free at last—saved from the ignominy of having to stay deep-frozen until the sun goes nova."

As I said this, I looked around at Finn, but he was studiously looking the other way. I took the opportunity to mutter under my breath: "Who told you to send the note?"

He was in too much discomfort to conjure up much of a look of blank incomprehension, but he did his best.

"What note?" he asked. Luckily his voice was too hoarse and his breath too feeble for the question to be loud.

"Nothing," I said, quickly. "Forget it." I turned round to face Susarma Lear. She was watching me like a hawk, and though she couldn't hear what had been said, her powers of deduction were easily equal to the task of figuring it out. "By the way," I added, "have any more humans arrived in the camp—more of the Star Force people, perhaps?"

"I've seen no one," Sovorov assured me. "And I really don't care."

"Do me a favor, Alex," I said. "Go to sleep—just go to sleep, and ignore everything that happens."

"I intend to do just that," he informed me, miserably.

The way he looked, there was little doubt that we could trust him to do it.

I waited for another opportunity to talk to Susarma Lear while Finn was lying in his bed and taking no notice. He had probably guessed by now that something was up, but he didn't know what. It didn't seem to be a good idea to tell him.

"Alex didn't write the note," I told her—confirming what she'd already guessed.

"It doesn't change anything," she said. "We still have to go. There might be other humans here—ones that neither you nor he knew about. Hell, it might be one of our boys—we don't know how many were picked up, where, or when. Serne and I were ambushed along with Joxahan when we went to a meeting-place we'd named on one of those stupid handouts Tulyar prepared. I knew that was a ridiculous idea."

She was right, of course. There could be other humans here. There certainly seemed to be humans collaborating—or pretending to collaborate—with the invaders. Maybe Sigor Dyan had other informants here, who were trying to play a double role just as I had. There must have been two hundred humans in Skychain City when the melodrama got under way, and there was just a chance that one of them had enough up top to be the Scarlet Pimpernel. If so, I couldn't wait to meet him.

No doubt we would find out the truth, when the time came.

In the meantime, though, there was nothing to do but twiddle our thumbs and try to build up our strength for the coming ordeal.

CHAPTER TWENTY-THREE

Everything was dark and silent for hours on end while we waited, pretending to be asleep. Sometimes, I actually dozed off, but every time I caught myself relaxing too much, I snapped myself out of it. The slightest noise was enough to wake me. Once or twice I was sure that the door had opened, but it was just nerves. Long before the appointed hour actually arrived, I had become impatient with the suspense.

When the door finally did open, the only light that came on was a tiny torch in the hand of a person who remained virtually invisible. The person handed me some clothes, and directed the light at them to show me what they were. My hand brushed the proffering fingers slightly as I took them. The fingers were hairy, with nails like claws. Not human, nor invader.

"Put them on," said an unfamiliar voice, in a purring whisper. The words were spoken in badly-accented *parole*. A barbarian, then—certainly not a Tetron.

I could see other bobbing pinpoints of light, and deduced that there were more of the visitors. I couldn't count properly, though, because the pinpoints were continually eclipsed by the bodies of the people who held them. I shoved my legs into the trousers I'd been handed, and swapped my nightshirt for a lighter garment. Then I dropped lightly from the bed and groped underneath it for my boots.

When I was ready, the hairy hand took me by the arm, and guided me toward the door. The others seemed to be ready too. They were bringing Susarma Lear, Serne, and Finn. I heard

Serne suggest to Finn that if he made a sound, or slowed us down, or did anything other than what he was told, he would end up dead. Serne could be fearsome when he was in that sort of mood, and I didn't doubt that Finn would obey. In any case, he might be just as keen as the rest of us to get out of here.

"I lead," said one of the furry humanoids. "Follow quickly. Make no sound."

Outside, the corridor was dark, but the firefly torches gave us something to follow. There were no lights on at all in this part of the camp, but we came quickly enough to a curving corridor which led past several of the observation windows, through which faint streams of colored light were filtering.

As we hurried past these windows, I was able to see that our guides were tall and thin, long-limbed like gibbons. I'd seen one or two of their race during exercise periods before I was laid low, and had assumed that they were one of the races conquered and displaced by the invaders while they were building their little empire. It seemed that the invaders' perfect prison wasn't quite as perfect as it had seemed, and that their dominion over the races whose habitats they had seized might not be entirely secure either.

We reached the relevant lock, and found that there were, as promised, a number of suits inside. They weren't heavy-duty pressurized suits of the kind that one would wear in a vacuum, but loose and lightweight plastic suits. They had no complicated life-support or waste-disposal systems—just a pair of oxygen-recycling cylinders apiece. The sight of them didn't fill me with enthusiasm or confidence. Their air-supply would be good for perhaps four hours, no more. When that time had elapsed, we had to be somewhere where the air was breathable. Racing out into the alien atmosphere, without knowing where we were going, or whether there was anywhere *to* go, suddenly didn't seem like such an attractive prospect.

"What's this all about?" I asked the furry humanoid who'd taken the lead in guiding us. "Where are we going?"

"No time," he said—or was he a she? I got the impression

that his or her *parole* was a trifle limited.

"Get into the suits!" snapped Susarma Lear, in a gruff whisper. She had got the bit between her teeth and nothing was going to stop her now. It was a philosophy of life that had already made her a hero. I hoped that today wouldn't be the day when it would make her a dead hero.

I had to take my boots off to put the suit on, but I put them on again afterwards, over the plastic feet of the suit—there might be a long walk ahead of me, and I didn't want blisters. While I was struggling into the suit the lock became even more crowded. There were several new arrivals, and although it was impossible to guess who was who in the near-darkness, I remembered what the note had said about Tetrax.

The inner door of the lock swung shut behind us, and the light came on automatically. I blinked furiously to dispel the glare, desperate to see what was going on. The tall furry humanoids had all stayed outside. There were, as promised, two Tetrax with us, just beginning to scramble into their suits. It's not easy to tell one Tetron from another, but one of them caught my eye and looked back with what seemed to be recognition.

"*Tulyar?*" I said, not entirely certain that it was he.

It's never safe to guess what a Tetron might be feeling by his expression, but the way he looked at me by no means gave me the impression that he was in control here. He looked bewildered—even frightened.

"Rousseau!" he said, forgiving me my indelicacy in addressing him without referring to his number. "Do you know...?"

That might have been a fascinating question, but he was only halfway through framing it when the alarm bells began to sound. The two Tetrax were already pulling their suits on as fast as they could, but the sound of the alarms panicked them into further haste. I jumped immediately to the conclusion that 994-Tulyar and his companion had no better idea than I did what was going on. The Tetrax weren't behind this break, after all.

I turned around to give the benefit of my sudden insight to the colonel, but she wasn't looking at me. She was puzzling over something that had been pressed into her plastic-clad hand before the furry men had faded away. As homing devices went, it lacked sophistication. It was just a glorified compass, with a swinging needle that always pointed the same way no matter how much the case was rotated. I knew it wasn't pointing to the north pole.

The lock worked on a double cycle—first the Earthlike atmosphere was replaced by nitrogen, and then that was replaced by the mixture outside. The pumps were quick, but the seconds were dragging by. Even inside the suits in the closed lock we could hear those alarm bells trilling away. I saw Serne looking at his hands, nervously, wishing there was something he could do with them. I had sealed my suit now, and so had the Tetrax, and though we could still be heard if we shouted the possibility of holding an intelligible conversation was remote. I looked at Tulyar's face, still trying to read it, though there was no longer anything in those alien eyes which I could call an expression.

Then the outer door was released, and we shoved it open, hurling ourselves through. We ran for the cover of the mist and the 'trees', and I prayed that the direction-finder the colonel had clutched in her fist would lead us to somewhere safe, and not just to a quiet spot where we could asphyxiate in private.

At first I reckoned we'd have a good four or five minutes start, because that was the time it would take to put the airlock through another complete cycle. I'd forgotten that there were a lot of locks, and that the neo-Neanderthalers could pile into any one of them. It can't have been more than two minutes before a dendrite to our left suddenly exploded, showering us with debris. It had only been hit by a single bullet, but the main structure of the thing must have been as brittle as glass. It didn't have to cope with any sharp impacts in the normal course of its affairs.

As we ran deeper into the 'forest', we had to let the colonel lead, because she had the device that was showing us which way to go. At first, she'd dodged around the twisting networks with their multifarious colored light-bulbs, but as she brushed the outer tips of the branches they broke, hardly impeding her at all, and she began to take a less sinuous course. She still couldn't go straight through the middle of one of the tangled bushes, but she became much less bothered about the fringes, despite the danger that sharp shards posed to our suits, and as we went we were virtually blasting a path for ourselves. The thought of all that wreckage in the delicate quasi-crystalline forest upset me, but the damage that was done by the bullets they were shooting at us was ten times as bad, so it was an angry kind of feeling rather than guilt.

The insectile gliding creatures were all around us, seemingly incapable of getting out of our way. In the misty semi-darkness it was like stumbling through a cloud of wind-swirled dead leaves and flickering candle-flames. When the dendrites shattered, their lights didn't go out as if they'd been switched off, but faded slowly into oblivion, so that the trail we left behind us was decaying gradually into grayness.

I was profoundly glad when we came out of the colored forest into a region where we didn't have to commit such evident vandalism as we moved, but the change of terrain wasn't greatly to our advantage in respect of the pursuit we were trying to evade. The mist was thinner here, and the ground became soft and muddy, slowing us down. The one consolation was that, instead of the trees, there were big bulbous mounds that could cut us off from the line of sight of the chasing invaders.

There was little color here: it was basically a monochrome landscape in shades of gray. Bioluminescent 'flowers' lived a more peripheral existence in this *milieu*, growing in small squat clumps between the fungoid mounds. I didn't doubt that the mounds were, in fact, life-forms, because their 'skin' moved in slow ripples, and seemed slightly moist, like the skin of a frog. There were very few tree-like structures, and they bore no colored lights. Their branches hung listlessly, and their paleness made it easy to think of them as dead, though there was no reason at all to assume that what would in another life-system be considered symptoms of morbidity might not here be signs of health and vitality.

There were fewer flying creatures here, too. The smaller firefly-like things were very scarce, and the greater part of the "animal" population consisted of gliders as big as an outstretched human hand, like butterflies and dragonflies made out of crisp crêpe paper.

There were fewer shots now—our pursuers rarely got a clear view of us, and now that the first recklessness of their excitement had cooled they were beginning to conserve ammunition. Serne, who had obviously been paying them closer attention than I, signaled to me that there were only half a dozen of them, but Susarma Lear extended the fingers of her left hand several times in rapid succession to remind him that there would soon be more. We could have shouted to one another even through the plastic of our helmets, but it would have been very difficult to make ourselves heard, so we settled for the kind of sign language that people use in vacuum. I could tell that the colonel was distressed by the stickiness of the going underfoot, and it wasn't hard to see why. If our pursuers could bring vehicles into the hunt, they could cover this kind of territory much more easily than we could.

Our problems were compounded by the fact that Tulyar and the other Tetron were already struggling to keep up. Even Finn was fit enough and fast enough to keep pace with the colonel, but the Tetrax are not overly devoted to physical culture, and Tulyar, at least, was a civilian used to all the comforts of advanced civilization. I saw Susarma Lear look back at them twice, speculatively, and I could imagine what was in her mind.

To what extent ought we to take risks ourselves in order to allow them to stay with us? Did we care if they became separated from the rest of us—and hence lost, given that we had the only direction-finder?

She didn't look to me for any advice. I didn't have any confidence at all in her eagerness to help them out, but I wasn't sure that I was eager myself. No one could have argued that I owed any favors to the Tetrax in general or 994-Tulyar in particular

Things didn't get much better in the course of the first hour. The shooting had stopped, but we had no reason to think that we had given our pursuers the slip. We were no longer sprinting and crashing carelessly through anything that got in our way, but we were still leaving a visible trail. Sometimes the gray mud was liquid enough to cover up our footmarks as soon as we'd passed on, sometimes it was set as hard as polystyrene, so that we didn't leave any noticeable imprints, but mostly it was somewhere in between. The invaders probably had no experience in tracking, but it certainly wouldn't have needed Cochise to read the signs and tell them which way we had gone.

By the time the first hour was up we were moving at a purposeful walk. Tulyar and the other Tetron were still with us, though they were showing signs of distress. We were surrounded by bulbous white growths, many of which were intricately patterned in dark gray and black. It wasn't easy to decide whether the dark tracery was specialized tissue belonging to the same organism or a kind of parasitic growth.

These globules seemed to me to be neither resting on the ground nor growing from it, but rather to be aggregations of the quasi-protoplasmic goo over which we walked, whose inner warmth I could feel even through my boots. It was as if we were walking upon a vast marbled-white tegument which welled up at irregular intervals into giant puff-balls.

It was easy to imagine that we were tiny endoparasites migrating across the skin of some vast scaly-skinned beast, and in my fanciful way I tried to enhance the illusion by trying to imagine the surroundings as verrucose growths on the hide of some albino giant. The globules varied in diameter from a meter to thirty meters; the larger ones towered above us and seemed almost to touch the ill-lit ceiling.

We dared not stop to rest, but Serne moved into step with Susarma Lear, touching helmets occasionally in order to be more easily heard. Their voices reached me as a low and distant murmur, and I couldn't see most of the hand-signals they were exchanging, but I knew they were discussing tactical options. I deduced that Serne wanted to try to get us some guns—feeling, no doubt, that two experienced Star Force commandos were easily the equal of half a dozen savages armed with vulgar popguns. I guessed that the further we went without reaching any sign of a destination, the more that idea might come to seem attractive to the colonel. She knew, though, that there wasn't time to lay an intricate ambush. We had no idea how much further we had to go, and our recyclers would supply us with oxygen for only three more hours.

Had I been fully fit, the pace at which we were moving would have been quite comfortable, but I had only just begun to recover from a bad bout of fever, and I was now beginning to feel weak at the knees. My stomach was sending me mutinous signals, and I became fearful that I might vomit. Throwing up inside a plastic suit is absolutely no fun at all, and can be very dangerous. You don't need a reducing atmosphere to choke you to death when a rebellious body feels like making its own arrangements.

The colonel and the sergeant were showing no obvious signs of similar distress, but as we went on I noticed a slight faltering of their strides. They might have been giving the Tetrax a fair chance to stay with us, but it seemed more likely that the sickness was beginning to take its toll on them, too. To my annoyance, Finn seemed to be having no difficulty at all.

I soon began to have distinct feelings of *déjà-vu*, remembering that last time I'd broken out of jail, I'd quickly begun to wish heartily that I'd never left the comfortable safety of my cell. I reminded myself that the invaders had been all set to treat me like a good friend, until they had been disconcerted by the plague I'd unwittingly unleashed among them. Now my ingratitude in opting out of their hospitality had persuaded them to try to kill me. And for what? We still hadn't a clue where we were going, or why.

I was seized by a distinct impression that ever since I had last been trapped deep inside Asgard with Susarma Lear and her loyal followers, with pursuers on our tail and the unknown up ahead, life had been one long bizarre dream.

Maybe, I thought, *I'll wake up in a moment to find my head aching from that stupid mindscrambler, and discover that I'm right back at square one.*

Unfortunately, it didn't happen. What happened instead was that a whole section of the sky got plowed up, and bits of it began to fall on the fungoid jungle like a black rainstorm. Just for a fraction of a second, it did look like the fancy mindscrambler Myrlin's friends had used during our final encounter, but it wasn't. The sound and the shockwave, arriving just behind the shattering of the sky, told us what it really was. The invaders had fired a shell at us from some kind of tank. They had miscalculated the attitude of the gun—the arc of the shell had been just a fraction too high and it had hit the ceiling.

It all struck me as being rather unsporting—it was like spearing fish in a bathtub. But I could hardly doubt that it would be effective, even if they only kept hitting the sky and bringing tons of debris down on our hapless heads.

Terror lent strength to my legs which I had been sure they did not have, and I ran. So did everybody else. There are times when you just have to let panic take over, and deliver your future into the unreliable hands of fate, even when you know full well that fate is out to get you.

CHAPTER TWENTY-FOUR

I think it was the fourth blast that knocked me off my feet, although the bangs and the shockwaves and the solid black deluge were beginning to blend into an endless ongoing confusion, and my head was aching so badly I thought my brain might be about to erupt out of my skull like a gray volcano. I went face forward into a mass of off-white goo, which seized my plastic-clad limbs like flypaper. I struggled for a few moments to get up, but then another blast went off nearby, and more of the ceiling rained down.

I'd had enough, I tried to stick my head down into the glutinous protoplasmic mud, and hoped it would swallow me up entirely. I didn't care whether it cloaked me, choked me, or digested me. I felt quite bad enough to be careless about dying.

There was another blast, not quite so near, and my head rocked as something bumped into my helmet. With the mud all over my faceplate I was as blind as a bat, so I raised my head slightly and began to push the mud away with my fingers. Something knocked my hand away and forced my head down again.

"Stay low, damn it, you stupid bastard!" The words reverberated, as if I were hearing them under water. Despite the *basso profundo* tone, I recognized the charm and poetic diction of my commanding officer.

There was a lull then in the firing. I felt her squirming round so that we were side by side, and she put her arm around me so as to snuggle in close. It wasn't a sign of affection. She just wanted to get our helmets so close together that we could converse without undue difficulty.

"They don't know exactly where we are," she said. "But they know which direction we're going in. I think the bastards are actually trying to bring down the roof on our heads—puncture our suits with shrapnel."

I had another go at clearing the mud from my faceplate. It seemed much darker now, possibly because the area of ceiling directly above our heads wasn't glowing any more—not even faintly. I had a momentary vision of the whole thing coming down on us—of the macroarchitecture of the whole world making an infinitesimal adjustment, and squeezing level fifty-two entirely out of existence, eliminating it from the scheme of things Asgardian. I imagined the collapse leaving only an extremely thin layer of organic sludge in a sandwich of awesome solidity. It couldn't happen, of course. No feeble shell fired from a cannon could do more than knock a few chips off the outer surface of the sky. Behind that thin tegument was something utterly unscratchable.

After a minute passed, she said: "They'll send in the foot soldiers to mop up, now. Stay cool, Rousseau."

Then the brief touching of helmets was over, and she was gone.

I sat up, and looked around. It was difficult to see much, with the local sky out of action. There was a lot of debris in the air—the mists were supplemented now with heavy smoke. Contrary to proverbial wisdom, though, there was no fire at all. For fires you need free oxygen.

I staggered to my feet, and continued to clear my faceplate as best I could.

Six or seven meters away a figure emerged from the roiling murk. It could have been anyone—except that it was carrying some kind of rifle. He must have seen me about the same time I saw him, and his immediate reaction was to bring the rifle to his shoulder. I never knew whether he just intended to cover me, or to blow my head off—another body hurtled at him from the left, wielding a great jagged-edged shard that must have fallen from the ceiling. The shard's battle-axe trajectory nearly took the armed man's head from his shoulders. The rifle spun away, unfired, and Susarma Lear fell upon it hungrily. She tossed the club to me, and pointed in the direction in which we'd been traveling. Her forefinger stabbed the air urgently, and I realized that she was telling me to get the hell out of it.

Behind me, as I lurched once again into a ragged run, I heard her firing.

With every minute that passed I expected to hear the tank open up again, and the images my mind produced of the sky erupting again spurred me on. I was no longer coherent in my thinking, but in a state of profound trauma. I had forgotten my stomach and the danger of vomiting, forgotten the agony in my unready limbs. The headache was still there, the blood booming in my temples, but there was no thought in my mind that it might all calm down if only I could stop running.

I got away from the smoke and the darkness, back to territory where the sky still glowed, and where the ground was firmer and flatter. In retrospect, that was a lucky break, because if I'd had to run around and between the black-patterned deathcaps for any length of time I'd have completely lost the direction that was indicated by the colonel's stabbing finger. As it was, I was soon back among dendritic forms again—but not, this time, the faintly-lit tangled things that grew around the prison. These were much bigger and more angular, growing floor-to-ceiling like heaps of scrap metal, intricately bedecked with spiky thickets of branches. Fortunately, they didn't grow close together and their most extensive branches grew above head height.

It was like running through a vast vault filled with gigantic decorated pillars—the fact that these trees were rooted at both top and bottom made the ceiling seem so much nearer.

I looked back once or twice, and to either side, but as far as I could tell I was completely alone. I could still hear the occasional crackle of gunfire, but it sounded surprisingly faint and far away. I wasn't in much of state to think about that. I just kept running and running. I fell three or four times, but each time I just jarred my bones on the hard ground, picked myself up, and kept going.

I kept going, in fact, until I reached the wall.

The levels of Asgard are full of walls. They have to be—after all, something has to hold the levels apart. In the topmost levels, with which I was most familiar, the walls were usually the walls of cities, with many doorways, because the supporting pillars were honeycombed with passages. Up there, though, even the more open spaces tended to be small in scale, continually cut up and blocked off by sections of structural material. This level seemed to have bigger spaces, and it also seemed to have thicker supports, because the wall I came to was smooth and black, and there was not the least sign of a door or a window or anything else in the thirty meters or so that I could see to either side.

I staggered right up to the wall, and put my spread-eagled arms upon it, as if appealing to it to be sucked in and dissolved. It was as hard as adamant, and surprisingly cold. Unlike the ground, which I judged to be close to blood heat, it felt as unfriendly as ice. I flinched away from it, and stood still, having not the faintest idea what to do next.

I was breathing in great ragged gasps, and my heart was pounding. I could feel no immediate sense of recovery as I turned around and looked back the way I had come. Seized by exhaustion at last, I sank to my knees, and then slipped sideways into a half-sitting sprawl, my upper torso propped up by my left hand. In my right hand, I was surprised to find, was the makeshift club that Susarma Lear had thrown to me before commanding me to run. I had carried it, without being aware of the fact, all the way from the scene of carnage.

I had no idea how much time had passed, and I became fearful that I might run out of oxygen at any moment. The recycler was still working perfectly despite the battering I had taken, but I had no way of knowing how much longer it would do the job before coming to the end of its resources.

My capacity for intelligent thought was restricted to the

consciousness that there were only three things I could do. I could go left along the wall; I could go right along the wall; or I could stay put.

I stayed put. I can now think of three or four good reasons why that might have been the correct thing to do, but I cannot honestly claim that any of them was the true reason why I did it. I did it because I felt completely and utterly finished. I was probably underestimating myself—after all, it wasn't the first time I'd felt that way—but I couldn't for the life of me get back to my feet.

Even when the other suited forms appeared between the spiky pillars, I couldn't get up. First there was one...then two...then half a dozen. I saw the nearest one pull up, turn and go down on one knee, firing twice before hurling aside what was presumably an empty rifle and coming on toward me. I saw one of the others fall, and two or three others returning fire, but there was no sustained firing, and some of the pursuers were hanging back. Obviously, the shortage of ammunition was universal.

The first one to reach my side was Susarma Lear. She took one look at me, and then reached down to grab the club from my hand. I could barely lift it to meet her partway. When she turned back, I realized that she was the only good guy who had made it through. Serne was not with her, nor Finn. There was no sign of the two Tetrax. All the other suited figures I could see were the enemy.

Now they knew they had us cornered they weren't chasing... instead they were fanning out, and approaching very slowly indeed. I realized that they were waiting for further support. There were five of them, but they were staying thirty or thirty-five meters away, awaiting reinforcements. I didn't take any pleasure in the implied compliment which they were paying to my heroic commander.

Seconds drained by, and nothing happened. The approaching Neanderthalers had all stopped, apparently just as drained by it all as we were. I stayed sitting down. Susarma Lear stood beside me, battle axe at the ready. I wondered whether she would carry the fight to them, if discretion kept them back for too long.

Then I saw the tank, maneuvering round one of the pillars. It was a great ugly thing, with caterpillar tracks and an absurd plastic-shielded turret. Forty meters away, it stopped. The turret-hatch opened, and a suited man climbed down, followed by two others. They carried pistols, and they began to walk in a leisurely manner toward us. I watched them approach, their lazy measured strides in sharp contrast to the staggering steps which were all that their companions had been able to manage at the end of the long chase.

She waited, without moving a muscle, until they were only three or four meters away. She stood in a slightly slumped position, as though she had given up.

But she hadn't.

She hurled the battle axe with all her might at one of the approaching men, and it took him full in the chest. He fell backwards, spilling his pistol. She hurled herself at the next in line, and though she moved faster than I could have imagined possible after everything she had been through, it had all taken just a little too much out of her. He was too quick on the trigger.

The shot, fired without aiming, must have gone through the flesh of her thigh, and I saw blood gush out into the cavity between her transparent plastic suit and the leg of her pants. I heard her scream of anguish, and I dived after her, trying to get my hands around her leg, in a desperate attempt to seal the rent in her suit. I knew that she'd be dead in a matter of minutes, even disregarding the bullet-wound, if the suit wasn't patched.

My own attempts were futile anyway—it didn't matter that the guy who'd been hit in the chest by her missile came to his feet in a temper and lashed his pistol across my helmet. In fact, if *they*'d been ready with some kind of patch or tourniquet, it might even have been the best thing for them to do, to clear me away while they took effective action.

They weren't interested in applying any first aid, though. They were more than happy to see us both die. The blow landed just about where Trooper Blackledge's punch had landed, and this time I felt as if it had really broken my jaw. I sprawled over, while he got ready to hit me again, and I saw that they weren't going to do a damn thing for the colonel. In fact, one of them tried to roll her away with his foot. I was watching him, not the man who was hitting me, so the second blow came right out of the blue, smashing into the other side of my helmet.

If the plastic had been rigid, it would have cracked, but the soft suit could take any number of blows like that. Unfortunately, the recycling apparatus inside the suit couldn't. I heard a kind of splintering sound, and I knew that the next few breaths I took would be the last ones from which I'd get any real benefit.

I lashed out with my foot, but didn't connect with anything, and then was flat on my back, gasping for air that wasn't coming through. Above me, silhouetted against the glowering sky, I could see three helmeted heads—our murderers.

And then, in what I thought at the time was a vengeful hallucination, I saw those three helmeted heads *dissolve* into murky black vapor.

For a few seconds there was nothing but the sky, and then something else floated into view. It was silvery and even in the faint light of that dreadful underworld it gleamed and glittered like something magical and marvelous.

Mon Dieu! I thought. *There is light beyond death after all*!

And then, it seemed, I died.

CHAPTER TWENTY-FIVE

You, of course, will not be in the least surprised to discover that I didn't die. I would hardly be telling you the story if I had. I, on the other hand, was in no position to prejudge the issue. It came as something of a surprise to me when I woke up again, and the shock was most definitely not ameliorated by the circumstances in which I found myself.

I was floating.

At first I thought it was a purely subjective impression; I leapt from that idea to the conclusion that I was in zero-gee. Eventually, though, the tactile messages arriving in my brain sorted themselves out into reluctant coherency, and I knew that I was *literally* floating on some kind of thick liquid, which wasn't wetting me. The only kind of non-wetting liquid I knew was mercury, but I was too deeply immersed for it to be mercury.

There was sound in my ears, but it was only the thin hiss of white noise, completely featureless.

I tried to open my eyes, and found it difficult—not because there was any tiredness left to make me want them shut, but because there were two wire-ends stuck to my eyelids. I had to pull my right hand out of the glutinous fluid to snatch them away. There were other wires secured to my forehead, and more on my skull. They weren't just glued down—in some peculiar fashion they seemed to be extending roots into my skin. I ripped them all away, not caring what kinds of sensors were on the ends. The 'roots' snapped easily, causing no more than mild discomfort, and leaving only a faint itching sensation in my skin.

The white noise ceased when I pulled the wires from my ears, and I was left in silence.

Opening my eyes brought me little immediate profit, because the light was as numinous and devoid of information as the sound in my ears. My visual field was filled with gray. I reached forward with my hand, and touched a surface about fifteen centimeters in front of me—above me, that is, given that I was floating on my back. The surface was concave.

I knew where I was, now. Not in Hell, and certainly not in Heaven. I was in a sensory deprivation tank.

I pushed at the concave surface, which was neither warm nor cold to my touch. The force of the push sent me back into the liquid, in accordance to Newton's third law, and then the liquid buoyed me up again, sloshing around the interior of the tank. The surface above me didn't yield.

I made a fist of my hand, and rapped on what I assumed to be the lid of my tank. The non-wetting liquid slopped around me, agitated by my movements. I tried to change my attitude, thrusting my leg down, and touched the floor of the tank, also concavely curved.

I'm shut up in a bloody egg!, I told myself, with deliberate vehemence. *Or in some kind of hi-tech make-believe womb!*

I remembered, then, that I ought not to be feeling too good. I moved my jaw from side to side, and touched my fingertips to the place which should have been injured. There was no break, and no sign of a bruise.

I had a pretty good idea where I might be, by now. I was down to my last hypothesis, and as Sherlock Holmes always used to remind us, when you have eliminated the impossible, whatever remains—however improbable—must be the truth.

I still wanted to get out of the tank. I don't suffer from claustrophobia, but there was something about that perverse liquid that I didn't relish. In addition to which, I was no longer deprived—I was conscious, and my mind was sharp and clear. A sensory deprivation tank is no place to be when you want to get on with your life.

I banged again on the inside of the lid, and suddenly felt it move beneath my hand. It was moving sideways, in an arc following its curvature. It was as if the upper, transparent half of the egg were being rotated about a central axis, disappearing into the lower, solid half.

I pulled myself free, not wet at all. I was naked, but the air was neither warm nor cold on my skin.

The light outside the tank was just as numinous, just as gray. I could barely make out the shape of the room. The walls seemed to be utterly without color, and were featureless. I looked back at the half-egg behind me, where the liquid had already become calm. Wires attached to the rim of the egg trailed in the liquid. There were more than I'd thought. They weren't metallic; they looked to me as though they were organic. The egg-thing looked like a giant woodlouse tipped on its back, with spindly legs everywhere.

The only thing I could feel was my own body. That was lighter than it had been for a while. The gravity here was nowhere near Earth-normal, or what passed for Asgard-normal in the upper levels.

I was just wondering where I might start looking for a door when the grayness of the walls was disturbed. White clouds, vague and almost formless, began to appear—not *on* the walls, but within and beyond them, as if the walls were windows looking out into a world of ghosts.

The clouds became humanoid faces, but in a strange unfocussed way. Their clarity wasn't enhanced by the fact that the faces overlapped, and passed through one another as they moved around the room. It was quite a fancy effect, but I wasn't unduly upset or surprised by it. The walls were obviously screens, and the cloudy faces were some kind of video-holographic display. The holograms looked very primitive and rough-hewn, but I wasn't convinced that it was poor technology that was responsible for their incoherency. There was something else...something not quite right.

The voice, when it came, was just as fuzzy. In a way, it was even more blurred, and multilayered—as if many people were trying to speak at once, and weren't quite managing to synchronize their voices.

"R-r-rouss-ss-ss-eau," they said.

"The ghost routine's no good," I told the walls, trying to inject some heavy contempt into my voice. "I know where I am, and I know who you are, too. What the hell are you trying to prove?"

The faces were huge—two meters tall from chin to crown—and the room seemed quite small as they drifted in and out of one another. They were becoming gradually more focused. They seemed to me to be a creditable imitation of human faces—female human faces. But I couldn't imagine what it was all for. Almost without meaning to, I counted the faces. There seemed to be nine. Nine didn't seem to me to be a very round number, so I recounted, trying to make it ten, but there were nine.

"P-p-pleas-s-se w-w-wait-t-t," they said. Their voice was slow and drawn-out. They were speaking in English. In spite of what I'd said, it really was rather spooky, not because of the nature of the apparitions, but because it didn't make any sense.

"How long for?" I asked.

I paused for an answer, but when they spoke again, they were on a different wavelength.

"Ap-p-pologiz-z-ze," they said. "S-s-sorr-rr-rry. W-w-will y-you ans-s-swer qu-qu-qu-quest-t-tion?"

Waiting for them to finish a sentence was distinctly tedious, but I decided that I probably had all the time in the world.

"Sure," I said.

"Ar-r-re y-you l-l-lonel-l-ly?"

I blinked in surprise. It didn't make any sense. I tried to concentrate on one of the faces, pretending that it was really looking at me, trying to meet its eye. I realized that it reminded me of someone. It wasn't quite right, but the features were obviously modeled on Susarma Lear. I looked at the others, then, scanning them quickly to confirm the hypothesis. They weren't all the same. Indeed, it was almost as if they were trying to be different—with difficulty, because they were all based on the same model. The pattern of modification wasn't random, either. It was as if they were borrowing just a little from someone else's face. I tried to remember what I looked like in a mirror, looking for bits of my own face, but that didn't work. I had to think quite hard before I finally realized whose features they were borrowing from to make their Susarma Lear-faces look different.

They were borrowing bits of John Finn.

"Loneliness isn't one of my vices," I told them. "But I would appreciate a little company right now. I know you can arrange it. I'll settle for Myrlin, or even one of your furry friends. I've been here before, I know, but you put on much better special effects then. Landscape with lions, bright and sharp—I couldn't see the walls at all, remember? I guess this is where you live. You don't have to put on human faces just for me. I don't care if you look like giant spiders."

Pause. Then: "M-m-must-t-t t-t-talk t-t-to y-you...int-t-teres-s-sted."

I couldn't quite work out where the voice was coming from. There was no obvious microphone, and it was diffuse, like everything else, as though they were having difficulty focusing it.

"I'm interested in you too," I told them, "but I had the impression that you didn't need to talk to me. I thought you picked my brain fairly thoroughly last time I was here—and all those wires suggest that you've been at it again."

"C-c-can't-t r-r-read m-m-minds," they told me. "S-s-so m-m-much of p-p-person-n-n on-nly at c-c-conscious-s-s l-l-level-l-l. C-c-can't-t und-derst-tand-d s-s-s-solit-t-tude."

I didn't get a chance to explain solitude to them. The door finally opened. I couldn't see whether one section slid behind another, or whether the hole just appeared. One moment there was nothing, the next there was a black rectangle more than two meters high.

Even so, he had to duck as he came through it.

Mercifully, he had brought my clothes. He even had my comfortable boots.

"Small universe, isn't it?" I said, as I pulled my pants on. The faces hadn't disappeared; they were still floating around, merging and coming apart. They didn't have to go around the door—they just disappeared at one edge and reappeared at the other. There was something very odd about their unseeing eyes. They had synthesized human features, but human expression was quite beyond them. They weren't quite my idea of immortal supermen.

"Hello, Mr. Rousseau," said Myrlin.

"You can call me Mike," I told him, not for the first time. "Especially as you just saved my life. I deduce that you saved Susarma, too. Did Serne make it?"

"No. But we got one of the Tetrax."

"994-Tulyar?"

"Yes. The other was 822-Vela. He was irredeemably dead when we got to him, like Serne."

Not just dead, I noted, but *irredeemably* dead.

"I suppose Tulyar was the one you really wanted," I observed. By this time I had my shirt and pants on, and I was pulling on my boots.

"In a manner of speaking," he said. He stood aside and indicated that I should precede him through the door. I went out into a gloomy corridor, lit by tiny electric bulbs strung along a wire. It seemed strongly reminiscent of the makeshift lighting the invaders had rigged up, none too cleverly, in the dark corner of Skychain City where they'd captured me. The walls were black and featureless. The corridors meandered left and right, with curves, corners and intersections, but Myrlin led me through the maze without hesitation.

"Why did you pull me out?" I asked him.

"Two reasons," he told me. "One—I thought I still owed you a favor. When I found out you were in the prison, I put you on my list. Two—they really are interested. In you, and in your companions. They already had records of you, but the records were damaged; the opportunity to have a second look was both a chance to renew their acquaintance, and a chance to assess how bad the damage was that they had sustained."

"There's something wrong with them?" I said—uncertain, though it certainly confirmed the impression I'd received.

"Something badly wrong," he confirmed. "They're still functioning, but...I'll explain it to you later. Who's the fourth one we pulled out?"

"Man named John Finn. Said to be good with electronics. We only brought him because we were afraid he might be useful to the invaders if we left him behind. They interested in him, too?"

"Oh, yes."

"Are the others awake?"

"Not yet. They're still probing the Tetron and Finn. The star-captain will take a little longer. She has a bullet wound in the leg and is suffering from tissue-necrosis."

The corridors were beginning to seem endless. Some of the side-branches were unlighted, and showed no sign of ever having been lighted.

"This isn't ancient biotechnics gone wrong, is it?" I said. "There never was light in these corridors."

"They don't use visible light much," he said. "Not in here, anyhow. The lighting's just for me. They used to be able to light the ceiling itself, but that was lost along with most of their other capabilities."

"I should have expected you," I said. "That note. It was stupid of me to assume that it came from Alex Sovorov. Your bosses—the super-scientists—must have been keeping an eye on the invaders all along. I should have realized."

He shook his head. "Actually," he said, "we'd only just begun to keep an eye on Skychain City. We were every bit as surprised as the Tetrax when the Scarida appeared. We weren't in a position to take a hand, then. Things had already gone wrong. I've had to take charge of a lot of things. We need to talk to the Tetrax, and to the Scarida too. The scions I planted in the prison to gather information will have declared themselves by now, but the Tetron virus has disrupted the chain of command both there and in Skychain City—it's a pity that you managed to infect a man as important as Dyan. It's a pity that the alarms went off so soon, as well; that might make it more difficult for the scions."

"It was hardly my fault," I reminded him. "Who are the scions?"

"The furry humanoids. The Nine made them—much as the Salamandrans made me—in the image of one of the races that the Scarida displaced. It wasn't too difficult to get them into the prison, once we'd found a way to that level. Our route up to fifty-two is direct and efficient—there are such routes available, once you know how to get access to them."

At last we came out of the corridors, and into what qualified as open space in Asgardian terms. But it wasn't like coming into the fresh air. There was a thirty-meter ceiling here, but it was lighted in the craziest way imaginable, with formless masses of silvery lights drifting and coiling like clouds against a gray background. And beneath this gloomy sky there were no "fields"—not even the kind of artificially-photosynthetic factory fields that the Tetrax had resurrected under Skychain City. There was a roadway, and a railway, extending side-by-side into the gloom, and there were buildings like metal igloos, but there was nothing alive at all.

I realized, belatedly, that the "sky" was no different from the "walls" in the room where I had awakened. It was like a vast video screen, and the clouds that moved across it were the traces of some kind of electronic activity. It suddenly dawned on me that Myrlin's masters had not simply rigged the sky to function as a big mindscrambler on that long-ago day when they had kicked me out of their little corner of manufactured paradise.

Myrlin's masters *were* the sky, just as they were everything else in this weird place.

They were everywhere.

No wonder, I thought, *they have difficulty producing manifestations of themselves in a particular location. And no wonder they don't understand "solitude".*

I turned to face him, able to see his face clearly for the first time, in spite of the dim light.

"Did they make you immortal?" I asked him.

"Yes," he said.

"You don't suppose they could do the same for me?" I enquired, tentatively.

"They already have," he assured me.

When destiny accepts you as a plaything, anything can happen. One minute, you think you're dead; the next, you might live forever.

CHAPTER TWENTY-SIX

It wasn't quite as good as it sounded. I could still be killed, violently. I could be stabbed, strangled, poisoned, burned, or blown up, and unless they could get me into one of their home-repair kits very rapidly, I'd be finished. But I wouldn't age. They'd repaired that little fault in my design.

Or so Myrlin said. I didn't feel any different.

"They might do more for you," he told me, "given time."

"Well," I said, "if they want to make deals with the Tetrax and the invaders, they certainly have some attractive bait on offer. But would they really want to offer immortality to twenty billion Neanderthalers?"

By now we were in a more homely environment. The steel igloos were houses, built for Myrlin and his furry friends. They had proper lighting, furniture, and all the usual amenities. Myrlin offered to feed me, but I wasn't hungry yet. While I'd been in the egg, all my needs had been taken care of—and then some, if reports of my newly-acquired gifts were really to be taken seriously.

"The situation is complicated," said Myrlin, "but I'll strip the story down to the bare essentials. I'd better start at the beginning."

"Please do," I told him.

"They call themselves the Isthomi," Myrlin said, settling back into an outsize armchair. "And they're personalities encoded in machines. Artificial intelligences, of a sort—but they were initially created as a result of the attempted duplication of the minds of humanoid individuals. Those humanoid ancestors lived in an enclosed environment not too different from this one, but the Nine don't know whether it was in Asgard, or in another artifact of the same kind."

"The Nine?" I said, remembering my counting. "You called them that before. Does it really mean that there are only nine of them?"

"Only nine," he confirmed. "The Nine's ancestors evolved from preliterate primitivism within their sealed environment. They had legends, which told them that their own remote ancestors had lived in a different kind of world, but until they discovered the universe the Nine had always considered those legends to have no basis in fact.

"Within their closed world, the humanoid Isthomi followed a path of technological sophistication not too different from the one that appears to have been followed by the Scarida—the invaders of Skychain City—except that they never found a way out of their closed world. They had no more reason to suppose that the light of the sky and the heat of the ground had been built in order to sustain them than men of Earth have to suppose that the sun was designed to light the Earth and placed there for that purpose, so they took their enclosed cosmos pretty much for granted.

"The humanoid Isthomi fought many wars, and despite relative shortages of certain heavy metals, they managed to develop an impressive technology of destruction. The time came when they had the power in their hands to destroy their world. They managed to avoid that eventuality, joined their nations and factions together into a single world community, and became, as your jargon has it, 'biotech-minded'. They also developed an elaborate silicon-based information technology, but more slowly than similar technologies have been developed by cultures like the human, whose progress in inorganic technology was aided by a relative abundance of appropriate raw materials.

"The humanoid Isthomi developed technologies of genetic engineering applicable to the transformation of somatic cells in mature bodies, and to the manipulation of egg-cells. They developed a technology similar to the one by means of which I was constructed—accelerated growth coupled with a kind of transcription of personality. Their experiments in the creation, modification, and transcription of personalities eventually led them to try to recreate personalities in different forms, including duplicating the minds of humanoids in silicon-based electronic systems. Thus were born the software Isthomi.

"It's impossible to guess how accurate, as copies of humanoid minds, the Nine were in the days of their infancy, but the question must have become irrelevant very soon. Minds they certainly were, and from the moment their new incarnations began they were able to undertake a whole new process of growth, maturation, and evolution. They changed very greatly, once they were no longer limited by fleshy bodies. They inhabited a vast complex of linked machines, sharing the new 'space' in which they were distributed with countless non-sentient programs as well as with one another.

"At some stage in history, however, the Nine—or perhaps fractions of the original Nine—were removed from their original environment and placed in another, of which they were the sole intelligent inhabitants—and which appears, in fact, to have been designed specifically to accommodate them. Their memories have no record of what was done to them. They don't know why it was done, or how, or by whom.

"The Nine don't know how long a lapse of time was concealed by the gap in their memories. They're not entirely certain that the memories they have that relate to their existence before they came here are to be trusted. They know how easy it is to create a new individual—robotic or organic—with a wholly synthetic 'past', and they wonder whether they might not have been created likewise, with a synthetic history inbuilt into them. But the essential questions still remain: By whom? And why?

"The Isthomi are by nature patient. They live their lives, normally, at a slow pace. Their sleep, and other trance-like states, may last for time-spans which would be many lifetimes in humanoid terms. They had no urge to be fruitful and multiply, to replenish this new world in which they found themselves. But they did set out to explore it, and eventually, to *fill* it. Their machine-bodies had the means to produce robotic extensions, and through those extensions they began to increase themselves still further. They undertook a process of colonization parallel to the process of colonization by means of which a handful of humanoids might set out to populate a world and build a civilization there, except that they manufactured no new individuals, but simply extended and complicated their own bodies. Their mobile robots were simply parts of a much greater whole. The analogy of an ant-hive will probably spring to your mind, but it is a misleading one; it would be more appropriate to compare the robots to motile cells within the body of an individual—white blood corpuscles, perhaps.

"For many thousands of years this process of expansion continued. The Nine did not compete with one another, but operated always in concert. Each of the Nine considered the companionship of the other eight to be infinitely precious. The Nine are not egotists—rather, they fear loneliness and excessive individualism, and they value community above all else. They're not Nine so much as Nine-in-One."

With an attitude like that, I thought, *they should certainly get on well with the Tetrax*. But I couldn't help wondering whether the Tetrax might not find them a little too clever to be entirely welcome.

"At some stage," Myrlin continued, "the Nine made the startling discovery that their enclosed habitat was not the only one in the world—that there were other environments above, below, and beyond it. They also made the discovery that there was a pre-existent technology connecting the levels, supplying them with energy in an ordered and controlled fashion.

"They concluded, of course, that the world in which the humanoid Isthomi had lived must have been a similar artificial environment, and that it might be nearby. By finding it, they supposed, they could find out why they had been removed from that world and placed in another. Naturally, they set out to investigate the technology which had been used in the design and construction of Asgard, and they also set out to explore the neighboring levels, at their own characteristic pace—which would seem rather leisurely to our species.

"They did not find the world of the humanoid Isthomi—although it might, of course, still exist somewhere in the bowels of Asgard. They did find many other levels with humanoid inhabitants, but in most cases the humanoid races were not thriving. They inferred, after considerable study, that their neighboring levels were like their own, in that a few individuals of a civilized species had been introduced in the distant past and left to their own devices. But they found no individuals like themselves—only humanoids and other fleshy creatures.

"Many of the humanoid species had made some progress in rebuilding the civilizations from which they had presumably been taken, but for almost all, the process of social evolution had been interrupted. Whatever legacy of memories the original colonists had brought with them had been lost, so that their descendants reverted to savagery, sustained by elementary agriculture or by hunting and gathering. In some, there was a recovery after the initial decline, so that when they had increased to fill up their new world, they began again to follow the path of technological progress; but in no case that the Nine found was there any species which had done as they had done, and conserved the heritage which they had brought with them into their new world.

"The uppermost of these inhabited levels was the one to which Saul Lyndrach found a route—a route that was followed first by me and later by you. You know what we found there—a decadent population, living in the ruins of a city built by their remote ancestors, under threat from animal predators which had evolved from less aggressive ancestors under strong competitive pressure. You know, too, that the Nine had begun to supply the inhabitants of that level with materials, fearing that they otherwise might become extinct. They had conceived of that project—as they conceive of all their projects—as a long-term matter, in which they could make plans for thousands of years.

"Our arrival changed their worldview very radically, and what I was able to tell them about the topmost levels of Asgard, and about the universe beyond, was a revelatory shock whose magnitude we cannot possibly imagine. We are young species, the humans and the Tetrax, and we are no strangers to surprise. The Nine are very old, and they had to make considerable adjustments in coming to terms with the knowledge that the universe is very different from what they had imagined.

"Their initial reaction, as you know, was to seal themselves off and give themselves time to think and to discuss. They told you that they would seal off the level which you had penetrated, and they did—but they left extensions of themselves on that level to continue the business of gathering information, and they opened new channels of communication between the levels they knew and the ones above.

"The Nine not only adopted me, as an informant who could tell them a great deal about the universe outside Asgard; they also began to use the technology by means of which I was created, to construct more humanoid bodies. You called me an android, and I suppose you might think of the scions as androids also, but I don't think that designation is correct in either case. I'm a true human, developed from a human egg-cell—albeit in unusual fashion. My new companions are true humanoids too. They were brought to adult form in a matter of months, and though the minds inside their heads are abridged versions of the minds of one or another of the Nine, they're entitled to be considered men and not machines. Because of the manner of their origin, they share just nine names, and distinguish them-selves otherwise by number, so that they can know one another as different versions of their parent personalities."

Again I noted how this made the prospect of a deal between the Nine and the Tetrax look healthy, and I wondered in my suspicious mind just how far the Nine had gone in making prep-aration for such a deal. The Tetrax had a long history of seductively playing the other galactic races for suckers, and I wasn't distressed by the thought that they might be due for a strong dose of their own medicine.

"The Nine," Myrlin went on, "were very disturbed by recent events in the upper layers. The Scarida, apparently, are an exceptional species; although they haven't completely avoided the pattern which reduced most of the other transplanted races to savagery, they've managed to transcend their primitivism more rapidly than any of their neighbors. They've multiplied more rapidly, and have continued their expansion beyond their own level. They've met very little opposition until now, and know full well that they face a desperate task now that they've set themselves up in opposition to technologically superior opponents. It might not be easy, though, to persuade them that the limits of their expansion have been reached.

"The Nine knew that the task of forming a community of species out of the three very different factions which are now involved—the Scarid empire, the galactic community, and the levels known to the Nine—would not be an easy one, but they had to face the idea that the entire future of Asgard was at stake, and that they have to play a role in the deciding of that future.

"That was the point at which the Nine decided to try a very daring experiment."

"And that," I put in, "is where things went seriously wrong?"

He nodded, slowly.

"What did they try to do?"

"They tried to connect themselves up to the software of Asgard itself—to extend themselves beyond the machinery of this particular habitat into the fundamental machinery of the macroworld itself. They projected their mind-group into the network of control systems that's built into the structure. The systems that impinge upon the habitats are, of course, simple ones governing the distribution of heat and light. The Nine presumed, though, that those systems must provide a means of access to further, more complicated systems, probably inhabited by machine-personalities like themselves. They believed that they could make contact with those personalities, by extending their own mind-group into the inner regions of Asgard's 'software space'."

"They thought they could set up a hot line to the builders," I said.

"In essence, yes," Myrlin agreed. "They hoped that at the very least they might find out about the true extent and nature of Asgard's electronic 'mind'."

"Why didn't it work?" I asked.

"Because the systems into which they tried to project themselves are themselves damaged. The Nine weren't just sending a message out into the hardware in Asgard's walls. They were transmitting themselves. All nine of them—because, although distinct, they're essentially inseparable.

"If the systems controlling Asgard had been simple and automatic, those systems would just have become part of the Nine's extended body. If those systems had their own highly-refined artificial intelligences within them, then contact would have been made—albeit a kind of contact for which you and I have no ready-made analogy. It wouldn't be like two humanoids meeting at a conference table—more like two immiscible liquids flowing together. The Nine didn't think there was any real danger in what they were doing, even though they couldn't know what kind of reception they might get from the intelligences they were trying to contact. They were wrong."

"What happened?"

"I'm not entirely sure, and the Nine can't explain it to me. I don't know whether they were the victim of actual hostility or unfortunate circumstance. But whatever it was, they made contact with down there, it went through their electronic selves like a bomb blast, injuring them very badly. They're not dead, and they're not quite incapable, but they're seriously hurt. They may well have lost aspects of their own personalities, and—more ominously—they might have unknowingly picked up parts of other personalities. They're no longer entirely coherent. Again, it's difficult to find an analogy, but it's as if you were to wake up feeling very weird, unable to access large chunks of your memory, occasionally acting without knowing what you were doing and why, maybe hearing voices too—as if your mind were no longer fully in control of itself or your body, and as if there were bits of other minds somehow lodged in your brain."

I thought about it for a few minutes, trying to figure it all out. It didn't quite come together to make a coherent picture—I thought I could see what he was getting at, but it was as dim and strange as those not-quite-focused faces, in which guise which they'd appeared to me. Anyhow, it seemed that our software supermen were no longer as super as they once had been—which could make things complicated, if their grand plan still involved bringing peace and harmony to the whole of Asgard.

"It's not at all clear what we can conclude from the Nine's unfortunate experience," said Myrlin. "But I'm rather afraid that there are two available ways of looking at it, neither of them encouraging."

"Go on," I said.

"*If*," he said, emphasizing it heavily to let me know what a big if it was, "the builders of Asgard—or the guiding intelligence the builders left behind to look after it—is an entity like the Isthomi instead of a humanoid species, then what happened to the Isthomi when they tried to contact it can only be interpreted in two ways. Either it's hostile—or like everything else in and of this macroworld, it's badly decayed: mad, senile, or incompetent.

"If the first hypothesis is true, we could all be in deep trouble—you, me, the inhabitants of Asgard, and the inhabitants of the galactic arm. There's no way we can fight something like that. If the second hypothesis is true, the situation is even worse. All the aforementioned are still in trouble—and so is Asgard itself."

"Not necessarily," I countered.

"Oh no," he said, "not necessarily. But think about this: if the Nine experienced the contact they made as a kind of bomb-blast, which has all but reduced them to helplessness, how do you think the other side experienced it? *If*"—that big if again—"it did the same to the indigenous systems, it might have done untold damage to Asgard. And you know what has to be in the middle of Asgard, to produce the energy that runs all the levels, don't you?"

I did indeed. At the physical center of Asgard, whatever was wrapped around it, there had to be a little star. The biggest artificial fusion reactor in the known universe.

"And you think...?" I began.

"I don't know," he said. "But I do think that we'd better make every effort to find out."

CHAPTER TWENTY-SEVEN

Later, Myrlin had to leave. It was time for 994-Tulyar to awake, and he wanted to be there, in order to begin the lengthy business of explanation all over again. He wanted to put Tulyar into direct contact with the Nine as soon as possible, so that Tulyar could begin the work of bringing peace and harmony to the upper levels.

"I'm hoping that the scions will be able to bring some of the Scarid leaders down here soon," Myrlin told me. "The Scarida will have to put themselves in the hands of the scions, of course, and leave their hardware at home—but if they have any notion at all of the realities of the situation, they'll come. We can bring them swiftly and directly here—one thing the Nine did get from their excursion into the structural systems was a much more elaborate picture of the connections between the levels. As I told you, we now have access to a shaft that goes directly from this level to fifty-two, with a working elevator still in it."

"What do you want me to do?" I asked.

"Stay out of it for the time being. The Nine do want to talk to you, though. They'll probably send a couple of the scions over to do the talking, but they'll hear everything themselves. Don't be alarmed by the scions—they're partial personalities of members of the Nine, modified for life as humanoid individuals, and they're somewhat weird, but they've made a lot of progress during the last months. We can't make any more for the time being—we just wouldn't be able to fill their heads effectively now that the Nine have been injured. We daren't run the risk of producing madmen. A great pity—we should have made hundreds more, in a dozen different forms, while we had the chance. We may need them. By the way: Finn should be waking up too—or would you rather we kept him in the tank?"

"It's okay," I said. "Send him out. I'll look after him. What about Susarma Lear?"

He shook his head. "Another twenty-four hours, I should think," he said.

After he had gone, the furry humanoids came to visit. There were two, and they were certainly somewhat weird.

"We are Thalia-7 and Calliope-4," said one of them, peering at me with big brown eyes. They looked more like Tetrax than humans, but their hair was shaggier and much lighter in color, and their faces weren't as compact. They had wide mouths and rubbery lips, and put me in mind of steep-faced orangutans.

"Thalia and Calliope?" I queried.

"The Nine have no names; they have no need of them. When they created our partial personalities, we adopted names suggested by your species-cousin Myrlin, and numbered different versions of each parent personality in a fashion similar to your more distant species-cousins, the Tetrax."

They sat down together on a sofa, moving almost in unison. They could easily have been twins, and I would have inferred from the way they stuck so close that they were aspects of the same personality rather than different ones, but I guessed that it might take two to make a crowd, and remembered that they didn't like "solitude". I couldn't tell what sex they were, but in view of the fact that they'd chosen to name themselves after the Muses, I decided to think of them as being on the female side of neuter.

"Why are you so interested in me?" I asked them. "Paradoxical as it may seem, Myrlin probably has more of the heritage of human knowledge locked up in his mind than I do, even though he's never been to the solar system."

"But you have seen so much more of the universe—and you know much more than he does about Asgard. In any case, it is good to talk as well as to know. To express knowledge...." She groped momentarily for words, then concluded: "...is to create being."

I looked at them both, uneasily aware of the fact that these were beings more alien than any humanoids I had ever before encountered.

"I thought the Nine's machines had picked my mind clean," I said. "I thought you knew more about me than I do."

Calliope shook her head, obviously intending the gesture to be read as a negation. "We know much," she assured me, "but there is a sense in which we also know little—so very little. We can only know about you by hearing your own account. In one sense, that is the only real account that can be given. Do you follow?"

I thought I did. The real person is the active, thinking, talking person. I was the only one who could tell them about me. And it was something that had to be told, not extracted by neuronal taproots plugging into my brain. They might have copied my brain's software in some arcane fashion, but that wasn't the same thing as knowing the person who belonged to that brain.

"What do you want to know?" I asked.

They wanted to know a great deal. About myself; about the history of mankind; about the evolution of life on earth; about cosmology and cosmogony and atomic physics and things that go bump in the night. In some sense, they knew it all already, but they wanted to hear it. There was a great deal that I couldn't tell them, and much that was very difficult for me to put into the proper words, given my own ignorance and lack of expertise, but I tried.

All the while, they watched me. It was as if they were studying me, learning how to be human....how to be humanoid. They were unfailingly courteous in asking questions—like great grave children anxious for the lowdown on the business of adult living.

And in the end, of course, they asked me about Asgard— about who might have built it, and why, and what I thought about it, and what my reasoning was.

So we were back to the heart of the matter again, back to the thing that could hardly help but fascinate us all—except that the matter was more complicated now, because the Nine had their own unfortunate experience to add to the register of perplexing evidence.

We talked for a long time, and much of what we said even about Asgard simply went over old ground. I told them about the galactic races, and about all the things I'd discussed with 673-Nisreen aboard *Leopard Shark*—all of which was news to them. We had a sense of getting nearer to the whole picture, but we still didn't have enough to put it all together.

"The Ark scenario still looks most likely," I told them. "The way I had it figured, on the basis of what I saw in the levels while the Scarida were taking me to prison, was that the builders of Asgard were making an object to contain thousands of environments, reproducing the conditions of a whole galaxy full of inhabited worlds. From each world they then took a series of ecosystems, and a handful of indigenes. But what Myrlin told me about the Isthomi doesn't quite square with that. There, it seems, the parent culture was living in a macroworld like Asgard, with no memory of any worldly existence. So maybe Asgard is a daughter macroworld, reproducing the structure and cultural diversity of an earlier model. In which case—was the earlier model an Ark, or do we face an infinite regress?"

"We are more anxious about the disaster which appears to have overtaken the world," said Thalia-7. "What we have discovered about the outermost levels of Asgard is puzzling. For one thing, the outermost levels seem once to have had a level of technological sophistication that few of the levels below have reproduced, even though they were evacuated long ago. Wherever the inhabitants of those outer levels went, it was not to the levels immediately below. But the mystery of where they went is perhaps a lesser matter, compared with the mystery of why?"

"The standard theory is that Asgard lost most of its atmosphere passing through a dense, cold cloud, and that the levels had to be evacuated because of that. We always supposed that the outermost levels, unlike the levels below, relied upon an external source of energy—an outer sun rather than an inner one."

"That is a possibility," conceded Calliope-4—the two scions tended to take it in turns to speak—"but given that levels just below the outermost ones are equipped to draw energy from the distribution-system that exists in the walls of the macro-structure, we find it difficult to believe that the outermost levels could not have been sustained through any such disaster. We also cannot understand how the temperature in those outer levels fell so very far. We think it could not have done so by virtue of any natural process. We tend to favor the hypothesis that the outermost levels were deliberately cooled, and that the regions whose temperature was reduced almost to absolute zero were set up as a kind of defensive barrier."

"A barrier against what?"

"Some kind of invasion." Thalia took up the thread again. "Not by entities like you or us, but by something microscopic, on the same size-scale as bacteria or viruses."

I remembered all those bacteria, frozen in the rings of Uranus for four billion years, and still viable. But the temperature in the vicinity of Uranus was still tens of degrees Kelvin. Cold preserves, but not *absolute* cold. Maybe it was easier to freeze the outer layers of the macroworld than heat them up or irradiate them to the level needed to destroy a microscopic invader. But it was difficult to believe. Bacteria are no threat to an advanced biotechnology, and viruses can be combated too. Myrlin had assured me that neither he nor I now had anything to fear from that kind of attack.

I explained to them that there was yet another aspect of the problem that interested me, and that the existence of entities like Asgard might help to explain why all the galactic star-faring races were about the same age. I pointed out that one could easily invert the story about Asgards—it seemed that we were now entitled to speak in the plural—being populated in the first instance by borrowing from the ecospheres of worlds. Perhaps, instead, the ecospheres of worlds were populated by borrowing from Asgards. I explained my gardening analogies: Asgard as a seed-nursery, its builders as planters, engaged in a project of colonization whose time-scale ran to millions of years. They thought the story more plausible and more palatable than Nisreen had—but they were used to the idea of personalities inhabiting inorganic hardware, whose sense of time was very different from that of planet-born humanoids.

The galactics had always imagined the builders of Asgard in their own image—encouraged, of course, by the fact that the one-time inhabitants of the outer layers had been humanoid. The Nine, obviously, had always thought of the builders as beings more like themselves—beings whose personalities might be distributed through the systems of the entire macroworld. That would have looked like the more likely hypothesis, now I knew that it was on the map of possibilities, except for two things. How could we explain what had happened to the Nine when they tried to contact these hypothetical master-builders? And why would beings like the Nine, only more so, be interested in seeding whole galaxies with the kind of DNA that eventually produced humanoid beings?

"If the chronology of the Nine is anywhere near accurate," I said, "then it can't have been *this* Asgard that seeded the galactic arm with the genes of my remote proto-mammalian ancestors. Perhaps the one that did has gone away again. On the other hand, there's every chance that there are other Asgards lurking about in the galaxy—even in the local region of space, which has been very imperfectly explored. If the others aren't in solar systems, we wouldn't have a snowball in hell's chance of locating them. We travel between star-systems in wormholes—for all we know, the depths of interstellar space might be lousy with macroworlds. Maybe we only found this one because something *did* go wrong with it."

I think we could have gone on for several more hours, but

we were interrupted by a knock on the door. It was a curiously homely sound to be hearing in that bizarre place.

"That'll be Finn," I said, as I went to answer it.

I was due full marks for deduction. When I opened the door of Myrlin's little igloo, I found that it was indeed John Finn who was standing on the doorstep. But he wasn't quite as I had expected to see him.

For one thing, he had a gun, which he was pointing at my chest. I could tell by his expression that he wouldn't be at all averse to using it. It wasn't a mud gun either—it was the kind of gun the invaders used. Given that, the second surprise dovetailed perfectly with the first. As well as the scion who'd presumably been appointed by Myrlin to guide him here, he had three Scarida with him, one of whom was my old adversary with the sky-blue eyes.

They were all carrying guns.

Only a soldier, I reminded myself, as a sinking feeling took possession of my stomach. *He's only a soldier.*

It seemed that these particular enemies weren't quite ready to negotiate on our terms. In fact, it looked as if they weren't in a negotiating mood at all.

CHAPTER TWENTY-EIGHT

When we were all safely inside, with the door closed, I relaxed a bit. Not that it was a very relaxing situation—the gleam in John Finn's eye suggested that he would like nothing better than to blow my head off. He still blamed me for everything. The three invaders with him were as nervous as cats, though. I guessed that they hadn't the slightest suspicion of what the real situation was.

Thalia-7 and Calliope-4 stood up, anxiously. "What has happened?" asked one of them.

The invader officer looked at them, but didn't answer. He seemed very uneasy indeed, as if none of this was making much sense to him. That was hardly surprising.

"What's happening at the prison camp?" I asked him. "The negotiations between the scions and your superiors must be under way by now."

I got no response save for a blank stare. He didn't know anything about any negotiations. He didn't know that Thalia, Calliope, and all their siblings were scions of the Nine. To him, they looked like members of a conquered race, and he couldn't figure out what they were doing here. He was out of his intellectual depth.

"Who brought you here?" I asked, trying to take the initiative in what was sure to be a difficult conversation, and hoping that I could explain it all to him.

"As a matter of fact," said John Finn, "you did."

I looked at him in puzzlement, thrown out of my conversational stride. He was grinning with smug satisfaction. I could only wait for him to explain.

"You were right about me," he said. "I know what you told the blonde while we were sick in that hospital. You told her I couldn't be trusted. Dead right—I don't owe one damn thing to the Star Force, or Mother Earth, or the whole human race, let alone the Tetrax. When the invaders picked me up, I told them everything they wanted to know—and then some. I told them about all the little gadgets the Tetrax gave me, about which I knew a little bit more than the Tetrax thought I did. I told the Scarids how to start searching for all the bugs that were already in place. They found lots of them in the city—and we found some in places we never expected to. It took me a while to realize that I was carrying a bug myself, but I figured it out. My boot heels were leaking some kind of organic muck, leaving a trail for an olfactory sensor. Guess who else has a couple just like them."

I remembered what had happened last time I had been followed into the deeper levels.

"Oh *merde*!" I said. "Not again!"

He nodded.

"But why?" I asked. "It doesn't make sense for the Tetrax to bug their own agents."

"Maybe they didn't trust you," said Finn. "Want to know what I think? I think they expected us to defect to the opposition—if not immediately, as soon as we found out what we were really carrying. They knew we'd be in trouble when the invaders found out that we were carrying that damned virus. They expected us to take the obvious way out. And they wanted to be able to find us again when the war was over."

I suppose it was just about plausible, but I didn't believe it. The Tetrax had no interest in persecuting us. My theory was that they had tagged us for our own good—so that they could save us from the wrath of the invaders, if they got the chance. The Tetrax fight dirty, but they do have that curious sense of obligation, and in their own weird fashion they do go in for orderly moral book-keeping. A man like John Finn wouldn't begin to understand things like that, though, so I didn't try to argue with him. Anyway, he hadn't finished bragging yet about how clever he had been."

"The Scarids don't know anything about electronic security," he told us all, "but it didn't take me long to show them what was going on in Skychain City. I was a lot sharper than the Tetrax gave me credit for, that's for sure. Then I fell ill, and they shipped me downstairs with the others. When we all broke out, though, they discovered just how useful the information I'd given them was. Tracked us here—no more than a couple of days behind."

It was interesting enough, in its way, but it was distracting us from the issue at hand. I turned back to the man with sky-blue eyes.

"The situation's changed now," I told him. "The Isthomi in the camp...."

"You bet the situation's changed," Finn interrupted. He wanted to be in charge—to call the tune. "Skychain City is in the hands of the Tetrax again, and they're shipping in war materials just as fast as they can."

I ignored him, and continued to appeal to the man with blond hair. "Lives are being lost," I told him. "The Tetrax will run right over you if your people don't capitulate. There's no help for you here—not the kind of help you're looking for. These people aren't your ancestors, and they can't give you any superweapons to help you turn the tide of battle. All they can do is make their own peace with the Tetrax—and they have a great deal to offer. They've already begun to talk to your people, back in your own levels. You can only foul things up by running around with guns down here. Believe me, it's all out of our hands."

It was no good. He was only a soldier. I might as well have been talking to a brick wall. It wasn't just that he didn't believe me—I just wasn't making any sense at all. I had to try harder, but I didn't even know where to start.

I glanced sideways at Finn, wishing that he wasn't there

to complicate matters. "What exactly do you intend to do?" I asked, in a tone as gentle as I could manage

"We want weapons," said Sky-blue, as though it were perfectly obvious. "We want the mindscramblers that you described to Dyan. We want weapons powerful enough to stop the Tetrax and drive them offworld again. We want to take control of Asgard, and keep it."

"And how do you intend to proceed?" I asked, trying not to be sarcastic. I turned briefly to look at the scions, who seemed utterly bemused by it all. They were content to leave it to me for the time being, it seemed. I was flattered by their confidence, but I couldn't believe that I was actually making any headway in this crazy discussion.

"We want to speak with the immortals," said the blond-haired soldier, in his best heroic manner. "We want you to take us to the people who rule this habitat."

"I don't need to take you to them," I told him. "They're here. Not just Thalia and Calliope—the walls, the floor, the ceiling. They're not people like you and me—they're electronic person-alities. Sentient computer programs. They don't have bodies as you understand them. They're all around us." His eyes were blank, and I knew that I wasn't getting through. "I can't help wishing that they'd take a more active part in all this," I went on. "I wouldn't object in the slightest if they put us all to sleep with one of their fancy tricks, and let us sort things out without those guns you're waving around."

I was assuming, of course, that the Nine were quietly observing all this, as they'd quietly stood by while the Star Force settled accounts with Amara Guur on my last visit. I assumed that they had the situation completely in hand: that these cowboys had been detected and closely watched ever since they had penetrated this level, and that the only reason the Nine hadn't yet acted was that there was no need to panic. I wished, though, that they could take a hint.

But nothing happened, and I couldn't help casting an anxious glance at Thalia and Calliope. I realized that I didn't really know how badly the Nine had been injured by their software skirmish. Maybe they hadn't been paying attention when the Scarid soldiers sneaked up. I knew they were supposed to be paying attention now, because Myrlin had told me that they'd be eavesdropping on my conversation with the scions—but there was only silence and inaction.

Was it possible, I wondered, that the Isthomi no longer had sufficient control of their own systems to take effective action against the invaders? And if so—then where, oh where, was Myrlin?

"You're not in any position to make demands," I told Sky-blue. "Surely you must realize that."

"As it happens," said the Scarid, "we are in a stronger position than you think. I believe you were wounded when they brought you down here. You did not see the machine or the shaft connecting this level to the ones above. It is a very deep and unusually wide shaft. I do not know how many levels it extends to below this one, but I know there are many hundreds above. The total volume of the shaft must be immense."

"So what?" I said.

"So it's evacuated," said Finn, with a sneer. "The warning signs aren't in any language we know, but whoever posted them intended them to be clear to anyone with an atom of intelligence. We had a long journey down here, and plenty of time to figure out the graffiti. That cage goes smoothly up and down in an evacuated shaft, which is deep enough to suck an awful lot of air out of this habitat. All it takes is enough high explosive to blow the lock. We can do a lot of damage with one big bang, and if the people of this level like air, perhaps they ought to talk to us, okay?"

I shook my head in disbelief. "You don't get it, do you?" I said, exasperatedly. "You have no idea what kind of a universe we're living in. I don't know whether you really have enough explosive to blow a hole in this habitat—maybe you do—but you can't hurt the Isthomi. They don't need air any more than they need light, and you could blast away at them for years with your stupid popguns and not hurt them. Can't either of you get it into your heads that your firepower isn't any good any more?"

They looked at the guns in their hands, which were still pointed at my chest.

I turned again to Thalia and Calliope, appealing for some assistance. I felt that I had done all I could, and that it was their turn now. I had the uneasy suspicion that they were still observing, in fascination, the interactions of all these strange alien beings, as if they were watching down the barrel of a microscope as a culture of bacteria underwent some kind of awful crisis. Perhaps they weren't even wondering whether they ought to care.

"We can take you to a place where you may communicate directly with the Nine," said Calliope.

I wasn't entirely sure what she meant. Surely the Nine were here. They were in the walls; they were in the sky. They were hearing every word. We didn't have to *go* anywhere. Or was it me that didn't understand?

It was hardly for me to complain. I was only an innocent bystander.

"Haven't you seen them already, Finn?" I asked. "Didn't you see any ghosts when you woke up?"

"I don't know what you're talking about," he replied.

"I should have told Myrlin to let sleeping dogs lie," I said. "You did meet Myrlin?"

"The big guy who brought me out of that weird maze? Sure. He went back in again—that was just before I found my friends here."

"They're not your friends, John," I told him, switching from *parole* into English. "Compared to these guys, the Star Force is your father and your mother. You may be a piece of shit, but you're a piece of shit in Susarma Lear's command. Her you can trust. The Neanderthalers would shoot you in the back as soon as look at you."

Sky-blue was waving his gun, to suggest that he didn't like what I was doing.

"Shut up, Rousseau," said Finn, in *parole*.

"I want to be taken to someone in authority," said Sky-blue. "Now."

Thalia-7 intervened, and began talking to the invaders in what I assumed to be their own language.

The officer replied in kind, and all of a sudden he was launched into a dialogue with the two scions. I felt a little hurt about my sudden exclusion, and also a little anxious. The most obvious reason for switching languages was that Sky-blue's non-*parole*-speaking friends could now understand what was being said, but there was a nagging doubt in my mind that it might be because they didn't want me to understand. I reminded myself that the scions might look like elongated teddy bears, but there was no way to be sure that they cared one way or the other what became of me.

About three minutes went by before they switched back to a language I knew. Then it was Calliope who spoke—to me.

"We will do as this man wishes," she said, confirming the apparently-nonsensical suggestion she'd made earlier. "We will guide him through the corridors, so that he may speak directly with the Nine."

If she wanted to shoot them a line, that was okay by me. It was the Nine's world, and the rest of us, whether we knew it or not, were probably about as important to them as insects, no matter how interesting we might be. The Nine were in control— I didn't doubt that for a moment—and I was ready to play along with anything they said.

"Okay," I said. "If that's what it takes."

So we set out to retrace my steps into the maze of corridors that was one tiny part of the body of the Nine. As we went, I was uncomfortably aware of John Finn walking behind me, reveling in the fact that he had a gun pointed at my spine. I consoled myself with the one small measure of unholy glee that I could discover. If Finn had got away without facing ghosts before, I thought, he certainly wasn't going to get away without facing them now.

CHAPTER TWENTY-NINE

In order to go through the narrow corridors we had to string ourselves out somewhat. Thalia-7 and Calliope-4 walked together in the lead, with the Scarid officer and one of his bully boys behind them, guns in a threatening position. Then there was me, with John Finn sticking close, still getting a kick out of being able to hold the gun on me. Two more Scarid soldiers brought up the rear—there had been further reinforcements waiting outside the igloo. Another two remained outside, theoretically protecting the expedition's rear.

As we marched through the maze I kept expecting the walls on either side to come alive, wresting control of the situation from our captors with a mindscrambling flourish that would be as contemptuously easy as taking candy from a baby. But nothing happened, and the doubts continued to creep up on me. Somewhere up ahead were Myrlin and 994-Tulyar, but I had no idea whether they'd been warned about what was happening. Were the Nine just sitting back, like the audience at a play, waiting to see who would get shot?

Once, as we passed a dark side-corridor, I considered making a break, but Finn was just too close to me, and too obviously ready to punish any indiscretion. In any case, I had no place to go.

The walls on either side of us stayed black. There was not a flicker of a ghost. The life that was within them was quite invisible, and was seemingly content to remain in hiding. Confidently and without hesitation the two scions led us through the maze.

I could see that the man with pale blue eyes was becoming just a trifle worried, as it dawned on him that he'd never be able to find his way out unaided. Twice he lifted his radio to his lips, to contact the men outside, making sure that he was still in touch. I still couldn't decide whether or not Finn's story about the evacuated shaft and the explosives was anything more than a desperately inspired piece of stupid bluff, but the officer was taking it seriously enough to take pains about his presumed ability to send a signal to tell his men to arm the bombs.

I figured that the Nine could blank out his communications any time they wanted to, so that if it came to the crunch the message couldn't be sent, but there was still that edge of doubt. Nothing was happening, and I couldn't understand why. Gods and aliens move in mysterious ways, so the proverbs assure us.

I sought reassurance in telling myself, facetiously, that one would naturally expect the Nine Muses to have an acute sense of dramatic tension and suspense. There are times, though, when I don't find my own sense of humor very funny.

Finally, we reached Thalia and Calliope's intended destination. A hole opened in the wall, with a sufficiently magical flourish to make Sky-blue start with surprise, and we were able to pass through into a cornerless chamber whose ceiling was glowing with faint pearly light.

Thalia and Calliope went on through, but the Scarid officer hung back, eyeing the mysterious portal. In the end, he stepped through it, but he told the two soldiers who were bringing up the rear to stay outside and stand guard. That meant there were only three guns inside with us, but the odds were still far too high for me to want to try anything. I didn't think the scions were the types to be relied upon in that kind of fight. If Serne and Susarma Lear had been along, it would have been a different matter.

There were no sensory deprivation tanks here, but there were three 'chairs' hemmed in by all kinds of electronic hardware. They looked to me like the kind of chairs that medics use to take electroencephalographic readings and conduct SQUID brain-probes, or in full-scale biofeedback training. They had trailing nests of tentacular wires, like the ones which had sent superfine threads burrowing into my head while I was inside the egg.

I guessed that these were sophisticated interfaces by which conscious humanoids could hook themselves up to the Nine's main systems. They were probably the means by which the scions communed most intimately with their parent software personalities, and the means by which the Nine could enter into frank and full discussions with Myrlin, 994-Tulyar, and any other volunteers.

Myrlin and 994-Tulyar were already there, comfortably ensconced in the chairs. They didn't move or open their eyes when we entered, and even when I touched Myrlin on the arm, he gave no sign at all that he knew I was there.

That was the point at which I began to get very worried, having realized at last that something was badly wrong, and that the silence of the Nine was not simply a manifestation of their patience and curiosity.

Sky-blue didn't like the set-up one little bit, to judge by the expression on his face. I could see the expression quite clearly, because the room was well-lit by comparison with the gloomy corridor. The walls were screen-like, but they were solid gray. There was no console in front of the chairs to control their operation. It was all inside the big hoods into which the would-be communicants had to put their heads. The Scarid had never seen anything like it, but he too was beginning to realize that Myrlin and Tulyar were too quiet for their own good.

I stood back as the blond-haired officer came to stand by Myrlin, reaching out to touch him on the arm just as I had. I looked at Calliope, but her eyes were fixed upon the face of her sister. They wore very similar expressions, and it was an expression which spoke volumes, even upon an alien face. It was not a startled look, but a look which told us all that something they had already begun to fear was now self-evident in all its tragedy.

If I had any lingering doubts, that look dispelled them. I'd been coasting on all kinds of false assumptions. Something bad had happened—not something trivial and absurd, like the invasion of the habitat by the Scarid officer and his gun-toting comedians, but something truly desperate.

Ignoring Finn, I took Myrlin's burly wrist in my hand, and felt for a pulse. His body wasn't cold, but I couldn't find any evidence of a heartbeat. When I lifted his eyelid I could see only the white.

I went to Tulyar. I didn't know what kind of crucial tests you can apply to figure out whether or not a Tetron is dead, but he had no discernible pulse either. I looked back at Myrlin, remembering that this was the guy who'd promised me only a couple of hours before that I was as immortal as he was.

"What happened?" I asked Thalia-7.

She shook her head, to signify that she didn't know.

"What's going on here?" demanded Sky-blue.

To him, she said: "I think the Nine are not here."

He couldn't begin to understand what those few words implied. The nature of the Nine was way beyond the scope of his imagination. He still expected some bad-tempered authority figure like Sigor Dyan to emerge from hiding and say, "What can I do for you boys?" The fact that Myrlin and Tulyar were probably dead was something he could take in, but the fact that something had zapped the Nine—and what that implied about the nature and power of the something—was just so much noise to him.

I looked around at the gray walls. *Dead?* I wondered. *Can it really all be dead? Not just a set of persons but an entire world?*

"I want to know what's going on!" said Sky-blue. I almost expected to see him stamp his foot in petulant rage.

"Our hosts are indisposed," I told him. "They were already injured by something they made contact with—something at the Center. I can't believe that they tried again, so it must be the other way around. It must have come after them! Maybe it came to destroy them. Maybe it was only doing what they tried to do... trying to make contact. The Nine aren't here, but...." I looked around those still, silent walls, expecting that any second they would burst into furious life. "...Maybe somebody is," I finished, in a rather hushed tone. "Maybe *somebody* is."

Sky-blue's reaction was almost pitiful in its stupidity. He took three strides over to me and pistol-whipped me across the face. I rode with the blow, but it still hurt a lot. That right-hand side of my jaw seemed to be attracting so much violence I wondered if it had some kind of target painted on it.

"If you don't start talking sense," he said, "I'm going to get rough."

Thalia and Calliope looked shocked and pained by this outburst, and they moved even closer together than they already were. They weren't being much help. I wasn't entirely surprised. Solitude was threatening them now in a way it never had before. The possible extinction of their parent personalities was probably the most hideous thing imaginable, from their point of view.

I was tempted to advise retreat—to tell the moronic barbarians that they were inside the body of something alien and unknown, which might well mean them harm, and that if they could even begin to understand what was happening they wouldn't stop running until they were back home...and then some.

But that would be silly. If the Nine's systems really had been taken over by an alien *persona* of some kind, there was no way we could escape. If it had only been a destructive blast, wiping out the life of the systems entirely, there was no need.

I looked at the third chair—the empty interface. There might well be one way to find out. I looked again at the scions, and saw that they too were eyeing the chair, with no great enthusiasm.

By now, John Finn thought he had worked out what was going on. He took it upon himself to explain to his friends what the score was.

"The way I figure it," he said, "the computers were running the show. The machines were the ones in charge here, and these furry freaks are the hired help. The Tetron was making a deal when something crazy happened. Something else got into the machines—something that could hurt them. It looks as if the artificial intelligences have been ripped up, and these two got hurt in the crossfire. Rousseau thinks it's still in there. God only knows whether or not he's right. It might all be play-acting, but I don't think so. I think maybe we'd better get out of here."

Sky-blue looked at him frostily, and didn't budge an inch. Being only a soldier in his kind of army was ninety-nine percent courage and only one percent brains. I think he'd been accidentally short-changed on the intellectual side.

Unfortunately, he was obviously having great difficulty figuring out an alternative course of action.

"This is all a trick!" he said, eventually.

It was a nice idea. I wished I could believe it, but it was too much even for Finn, who seemed to be an expert at believing whatever happened to be convenient at the time.

The Scarid pointed at the empty chair. "Is this a device for talking to these machines?" he asked.

"Sure," I said. "Sit down, and they'll shout directly into your brain, without bothering with your ears—if they can still talk at all. You could be in line for a medal here. It might be posthumous, of course, but all the best-earned medals are." I nodded at the ominously still figures of Myrlin and 994-Tulyar.

Unfortunately, I must have expressed myself rather badly. He thought I was trying to be nasty. It's always dangerous to try sarcasm on aliens—even aliens who look like Neanderthal men. Either they don't understand it, or they take it in entirely the wrong spirit. He still wanted to believe that it was all a trick, and he didn't like the idea that I was treating him with undue contempt. At that moment, I think, he was feeling just as badly disposed toward me as Finn.

"Very well," he said. "You will please try it first."

Finn actually laughed.

I spread my arms wide. "Why don't you just shoot me?" I said. It was bravado based on desperation. I wanted to be out of the limelight, back on the sidelines where I belonged. But there was no one else handy to take over center stage. Myrlin was *kaput* and if Susarma Lear was still alive, she was slumbering in her sensory-deprivation tank, missing out on all the fun.

"If you don't sit in that chair," said the man with the pale eyes, "I will shoot you. You may be certain of that."

It was plain that he had had enough of me. He didn't even think that I was useful any more.

"Ah, what the hell," I said, bitterly. "I thought I was dead anyway, last time you bastards had me in your clutches. All this is so much borrowed time."

I certainly wasn't going to give him the satisfaction of shooting me, and I didn't want to wait for John Finn to volunteer to help him. Myrlin and Tulyar looked to be peaceful enough, and there was no sign that they'd died painfully. I even began to reassure myself that I wasn't at all sure that they were dead. If I was lucky, I would sit in the chair, activate the electronics, and nothing would happen: nothing at all.

I did glance briefly at Thalia and Calliope. Neither of them rushed forward to volunteer to take my place, but they did look concerned for me. They were hoping I'd be lucky, too.

I guess there's luck and there's luck. Of course I didn't die—the *of course* relating to your point of view rather than mine—but what happened was a very long way from being nothing.

The moment I sat down, before I could even begin to look for an activation-switch, I was engaged. The machine didn't need my help to come alive: it was ready and waiting. The neuron-worms began to burrow into the flesh of my scalp, searching for the axon-threads by which they could link up to my central nervous system. It was the first time I'd ever been conscious when such a thing happened, and it set up waves of rebellious nausea in my stomach. The sensation of being invaded like that is one of the most unpleasant I know, although it doesn't hurt at all. It doesn't even tickle.

What happens afterwards, of course, can hurt, maybe worse than any pain that could ever reach you in the natural way, sparked off in your nerves by injury.

I was already gritting my teeth against the pain that I feared, but what came made any such feeble reaction quite irrelevant. I felt my head tearing apart, my thoughts shredded by a searing blast of pure agony, and I screamed.

To make things worse—there's always some silly little thing that can make even the most horrible experience still worse—the last thing I heard before I lost contact with *that* reality was the sound of a gunshot.

CHAPTER THIRTY

I imagined myself to be Prometheus, chained to a rock, with an eagle's claw raking and tearing my ribs, the talons lunging at my heart. I became Sir Everard Digby, plunging from the scaffold, and then to the ground as the rope was cut, still conscious as the executioner moved to castrate me, and tear the entrails from my belly. I fused my mind with the sensations of Damiens, stretching on the rack, limbs ripped with red-hot hooks, wounds tormented with molten lead, with boiling oil, with burning pitch, with sulfur, the horses straining with all their might at a body which *would not tear....*

That wasn't mere melodrama, but an act of mental self-defense. I coped with the dangerously explosive firing of my neurons in the only way I could, by reconstructing even that most extreme of experiences into some kind of *story*, containing it with some kind of imaginative coherency.

I didn't know what I was doing, but I was saving my life and my mind from a shock that might otherwise have destroyed them.

It is said, although it must be the product of the corrupt imagination of yellow journalism, that it took ten horses several hours to pull off Damiens' limbs, one by one, even after his torturers had weakened his hip and shoulder joints by cutting partly through the ligaments, and that even then the man still lived, although he was unable to speak—and thus unable to repent of his sins and receive the last possible consolation. In my re-enactment of his drama, though, all that could be true, and was.

Reporters also said that Everard Digby was still conscious when they quartered him, but that is surely an observer's insistence on wringing the last drop of permissible horror from the tale he has to tell, to make the point that no man at any time ever did or could have suffered quite as much as the man in question. When I became Digby, though, it was the Digby of legend that I became, and limits of plausibility did not concern my fantasizing mind.

There were, of course, no eyewitnesses to tell us of the sufferings of Prometheus, and no one therefore with a vested interest in magnifying the importance of the incident. Perhaps that made it easier to be Prometheus.

I report now on what happened to *me*, not as an eyewitness but as a victim, and I find my own vested interests paradoxical. My memory is filtered; I can't remember the pain, but have instead to imagine it, and now that I *know* that it was in some sense not real pain (nothing, after all, happened to my actual limbs and heart), I cannot imagine it quite as it was then. My description of it certainly seems hyperbolic—any description would seem hyperbolic—in view of the fact that I survived the experience. Nevertheless, I can assure you that I suffered—*imagined*, if you wish—extreme pain, and that I did indeed identify myself briefly with those lurid attempts to describe the worst sufferings ever undergone by human beings.

Put me down, if you like, as a hypochondriac.

The pain, as I withstood it, made me try with all my might to become smaller, to shrivel myself up and hide myself in insignificance. I tried to wrap myself up in my own substance, like a worm eating its own tail with furious appetite...I tried to vanish into a fold of space like a starship into a wormhole, or like some devious subatomic particle strutting its vain appearance across the infinitesimal stage of the fabric of space for some unimaginable fraction of a picosecond.

Amazingly, that cowardly move seemed to work.

The hurt dwindled as I shrank, and by the time I was no

bigger, in my imagination, than an atom, I was no longer feeling pain. I felt curiously free; I was a world much tinier than a grain of sand, and there was a comfortable eternity extended within my hour. For the moment, though, I was paying no attention to anything outside myself.

Put me down, if you like, as an egotist.

Then, like the hero of some antique microcosmic romance, I suffered a kind of cognitive *bouleversement*, by which little and big were reversed. With a single elegant flip, like a move in zero-gee gymnastics, I became the whole universe, made of space and filled with stars, *flowing* as I expanded, clothed with a skin of paper-thin galaxies whose velocity of recession, relative to my stationary heart, was trembling on the brink of the magical c.

Inside me, streaming like amoeboid protoplasm, was a seminal fluid of nebular vapors, lusting for the vortical dance that would spin them into stellar spermatids, and the beating of my heart was the beating of the Heart Divine—the pulse and rhythm of Creation. Here too, there could be no pain, but only the crystal ecstasy of the music of the spheres.

Thus stabilized, safely, as some kind of *persona* no longer tied to my humanoid body and humanoid senses, I was ready to transfigure myself into some hypothetical *corpus* in which I might face other entities—in which I might be contacted.

Contact, after all, was what I was there for.

In the quaint romances of Old Earth, such intimate contacts as the one which I was set to make are usually uninhibited by the constraints of language. When the gods speak inside the heads of the heroes of myth; when the telepathic aliens make their crucial contact with the scientists of the twenty-first century; when the sentient computer programs first get to mental grips with their wetware progenitors, it is generally assumed that barriers of language are burned away, and that the protagonist's mind can automatically translate the messages that are being beamed at him into English—tortured English, sometimes, in the interests of dramatic effect, but English nevertheless.

In reality, alas, thought does not transcend language. When two humanoids meet, although they have not a word of any language in common, they may still hope to communicate with one another through gesture and mime, but when human and alien meet across some kind of neuro-artificial interface, brain-cell to silicon chip instead of eyeball to eyeball, it's not quite so easy. I presume that it is more difficult still when one of the parties seeking contact has not the least idea of what he can do in such a hypothetical matrix—so different from dear old spacetime!—or how to do it.

Take it from me, the business of contacting an alien intelligence through a direct neural hook-up is a bit like being required to appear on a TV quiz show immediately after being born, with horrible penalties to be exacted if the questions aren't answered adequately.

Subjectively, I began to conceive of myself again as something approximately human-sized. *What* I was I can't tell, and I assume that I wasn't provided with a shape or form; I only had to be a point of view. To what extent my own creativity was involved in the shaping of the environment which coalesced around me I cannot tell; I suspect that it was all done for me, but that those who formed it for the edification of my pseudo-sensory awareness drew upon the resources of my memory and imagination.

It was, if you like, a kind of dream—and thus, perhaps, amenable to some kind of psychological analysis, if only I knew how.

Let us say that I dreamed, then.

I dreamed that I was in a desert that once had been a sea, and that the life-forms which had filled the sea had been precipitated out in crystalline forms, which at night were still and white, like layered ices, but which sublimated in the heat of the day to become strange vapors and emanations.

I dreamed that I was in a forest of stalagmitic rocks, which had been eroded into edgeless smoothness, contoured with many curves as if they were molten statues. In the silver dawn the vaporous entities were stirring from their nightly sleep, floating upwards and writhing in a ceaseless but futile effort to attain fixed shape.

They began a slow, sinister dance around and around the coralline maypoles, beneath a purple sky slowly lightening to mauve. These shimmering shadows yearned for shape, for solidity, but their ambitions were hopeless. They didn't seem to react in any way to my presence, but were utterly self-involved, in pursuit of their own private purposes.

The rocks were colored gray and green, but as they were caressed by the miasmic vapor-creatures their colors were smeared, and a fugitive redness began to ooze, as if escaping from the core of each column through a porous epidermis. The more distant rocks began to recede, drawn backwards into gathering shadows of colored mist, but that took place as if at the very edge of attention, furtively.

The forest, having likened its warming air to water, began to repopulate itself with tiny sparks—transient flickers of light, which attempted the semblance of sunlight scintillating by reflection from tiny scales. The desert's memories of having been a sea were only impressionistic; it couldn't recall the mass of the water or the bodies of its former inhabitants, but it had their echoes imprinted in it. It had the spirit of a sea, and it knew how a sea felt in being a sea.

I didn't feel involved in any of it. Nothing seemed to be addressed to *me*. I felt, instead, like an invader, a trespasser in an autogenetic realm where I could not belong. I felt that the desert's dream was essentially a lonely one.

And then I saw the four eyes of fire, burning like red-hot coals, peering at me from the shadows, their inner light eclipsing sunlight and remembered sea alike.

As they moved from the limits of perception, closer and closer, it seemed that the desert stirred and muttered, complaining at the disturbance. The eyes glared, their fire a bloody radiance, which assaulted the forest like a hot wind, challenging and dispelling its dream.

The desert, angered, fought back. Whirlpools of vapor arose in an attempt to consume the eyes, but impotently. Writhing serpents tried first to swallow the eyes, and then to wrap themselves around the invaders, constrictor-fashion. Torrents of black rain fell from the sky, and lightning struck at the four eyes, again and again—hopelessly. The eyes *stared* at me. It was not the gaze of Medusa, turning me to stone, but rather the reverse. It was a stare in which I might dissolve or evaporate, becoming insubstantial.

Because I was no-where and no-thing, but simply a dislocated presence, the stare was inside me as well as outside. *I* wasn't staring, nor were the eyes of fire *my* eyes, but their searching was within me, through and through me, and I felt that I could never be apart from it again. I believed that I would always be under the scrutiny of those eyes, that there would always be something of that blazing stare in the way I observed myself.

The desert sighed, and I was not consumed. The womb-dream of a long-gone ocean began to reassert itself again, at the fringes of attention. The bulbous columns of rock still bled, and their blood became vaporous, taking flight as misty monsters—dragons and winged things. That dragonblood flowed *in me*, and I felt that if ever I had veins again, and blood of my own, then the pulse of the Heart Divine would send those dragons coursing through my being, for ever and ever.

I counted the columns, and numbered them nine, and for the first time my mind became thoughtfully active, striving for meaning, hoping for a key to the symbolism.

I was suddenly overcome by a floodtide of emotion, as if my metaphorical heart were bursting, but I didn't know what it was that I was supposed to be feeling. I couldn't tell rage from pity, grief from affection. I was moved, but I couldn't tell what it was that moved me, or what I was supposed to understand.

I clung to one conclusion.

The Nine are not dead!

I told myself that they had lost control of themselves, and of their systems, as if they had become unconscious, perhaps catatonic, but that they were not dead. That conclusion, that *thought*, was vital. It made me remember who I was, and what I was, and what the situation was. *Where* I was, or what *form* I had, remained questions unasked and unanswerable, but I knew that there were Nine and there were Four, and that the Nine were not dead, and that the Four were still present, still trying to achieve some mysterious end, not knowing how.

I realized, then, that it was not just me who was all at sea in this business of contact and communication. The Nine and the Four had their barriers to contend with, their walls of incomprehension. They, too, had no way to perceive one another save for the semblance of pain and the strangeness of symbol. They had exploded into one another with the devastating shock of first encounter, and their second encounter had been no less disruptive, but now perhaps their damaged selves were grasping at one another for mutual support—perhaps even for mutual inclusion. They were trying to touch one another so intimately as almost to *be* one another. But that was dangerous, as they had both discovered.

The eyes seemed now to be very close to me, in two pairs staring from either side, although I had no eyes of my own with which to meet their stare. They were still calling forth waves of feeling with their hypnotic insistence, but I still didn't know *what* to feel. Somehow, the feeling began to assume the nature of fear, but even as it did so, I felt a counterbalancing insistence that this was *wrong*. There had been a partial withdrawal, as though the eyes were struggling to become more remote, to distance themselves.

Terror grew inside me, and pain, and I felt again the urge to absent myself, to become small, to seek safety in the perverse world of the atom. But I also felt *not*-fear and *not*-pain, and I wondered whether those strange feelings might better have been translated into words, if only I had had the means.

Do not hurt! Do not fear!

Was that what the Four were saying to me? Or was it the Nine? Were the Nine and Four in conflict still—the Muses and the Seasons, competing to inform this private universe with frames of meaning? I couldn't tell.

The pain didn't reassert itself. No more legends of torture came to trouble and to save my soul. But the fear would not be gone. It ebbed and flowed, as though it were trying to undergo some metamorphosis of significance, but it couldn't quite make of itself what it wanted to become.

I tried to help.

Whose fear? I wondered. *Perhaps not mine. Perhaps....*

The thought did seem to inject something into the pattern of potentiality. The feeling seemed more confident, more nearly that which it was trying to be.

And then I guessed.

What you're trying to be, I said—to myself, because my thoughts were as difficult for them to understand as theirs were for me—*is a need! You're sending out a mayday!*

Once this was perceived, the feeling in which I had perceived the odor of fear now became sharper, as if it were no longer struggling to find form. The touching-point was there. I had made contact with a kind of mind which, as far as I could guess, might be the mind of Asgard entire, or might only be some tiny imprisoned thing, like the mind of a wordlet confined in one of its many levels. That mind and mine had not the encoded equipment to say anything at all one another—unlike the minds of the Nine, which remembered a humanoid incarnation and which were already equipped for interface with entities such as myself. *This* mind (or group of minds) was alien indeed; alien to the Nine and to me. It had learned to "speak" but a single word to me.

But I thought I understood the word. I prayed that I did, because if I didn't, this might all be for nothing.

I became the universe again, embodying all Creation. I took on the semblance of bodily form, albeit macrocosmically. I was four-eyed and nine-boned, and my eyes were eyes of fire and my bones the rocks of ages, and my heart was the Heart Divine, my blood seething with the venom of dragons and my semen with the ghosts of all men who had ever been and all who were to come.

As above, so below...and I felt this universe reflected in a mode of being much tinier, in a cage of absurd flesh. This was more than Creation. This was Encounter, and its beginning was a word.

And the word, I believed, was *help!*

Or, to put it more aptly: HELP!

HELP!

H-E-L-P!

It wasn't me who was screaming, but something much more terrible, and much more helpless.

It was Prometheus, and murdered Pan. In that scream was the waking of Brahma from his ageless dream. In that scream was the pain that Odin felt when he tore out his eye and sold it: the price of his godly wisdom. In that unbearable scream was the breath of *Götterdämmerung*, come to end the deep cold of the *fimbulwinter*, come to disturb Valhalla and bring the gods themselves to their meeting with destiny.

But when the gods cry for help, what strength can mere mortals bring to their aid?

CHAPTER THIRTY-ONE

I came round, and jerked forward convulsively, pulling my head away from the hood and its grasping spider web of intrusive connections. They slid from my skin with a dull tearing sensation.

My head was buzzing with confusion. I felt somebody grab me, but I wouldn't let myself fall back. Instead, I lurched further forward, thrusting myself out of the chair altogether. I would certainly have fallen if the other person had not been holding me, but the arms which had gripped me were strong, and helped me to stand.

I remembered the gunshot then, and gritted my teeth against the possibility of authentic pain, but none came. It was not I, then, who had been shot.

I opened my eyes, and looked around.

My eyes met other eyes—pale blue eyes, perhaps sky-blue eyes. But these were bright and warm, not pale and cold. There was yellow hair too, but in such abundance!

I blinked. I wasn't prepared to see *those* eyes, or that remarkable halo of blonde hair. I looked her up and down, to make sure that it really was *her*. All the curves were in the right place. The only thing that didn't make sense was that she was wearing the uniform of a Scarid trooper, a couple of sizes too baggy.

I looked around the room.

The Scarid officer was lying flat on his back, arms akimbo, with a bullet-wound in the middle of his forehead. The other trooper who'd come into the room with us was also quite dead, in a vast pool of blood which had leaked out of the chasm in his chest, apparently some little time ago.

John Finn stood looking on, a couple of meters away, leaning on the chair—now empty—which had earlier contained the body of 994-Tulyar. He was no longer holding a gun, and he no longer looked smug. He was watching me, seemingly less than delighted by the fact of my recovery.

It was sheer joy to be able to say, in real English words: "What the hell happened?"

"I disposed of the two outside," said Susarma Lear, "then borrowed one uniform and both their guns. These two weren't even watching the door. I'd have blasted *him*, too, but I wasn't quite sure which side he was on, so he had time to drop his gun and surrender. Wise move."

"How did you get out of the egg? Myrlin said you wouldn't be ready for another twenty-four hours or so."

"Search me. There was some kind of power failure, I think. Woke me up. For a minute or two, I thought I was trapped, but then I got the lid to roll back. I got out into the corridor, and started exploring. I just happened upon the two soldier-boys by sheer good luck."

"But you weren't armed!" I protested. "You didn't even have any clothes on!"

"That was the advantage I had," she said. "If you'd have been there, you'd have seen a colonel in the Star Force. But all they saw was a helpless naked woman. They didn't have a chance."

I shook my head in wonderment. Poor, stupid barbarians. I looked around again. "What happened to Tweedledum and Tweedledee? Not to mention the Tetron, and...." I didn't complete the sentence.

"Myrlin?" she said.

"That's the one," I confirmed.

"I thought he was dead," she said, in an ominously amiable tone.

"Isn't he?" I was able to counter.

"Apparently," she said, "that was touch and go. Your two furry friends rushed him away to one of those magic eggs. Tulyar too. They reckon that there's a very good chance of restoring them to health, despite their condition."

"They're good with things like that," I confirmed, disentangling myself from her steely grip now that I felt able to stand by myself. "Have they told you yet that you're immortal?"

She cocked a disbelieving eyebrow. "Am I?" she said.

When I nodded in reply she turned to look at Finn.

"Him too, I guess," I said. "Depressing thought, isn't it?"

Finn looked at us both as if we were making fun of him. The news should have cheered him up, but he just wasn't in the mood. I supposed that later, when it sank in—and when he began to believe it—it would make him feel quite elated, especially when he remembered how close the colonel had come to blowing his brains out.

The gray walls began to mist over. The ghosts were back. Susarma Lear and Finn looked uneasy as the silvery shapes began to coalesce, but I was pleased to see them. The Nine were back in control—in partial control, at least—of their body. Sailors on strange seas of fate, now safely back in port. I hoped that they were safe, though it seemed that they hadn't regained their former power and composure.

"R-r-rouss-ss-sseau," said the whispering voice, no clearer than before. "w-w-e kn-n-n-now-w-w y-o-o-ou n-n-n-now-w-w....."

Safe they were, it seemed, though by no means entirely recovered from their ordeal.

As before, the threads of light tried to settle into the forms of faces—nine faces, overlapping and drifting through one another, filling the room with their immensity.

They no longer had the face of Susarma Lear, though.

Now they had *my* face.

I heard the colonel's sharp intake of breath, and saw John Finn silently appealing for help to some nonexistent agent of mercy. I smiled. It was an impressive effect, and I felt curiously proud. But then I thought about what they'd said. They *knew* me, now.

They'd been inside me, and in some curious sense they were *still* inside me. A shiver ran down my spine, and I almost expected to hear alien voices inside my head...to discover my subvocalized thoughts turning into a weird dialogue, or worse—a Babel of confused conversations. But that wasn't the way it was. It wasn't that kind of "being *in* me". I was still myself, and as far as I could tell, I was still the self I always had been. Whatever extras I had acquired weren't yet manifesting themselves as other ghosts in my machine. I didn't doubt, though, that they *would* manifest themselves, eventually.

Like Saul of Tarsus on the road to Damascus, I had experienced revelation. I had been *converted*. The spirit was in me, and the *word* was in me. And the word was....

My senses reeled, and the colonel had to catch me again, to steady me. She was looking at me with genuine concern—almost as if she liked me. Not that I was about to believe *that*. I'd already taken in my ration of six impossibilities before breakfast, and now I was the hardest-headed skeptic of them all.

"What about the other Scarids?" I asked, freeing myself from her grip for a second time. "Can you disarm them now?" I was addressing the Nine, though Susarma Lear had opened her mouth to answer before they interrupted her.

"Un-n-nder c-c-control-l-l," they assured me.

I no longer felt impatient with the stuttering voice. I knew now how difficult a business communication could be.

"How about the battle for Skychain City?"

That, they assured me (I shall not attempt to reproduce the texture of their words, lest the typographical eccentricities become irritating) would take a little longer. It was a matter that was out of their hands, alas.

I stretched my limbs. They all felt as if they were in very good condition, and there was no reason to doubt that they were, though I couldn't help being surprised to find them so.

"Okay?" said Susarma Lear. "Can we get out of here?"

"We'll have to wait for the scions," I told her. Then I said, almost absent-mindedly: "Excuse me for a moment."

She looked surprised, but stood back, as if to let me go to the door. I turned the other way, and with a smooth efficiency that was surprising, given the weak gravity, I kicked John Finn in the groin. When he bounced off the wall behind him I lashed him across the face with the flat of my hand. I felt his nose break, but I didn't wince. I wasn't in a squeamish mood. When he was down on the ground I booted him twice more, as hard as I could.

Then I knelt down beside him.

"That," I hissed, in a suitably melodramatic whisper, "was just for the purposes of demonstration. I only want you to know that if you ever try to screw me over again, I'll hurt you so badly you'll be in pain for the rest of your fucking *life*. And that could be a *very long time*."

I stood up again, and met Susarma Lear's eyes. She was looking at me almost in horror—not at what I'd done, but at the fact that it was me who had done it. That was odd, in a way, because I would have thought that she'd be pleased to see me acting like a hero of the Star Force for once in my life. Sometimes, you just can't figure out how to please someone.

"Jesus, Rousseau!" she said.

I didn't feel anything. I didn't feel anything at all.

"I'm not quite myself at the moment," I told her. It wasn't true. I was entirely myself. I just felt that I had a license to act out of character for once.

Anyway, I was a hero. Not just a metaphorical hero, the way she was, but a real one. I had been summoned by the gods—or by the only kind of something which could pass for a god, in our thoroughly secularized universe. Destiny had put its mark upon my forehead, and beckoned to me with its bony finger. I didn't have the slightest doubt about that—not any more.

"Well," I said, "I guess we have time on our hands, now. We've surely had our ration of unpleasant surprises."

Looking down at John Finn, bleeding and gasping, I reflected coldly that he had probably had one too many—but no more, of course, than he deserved. The same was true of the Scarid officer, who had carried far beyond his ordinary conceptual horizons the dangerous and preposterous assumption that you can get what you want by threatening people with guns. There comes a time when it isn't sufficient to be only a soldier. I hoped fervently that his superiors might learn that lesson without it having to be rammed home quite so forcefully.

As things turned out, they did manage to learn it. They discovered the one and only possible defense against technologically-superior armed opposition.

They surrendered.

And then they sat down with both the Tetrax and the Nine, in order to try to overcome all the barriers that stood in the way of sensible communication, and to discover what there might be that they could discuss in a reasonable manner.

Which is what passes for a happy ending in situations like the one in which we all found ourselves.

CHAPTER THIRTY-TWO

Later, of course, the doubts began to creep back. Those magic moments of total conviction never do last. As I've observed before, the true gold of certainty is not to be found, and you have to settle for what there is.

What there is, alas, is the knowledge that one is always fallible. You never really know exactly where you're up to, let alone where it is that you need to go next.

For the first time since I'd put the final full stop to the first volume of my memoirs, things began to run smoothly for a while. The Scarid High Command saw sense; the Nine pulled 994-Tulyar and Myrlin out of the jaws of death; and a kind of balance was restored to the universe as I was privileged to experience it.

It didn't take much effort to persuade my commanding officer that our best interests lay in staying where we were. There was a great deal to be learned from the Nine which might prove to be of immense value to Mother Earth and humankind. She was quick enough to see that it might be a kind of intellectual treason to leave the task of collaboration with the Isthomi entirely to the Tetrax. Indeed, she was persuaded that the need to win what advantage we could from our fortuitous placement easily outweighed such minor considerations as her annoyance in discovering that her memory was a liar and that Myrlin was alive and well.

I figured that in time she might even learn to like him, once she was reconciled to the idea that she shouldn't try to kill him all over again.

I had my sacrifices to make, too. Even John Finn had to be put to work, and I knew full well that once he had absorbed a little of the new knowledge that was here to be gleaned, he would become utterly insufferable in his arrogance.

Inevitably, I began to regret having broken his nose. The memory of it still gave me a certain satisfaction, as well as a sense of having done my bit to preserve the moral balance of the universe, but I knew that I'd have to watch my back for as long as he was around, lest a stray knife should somehow become embedded between my shoulder-blades.

In spite of such minor difficulties, I soon began to enjoy myself. I was once again in my element, scavenging in strange places for unfamiliar things. The fact that there were other people around ceased to matter much—in all essentials I was alone with my insatiable curiosity, the only beloved mistress of my heart.

Which is not to say, of course, that I was completely uninterested in the big political picture that was slowly building around us. I was suitably enthused by the fact that for the first time ever, Asgard and the universe had agreed to communicate with one another. It filled me with optimism to know that the Scarida and the galactic community each decided that they had a lot to learn, and that they both stood to gain from an exchange of opportunities. The Tetrax (speaking on behalf of the entire galactic community) promised to teach the Scarida the joys of galactic technology; the Scarida promised to allow the Tetrax access to all the levels of Asgard which they controlled. The Nine, although facing an uphill task in the matter of self-repair, agreed not to seal themselves off from either side, and determined that they would hold the triple detente together. All very fine, in my view.

All these developments, as you will notice, solved the general problems within which context this chapter of my personal history started. Alas, they did not begin to touch the more personal problems that had arisen along the way. Nor, for what it is worth, did they provide any answers to the old, old problems that had been the Great Mysteries even before I got into the game.

Having emerged intact from my hallucinatory adventure in contact with alien minds, I had every reason to be pleased with myself, and in a way I was. For a while I was filled with zestful energy and a huge sense of pride, because I was convinced that I had achieved a great thing simply by surviving my encounter, and by virtue of what I thought that the contact implied.

Asgard itself had called out to *me*, to be its savior.

When I came down from my adrenalin high, though, I could hardly help but worry about what that implied, in terms of what I was now required to do about it.

That was when the doubts really began to gnaw away at me.

For one thing, I became increasingly less sure that it implied anything at all. How did I know, after all, that I had actually and authentically experienced anything meaningful? How could I be sure that my dream was not simply a dream—and my sense of importance nothing but a commonplace delusion of grandeur?

Then again, even if something *had* happened, how could I know for sure just what it was? Even if I was correct in believing that a message had been sent, which I had received, on what grounds could I assure myself that I had read it *right*?

And yet again, if all of it *was* true, and something in the depths of the macroworld—something great and fine and utterly mysterious—had cried out to me for aid...then what the hell could a mere human being be expected to achieve in rendering aid to beings who were apparently very different in kind, and far superior in their abilities?

What, indeed, could possibly be done?

I had begun this chapter of my life with a terribly sense of not knowing what I ought to do, but the progenitors of that feeling had been mere boredom and a superfluity of trivial opportunity. Now, I was faced with another uncertainty about what I could and should do next—an uncertainty infinitely more terrible in aspect.

It was at least possible that I had been singled out for great things—but I had not the slightest idea how to go about them.

I and I alone had stood four-square with the Nine when that anguished cry for help had surged from the depths of Asgard to blow through us like a hot wind. Myrlin and 994-Tulyar had been so badly shocked by the first instant of their contact that they had been thrust into the valley of the shadow of death—I was soon able to ascertain, once they were well again, that they had no memory of anything that might have happened to them while they were at the interface. If their being had been polluted with vestiges of an alien soul, they knew nothing of it, and manifested no stigmata of any such infection.

The fact that I had fared differently reflected no credit upon me. I was inclined to presume that by the time I entered the game the 'creatures' who were manifest in my dream as eyes of fire had learned to be more gentle, and had moderated their approach, so that their touch became something that a frail and tiny humanoid mind could cope with.

It was, of course, to the Nine that I turned in the hope of enlightenment, but they too were unable to offer much insight. The contact had affected them as severely as it had affected Myrlin and Tulyar, and in their fashion they had been much more severely wounded by it. They could not confirm or deny what I told them about my interpretation of the contact as a cry for help. Even when I interfaced with the Nine again, to give them more intimate access to my memories and interpretations of the experience, they could not judge what it was that I set before them. Their knowledge was no more secure than mine, their skepticism no less corrosive.

Perhaps, if they had been *well*, they would have had more powerful resources on which to draw, but in their injured state, they had to devote all but the tiniest fraction of their attention and endeavor to the business of self-repair.

Of course, I now had a relationship with the Nine more special than their relationship with Myrlin, or any other being of my kind. They and I had secrets in common; circumstance had forged a bond between us, and that bond was far from being merely metaphorical. In some sense, the Nine were in me...just as the eyes of fire and whatever consciousness lay behind them was in me.

It mattered very little that I could hardly begin to understand the Nine: what kind of beings they were, what view of the world they had. The Nine had taken the natural course in choosing my face as the medium of their new visual manifestations. They accepted that in some subtle but crucial fashion, they and I had exchanged parts of our personalities, and that I now lived in them and they in me. Their acceptance was a foundation-stone on which we could build trust, and perhaps a common cause.

But they, like me, had no idea what could and should be done to answer the call which I might have received.

In our ignorance, we hesitated—waiting, I suppose, for something more to happen. It was not that we were hoping for a third contact—the Nine felt that they could well do without another such traumatic experience. It was more that we were expecting some process of change to complete itself in *me*. We hoped and feared that my experience might have consequences which were yet to unfold.

After all, I did have a strong sense of being different from what I had been before, though it is not easy to describe exactly what that sense was like.

In my waking moments, I was myself, and once my elation had evaporated I seemed very much the self I had always been—stubborn, self-contained, frequently facetious, some-times churlish, but always with my heart in what I thought to be the right place.

In my dreams, though, I sometimes found strange sensations lurking within a deeper self than the one I knew and was in my everyday intercourse with the phenomenal world. I never went back to that dreaming desert, nor saw those eroded monoliths, nor faced those eyes of fire, but there were *feelings*, and more than feelings. Sometimes, there *were* faint and fragile voices, which spoke in querulous whispers, which seemed to be hunting for something to say, as if they were trying to remember—or simply trying to become.

I began to fear that those dreams would eventually intrude upon reality, but I waited, and they didn't.

I often went back to the room with the hooded chairs, to interface again and again with the wounded Nine, to dream more exotic dreams awake than those I dreamed in sleep. But it wasn't easy, as I've explained, to begin the serious work of communication.

Although the Nine already knew *parole*, and English too, there were still many barriers to the kind of speech that was necessary in that curious spaceless 'world' of electronic information. But the Nine did want to talk—they wanted, in fact, to bring me to the edge of their own community. There was no sense in which they could welcome me *into* that community, and become the Ten, but they did want to know me in a fashion very different from the way they had known Myrlin.

I think the waiting, and the work that we did while we waited, was valuable. I think even the uncertainty was valuable, in its way, in making us question what it was that we must do.

This time, though, there was no possibility of turning my back and deciding to go home. Although the Nine and I did not know what it was that we had to do—or what it was that *I* had to do—we did know that the way forward was the way downward, and that whatever was in the heart of Asgard *had* to be found.

As the wise man said: *Si Dieu n'existait pas, il faudrait l'inventer.* He might have added that there comes a time when it is no longer enough merely to invent. It is necessary, also, to *confront.* Even if our gods are invented, we still need to know what it is that they require of us.

And so, when I have finished recording this second volume of my adventures—which I have been doing, I candidly admit, as much to straighten out my thoughts as in the hope of entertaining readers—I intend to set out yet again on my journey to the center of Asgard, to discover whether, in truth, there is a place for me in the halls of Valhalla—and a task for me to do, in order to earn it.

I will be, as ever, a reluctant hero—and I leave it to you to decide whether that is the best kind, or the worst.

ABOUT THE AUTHOR

Brian Stableford was born in Yorkshire in 1948. He taught at the University of Reading for several years, but is now a full-time writer. He has written many science-fiction and fantasy novels, including *The Empire of Fear*, *The Werewolves of London*, *Year Zero*, *The Curse of the Coral Bride*, *The Stones of Camelot*, and *Prelude to Eternity*. Collections of his short stories include a long series of *Tales of the Biotech Revolution*, and such idiosyncratic items as *Sheena and Other Gothic Tales* and *The Innsmouth Heritage and Other Sequels*. He has written numerous nonfiction books, including *Scientific Romance in Britain, 1890-1950*; *Glorious Perversity: The Decline and Fall of Literary Decadence*; *Science Fact and Science Fiction: An Encyclopedia*; and *The Devil's Party: A Brief History of Satanic Abuse*. He has contributed hundreds of biographical and critical articles to reference books, and has also translated numerous novels from the French language, including books by Paul Féval, Albert Robida, Maurice Renard, and J. H. Rosny the Elder.

www.ingramcontent.com/pod-product-compliance
Lightning Source LLC
Chambersburg PA
CBHW050412260626
47156CB00003B/976